Security Force of Two

by

Tena Stetler

Mountain Town Mysteries

Security Force of Two

Cover Art by *Kristian Norris*

The Wild Rose Press, Inc.
PO Box 708
Adams Basin, NY 14410-0708
Visit us at www.thewildrosepress.com

Publishing History
First Edition, 2023
Trade Paperback ISBN 978-1-5092-4796-7
Digital ISBN 978-1-5092-4797-4

Mountain Town Mysteries
Published in the United States of America

Candle Bearclaw stood in front of Carl's large mahogany desk, laid the unsealed white envelope face up on the polished desktop, and slid it toward her boss.

"What's this?" Carl eyed the offending envelope.

"It's what we talked about last week, my resignation." She swung her briefcase onto the leather chair beside her. Pulling out a laptop computer, a manila file folder, and a memory stick, she set them on the corner of her boss' desk.

"It's all here, including the passwords necessary to access the sensitive files, my work on the assignment, including my contacts, and it's a good stopping point for me. Someone else should be able to pick up exactly where I left off, seamlessly. I am requesting a no contact status by you and the agency."

She pulled out a .380 semi-automatic tucked into the waistband of her slacks, ejected the magazine, and racked the slide open. Gingerly setting the gun on the desk beside the other items, she sighed.

He looked across the desk at her, observing her actions. "I understand your position, but that may not be possible. How deep were you?"

Hands flat on the desktop, she leaned over and glared at him. "Deep enough to understand the assignment goes against every fiber of my being. You knew that when you assigned it to me, and yet, you did it anyway, knowing it would be my final act as an operative."

Praise for Tena Stetler

Dedication

To my husband my own personal hero for his support and patience when brainstorming each story.

To the staff, especially my editor, Lill, and authors of The Wild Rose Press for their unwavering support and assistance.

To my readers who I write the stories for so they may be whisked away into a fantasy world they may never want to leave. Thank you for your never ending support! Love you all!

Other Books by Tena Stetler
Published by The Wild Rose Press, Inc.

A Demon's Witch
A Warlock's Secrets
A Vampire's Unlikely Alliance
An Angel's Unintentional Entanglement
A Magic Redemption
A Witch's Quandary
An Angel's Wylder Assignment

Charm Me
Charm Me Again

A Witch's Journey
A Witch's Holiday Wedding
Hidden Gypsy Magic
Chocolate Raspberry Magic

An Enchanted Holiday
Mystic Maples
A Witch's Protocol

Chapter One

A Career Ends and Life Begins

Candle Bearclaw stood in front of Carl's large mahogany desk, laid the unsealed white envelope face up on the polished desktop, and slid it toward her boss.

"What's this?" Carl eyed the offending envelope.

"It's what we talked about last week, my resignation." She swung her briefcase onto the leather chair beside her. Pulling out a laptop computer, a manila file folder, and a memory stick, she set them on the corner of her boss' desk.

"It's all here, including the passwords necessary to access the sensitive files, my work on the assignment, including my contacts, and it's a good stopping point for me. Someone else should be able to pick up exactly where I left off, seamlessly. I am requesting a no contact status by you and the agency."

She pulled out a .380 semi-automatic tucked into the waistband of her slacks, ejected the magazine, and racked the slide open. Gingerly setting the gun on the desk beside the other items, she sighed.

He looked across the desk at her, observing her actions. "I understand your position, but that may not be possible. How deep were you?"

Hands flat on the desktop, she leaned over and glared at him. "Deep enough to understand the assignment goes against every fiber of my being. You knew that when you assigned it to me, and yet, you did it anyway, knowing it would be my final act as an operative."

She stood and raised her arms in a surrender motion. "For God's sakes, Carl, I'm a computer analyst turned hacker under your fine tutelage. I can't do it anymore."

Carl leaned back in his chair. "A replacement will be difficult to find, if not impossible," he said flatly. "You're the best."

"You should have thought about that before you forced me to take this assignment," she insisted, pacing around the room.

He raked his fingers through his thick salt-and-pepper hair, rubbing at the back of his neck the minute she walked through the door. "Thought you'd come around. You always have."

She shook her head, feeling a little sorry for the predicament she'd put him in, though it was of his own making. "Not this time. I'm through. And I'm taking you up on the promise you made when I agreed to become an independent contractor with the agency." She gave a half laugh. "That didn't last long, did it?"

"That was a long time ago before you were officially with the agency. I'm not sure you can just walk now. The director needs to sign off on this." He leaned forward with his elbows on the desk, fingers tented in front of him, and gave her a hard stare.

"I guess that's your problem. Unless, of course, you want me to have a little chat with the President." She shrugged, then returned his stare, refusing to look away. "Come on, Carl, cut the bullshit. I know you don't want me to go, but we both know I'm not cut out for what this assignment could turn into. I'm a computer geek, not a deep-cover operative."

Finally looking away, he sighed, reached for the envelope, and pulled out three pieces of neatly folded paper. The first was her handwritten resignation, signed and notarized. The second had one word typed on the entire page, a password to unlock her agency computer, giving access to the top-secret files stored there. "Only one password?" He raised a bushy brow in question.

"Yes, the rest you can get from my handler, Mark, along with anything you don't understand on the third page regarding my assignment." She turned on her heel and started for the door.

He stood and walked around the desk. "Candle. Are you sure about this?"

She paused and turned halfway around. "Positive."

The determined look on her face said it all. He sighed. "Ok, I'll set up your exit interview in one hour. That'll give me time to get HR briefed and up here."

"Thanks, Carl. I appreciate it." She pulled a single piece of paper out of her briefcase and laid it in front of him. "I need you to sign off on this, acknowledging receipt of my computer, weapon, phone, and files."

He pulled the paper toward him, scribbled his name at the bottom, then pushed the document back to her. "You know this is going to tarnish my reputation," he said gruffly, a small smile crossing his lips. "I just allowed one of our best geeks to cut her ties to the agency."

"No, it won't." One corner of her mouth turned up in a partial smile. "I'm not cut out for this. I want to live a normal life without looking over my shoulder." She picked up her briefcase, continued toward the door, turned, and paused. "I'll be back in an hour, and thanks."

Carl solemnly nodded his head, bringing his eyes up to meet hers. "I wish you'd reconsider."

She shook her head slowly. "Not a chance." She grasped the polished silver handle and yanked open the door. Walking through, she closed it quietly. Leaning her back against the door, she felt like a dead weight had just been lifted from her shoulders and let out a sigh of relief.

The squeal of Carl's chair wheels caught her attention. In her mind's eye, she saw him shoved back in his chair, rubbing his eyes as he did when stressed. Inheriting her mother's talent had saved her ass many times. However, she'd never be as good as her mother.

Pekabo Bearclaw had a way of knowing things before they happened and seeing things ordinary people shouldn't. The receiver tumbled onto the desk with a *thud* as he reached for it. She heard beeps as he punched in two numbers and then drummed his fingers while he waited for an answer. A late summer rain began to patter against the office windows.

"Director, I've set up an exit interview for Candle Bearclaw first thing this morning. I need to arrange for an HR representative to be in my office in an hour. She turned in her letter of resignation, the agency's laptop, and her service weapon." There was a pause in the conversation, then Carl snarled, "I know you thought it was a bad fit, but…Well, it doesn't matter now."

Another pause.

"I need a replacement ASAP. I can bring them up to speed and hopefully save the operation before anyone senses anything is amiss. Candle gave me her field notes, investigation information, and all contacts," Carl said, then added to the empty office, "Good luck, Candle. I hope you find what you're looking for."

Lips curved in a half-smile, she quietly pushed off the door. Her footsteps left imprints, but made no sound, on the plush navy-blue carpet as she made her way down the long hall and reached the security doors. She punched in her code and walked out the doors into the darkness. *I have an hour to kill before dawn.*

The early morning rain had turned to mist cool and refreshing against her face. She glanced at the darkening clouds and pulled out an umbrella as she strolled across the manicured lawn, then sat on a bench to wait. Another hour or two at the most, and she'd be free from the agency. She blew out a breath. Freedom and the open road were calling to her.

****

The roll-up door to the storage unit creaked when Candle pushed it up the final inches. She took a set of keys and an electronic device from her briefcase. Holding the device about waist high, she walked around the covered vehicle and then slid under the car. A quiet ping sounded, and she wriggled out from under the vehicle. *Old habits die hard.*

She shrugged her shoulders. *Better safe than sorry.* She pocketed the device, uncovered the copper and black sports car, pushed a button, and the driver's door swung up, like a wing, rather than out, so secret agentish. She liked that. The vehicle was a bonus for a challenging eighteen-month undercover assignment well done.

She shivered, laughing at herself, shoved her duffel bag behind the front seat, covered it with a towel kept folded on the floor, then climbed into the car and turned the key in the ignition. The engine roared to life. *Raw power.* A tremor of excitement danced up her spine.

Awesome sound. Reaching under the passenger seat, she pulled out her laptop, several peripherals, a tablet, and a cell phone, all bundled together. Leaning back against the seat, she rubbed her eyes and yawned. She'd spent the entire week planning her exit from the agency, making sure her bank accounts and documents were in order, leaving little time for sleep.

The first order of business, get lots of caffeine in her body, then put miles between her and the agency. Next, find a nice hotel with decent security and underground parking. She didn't want her vehicle to come up missing when it had less than one hundred miles on it. She planned to make up for the lack of vacations and personal time over the last fifteen years by taking her time traveling to her final destination.

The little cabin she'd bought didn't close for almost a month, allowing her extra time, in the event extricating herself from the agency took longer than anticipated, which it hadn't. Once Carl understood she wouldn't change her mind, HR's paperwork and the exit interview went smooth as silk. Everyone wished her good luck with life in the private sector. Only she figured Carl secretly hoped she'd get bored and come back. *Fat chance.*

****

Meandering cross country in her sports car was a kick. In the Catskill Mountains of New York, she enjoyed negotiating hairpin turns and hiking the trails. When she crossed the state line into Ohio, her heart skipped a beat. The excitement she'd tamped down for the better part of a couple of months bubbled to the surface.

In the southwest corner of Ohio, she planned to stop

at a kennel she'd been talking with and pick up her puppy. While working with the agency, she'd longed for a canine companion, but her time was not her own, and no way for a dog to live. But now, she'd have that puppy, and raise it to be her protector as well as her companion.

When she stopped at the gates of the small farm that housed the kennel, she was practically giddy. Several dogs greeted her at the fence as an older man strolled across the green lawn, opened the expansive gates, and motioned her to drive up the driveway.

When she swung the car door up and stepped out, the gentleman gave a low whistle and grinned. "That's quite a car you have, Ms. Bearclaw. Are you aware of what a puppy could do to that interior?"

"It's the one indulgence I allowed myself. Now I'm about to allow another. Only this one comes with fur and fangs. Yes, I'm aware. That's the reason I sent you the specific dimensions I needed for a kennel for Terrabyte." She closed the car door and noticed the man craning his neck to look inside the car. She smiled, extending her hand toward the man. "You must be Luke. Please call me Candle. Would you like to take a look at my car?"

He grasped her hand in his and grinned. "You bet." He released her hand, leaned through the open window, looked around inside, and sniffed. "Love that new car smell. How long have you had her?"

"Several years, but I didn't get to drive much, so the car might as well be brand new. Less than one hundred miles on her when I left."

Looking across the car to the passenger seat, he said, "We found just the size and type of kennel you were looking for, but first, I'm sure you would like to meet...what'd you name her?" He frowned as if trying to remember the name.

"Terrabyte."

"Okay, let's go into the house where she's waiting." Luke led the way into the one-story rambling ranch house painted blue with white shutters. While they walked toward the house, he instructed the dogs to leave her alone and go about their business.

"Wow. Well-behaved dogs."

He shrugged. "They know who their pack leader is. Gotta have a firm but loving hand with these dogs. Socialization is the key."

She nodded. "Understood."

A pleasant-looking woman opened the door holding a wriggling fur ball when they reached the home. "Come in, come in." She leaned down and put the puppy on the floor. Straightening, she reached out and hugged Candle. "I'm Maleah Davis. Feel like we know each other as often as I've communicated with you by phone and email."

The puppy barked, spun around, and wiggled, then sniffed at Candle's shoes, testing one with her puppy teeth. She reached down to pet the puppy, who backed away and then rushed forward. She scooped Terrabyte up, and the puppy rewarded her with kisses.

"Do you have time for a tour of the farm?" Maleah offered. "It's such a beautiful day."

"Yes, I would like that." She held the wriggling puppy close to her. "I've had enough sitting for a while. A walk would be wonderful."

After the tour, Luke seat-belted the kennel in the front seat, stowing a bag with puppy food, bowl, harness, brush, and leash on the floor in front of the seat, closing the door carefully. He stepped back, a smug grin on his face. "It fits perfectly." The puppy barked its displeasure at being confined.

Maleah gave her several sheets of puppy care instructions, having explained them all earlier as they toured the farm. "If you have any questions, don't hesitate to give us a call."

"I won't. Terrabyte and I won't be home for a couple more weeks, so I hope she likes to travel," she said with a laugh as her tummy gave a flip, hoping the pup wouldn't get carsick. She pulled out a chew stick and put it in with the pup. With a list of dog-friendly hotels that met her security requirements tucked in the console, she climbed inside the car and waved goodbye to Maleah and Luke.

****

She and Terrabyte wound their way down the coast and spent a week exploring Florida's dog-friendly places, careful to limit dog-to-dog contact. They spent a few days tasting the cuisine and soaking up the atmosphere in the bayous of the south. The Alamo was near San Antonio, Texas. A destination she had always wanted to visit. Upon arrival, she found a parking place, leashed the pup, and wandered around the site. It gave her goosebumps as she ran her fingers over the relics and saw a glimpse of the famous battle. Quickly, she yanked her hand away and stepped back. The visions all but disappeared during her time at the CIA and she'd rather not have them start up again. If she wanted to know the history of an item, she'd look it up in a book. She didn't need to see the actual event in her mind.

Protection of freedom made her sign on with the agency to make a difference. She considered that naive nineteen-year-old girl. *Did I make a difference?* She shrugged one shoulder, clicked her tongue, and held out a treat to get Terrabyte to follow on leash.

The pup rolled over, tangled in the leash, only to get untangled, plop down, and refuse to move, chewing on the offending strap. *Could be more of a challenge than I thought.* Stowing a squirming Terrabyte under her arm, she meandered her way back to the car.

Turning on Highway 10, she headed west. *Well, it's now or never.* A knot formed in her stomach. *Shouldn't have stayed away for so long.* She set the GPS coordinates for a little place called Aspen Ridge, high in the Rocky Mountains of Colorado. Before reaching her destination, she stopped in Aspen, Colorado, rented a storage unit in a secure facility, parked the sports car inside, and covered it up. She secured the unit with two combination locks.

The town of Aspen catered to movie stars, million, and billionaires from all over the world, so she figured an expensive sports car wouldn't draw much attention.

Across the street and down a couple of blocks, she found the rental car agency where she'd reserved a fairly large SUV. Returning to the storage unit, she transferred Terrabyte's crate and puppy stuff to the rental then drove the twenty-five miles or so to Aspen Ridge. The knot in her stomach tightened with every passing mile that brought her closer to her destination.

Chapter Two

Homecoming but My How Things Have Changed

Candle parked outside a modest two-story house. Yellow and orange leaves swirled and danced their way across the street. She sighed and reached for the door handle, ensuring the passenger side window was open for the puppy. *I might as well get this over with.* Wiping her sweaty hands on her jeans, she strolled up the sidewalk, stepped onto the porch, and drew in a breath of the fresh mountain air before knocking on the door. Her knees felt like rubber as she shifted from foot to foot. *Maybe I should've called first.*

A tall, muscular man with straight black hair graying at the temples opened the door. He stood rooted to the spot, speechless for several moments.

"Chief," she said quietly, moving toward him, her hand outstretched. "I guess it's been a while."

"Well, damn if you didn't find your way home." He grinned, squinting his eyes against the bright sunlight. Stepping forward, he swept her up in his arms and kissed her cheek.

All her doubts and nerves melted away as she wrapped her arms around her father.

"It's really you. Pek, you better come see who's here. You're never gonna believe it." He returned her to her feet inside the doorway. A brisk breeze sent fallen leaves whirling inside the door.

A tall woman with a long blonde braid that hung over her shoulder ambled in from the kitchen, wiping her hands on a blue striped towel. "Who is…Candle!" The woman squealed, rushing forward, and throwing her arms around her daughter. Unshed tears glistened in her eyes as she said, "It's been so long."

"I know, Momma, and I'm sorry." She wrapped one arm around her mother's waist and the other arm around her father's neck. She peeked over her father's shoulder into the warmly lit living room where a fire crackled merrily in the little hearth. *Nothing had changed since the last time I visited.* "Dad." She laughed. "The wind is scattering papers from your desk all over the floor."

Unable to take his eyes off his daughter, he tugged her and her mother inside, closing the door.

Her mother released her and tugged her toward the living room sofa. "How long are you here for? You're not leaving tomorrow, are you?" She giggled. "I had the strangest dream last night. You roared into town in a copper sports car, of all things." She shook her head as if to dispel the feelings the dream had left. "Had a feeling a big change was coming, but there was something else. I couldn't—still can't—put my finger on it." Pekabo stared off for a moment, then smiled at her daughter.

During Candle's childhood, her mother was known for her ability to tell when something was about to happen, among other things. But she'd never bought into the concept. She was far too centered in science to believe that hogwash. But she couldn't deny that a copper and black sports car had brought her to Colorado. *Then again, when the talent manifested itself in me while at the agency, I never told her. Probably need to rectify that situation.*

She took a seat on the sofa and looked from one parent to the other. "Well, probably a bit longer. In fact, I am planning on settling down here. If that's all right with you two."

"I'll get your room ready." Her mom pushed up from the chair, then spun around. "What? Here?" Pekabo Bearclaw pushed a strand of hair out of her eyes and looked over at her daughter. "Oh, you're messing with me."

"No, Mom, just sit down. I already have a place to stay, no furniture, but it should arrive in the next day or two, along with my belongings. I have an air mattress and cozy sleeping bag that will work just fine. I bought the old Hamilton place on the edge of town. Close on it tomorrow."

"We won't hear of it. You're staying here tonight. That's final. Right, Hunter?" Pekabo glanced toward her husband for confirmation. "Anyway, you'll have to make arrangements for utilities and telephone."

"The real estate woman should have taken care of that. But I have a puppy out in the car that would like to visit your backyard if that's all right with you."

"Why'd you leave it out there? Bring her on in," her mother said, starting for the door again.

"It's a gir—How'd you know?" She shrugged it off. "I figured my showing up here unannounced was enough without a puppy in tow." One of her mother's many claimed talents.

"Oh, don't be silly. Bring that puppy in here," Pek instructed.

She returned to the SUV, opened the crate, and attempted to put a pink harness on the wriggling puppy, twice, the third time being the charm, then attached the leather leash. She took Terrabyte out of the crate and set her down on the ground.

The puppy's paws crunched on the brown grass, she squatted for only a moment, then she yipped and dragged Candle across the lawn toward the house where Pekabo was waiting in the open door.

Once inside, Candle walked through the house with the puppy. As she opened the back door, a gust of wind caught the door and slammed it against the wall. Terrabyte jumped back and barked, turning circles on the floor.

She poked her head outside. Her warm breath clouded around her head as she stepped outside to walk the perimeter of the enclosed four-foot picket fence yard, checking for any holes the pup could wiggle through. Once she returned to the door and opened it, Terra raced outside into the backyard and did her business.

She tossed a small squeaky tennis ball and a stuffed red dragon out in the yard to keep Terrabyte busy. The puppy immediately pounced on the dragon's middle. It emitted grunting sounds while she grabbed the foot with her mouth, working the squeaker continually while slinging the dragon back and forth.

She returned to the living room, shaking her head. "Gonna be noisy out there for a while. Hope your neighbors don't mind."

Hunter cocked a salt-and-pepper brow and said, "The Hamilton place. Huh?" Then nodded. "Tonight, you and the puppy will stay with us. Tomorrow morning, I'll fix the blueberry pancakes you used to love so much. You still like blueberry pancakes?"

"Of course. But you don't have—" At the

determined expression on her father's face, she backpedaled a bit. "Thanks for the offer. We accept. If you don't think it's too much trouble." She looked at the clock, frowning, and turned back to her father. "Dad, I didn't expect to see you 'til later this evening. Are you all right? You never used to be home before six or seven. And you're out of uniform."

Hunter chuckled. "No trouble. A lot of things have changed in the years you've been gone. I retired last month. The town hired a new Chief of Police a couple of months back. His name is Roark, comes from Montana. I'd been training him, but now he's ready to handle it on his own, so I stepped down."

Completely dumbfounded, she could only think of one thing to say. "Why?"

He glanced at his wife and back at his daughter. "Well, because I'm getting older. Reflexes aren't as quick as they used to be. Your mother and I thought we'd do a little traveling. Maybe visit you. But as luck would have it, you came to us. Aw hell, Candle, law enforcement is a young man's profession. Especially in a small town where you do it all."

"Oh, I understand. Just surprised the town council agreed. It's been what—thirty years?"

"It was thirty-five years the end of August. They had no choice, been trying to retire for three years. Finally, I guess they decided I meant business." He chuckled and shook his head.

Wow, thirty-five years. I've been away too long. She gazed into her dad's weathered face.

"The new Chief is competent and experienced. He'll do fine. Besides, he's got Blake and Sean, the two deputies, to answer any questions that come up. Jim

Gantry is the mayor now, and Sally, head of the city council, still wants me to stick around in some type of advisory position. We'll work that out."

"You have two deputies now? It was only you when I left."

"Like I said, things change," her father said with a sigh. "Pek, how about you warm up some of that chili we had for lunch? Your daughter is just skin and bones. Needs a little meat on her."

"No, don't bother," she said, waving her hand in dismissal. "How about I take you and mom out to dinner? Where's a nice steakhouse?"

Laughing, Hunter asked, "Do you have any idea what will happen in a restaurant once the locals figure out who you are? You'll be mobbed. Besides, you don't want to leave that pup alone."

"I can put her in the crate. She'll be fine. I highly doubt I'll be mobbed. Doubt many remember me. Anyway, I'd really love a porterhouse steak, baked potato, and chocolate pie for dessert." She licked her lips.

"And we can fix all that right here. I'll just start the barbecue." Hunter shoved up from his chair.

"Oh, I don't want to put you and Mom to any trouble."

"We're not ready to share you yet, and you aren't any trouble. We gotta eat, don't we?" Pekabo said firmly, winking at her husband. "Now come on out to the kitchen. You can scrub the potatoes and wrap 'em in foil, so they're ready to pop in the oven while I make the pie." Her mom gave her another lingering hug. "We're so glad you're home."

"I'll be right there." She stepped to the back door and saw the pup happily playing with her toys. "I'm going to run out to the car and get Terra's things. She needs water after chasing her ball and the wildlife along the fence line."

"Okay, dear," Pek said. "Need any help?"

"No, I got it."

Hunter went out the garage door and came back in carrying a large half-open bag of charcoal in one hand and an electric starter in the other. "We can discuss what brought you home tomorrow," Hunter said to his daughter's back as she strode toward the front door.

"Oh, Hunter, I don't care why she came back. She'll be home for the holidays. That's all I care about." Pekabo gave his shoulder a shove. "Leave her alone."

"I care," Hunter muttered, and the back screen door banged closed behind him.

She felt her mother's eyes on her as she walked down the sidewalk to her car. When she returned to the house her mom's gaze washed over her.

"Seems like only yesterday that you skipped down that same sidewalk on your way to Gabby's house." Pekabo sighed. "Time passes so quickly these days."

She carried Terrabyte's fleece bed, wire crate, and food and water bowls inside. She filled the water bowl at the kitchen sink and walked out back onto the porch. "Terra, come get a drink." The fur ball stopped mid-bark and rushed up the stairs to the porch. She lapped up water, backed away, and plopped her front feet in the bowl, splashing water everywhere. Candle snickered. "Terra thinks she's a water dog."

The pup turned her head and caught sight of a rabbit scampering on the other side of the fence and bolted down the steps, barking wildly.

Wiping her damp hands on her jeans, she sighed,

walked back into the kitchen, and closed the door.

"Candle, wait 'til I tell you the latest." Pekabo picked through several large russet potatoes on the pantry shelf. She handed three potatoes to Candle along with the vegetable brush. "Remember that Zane boy? He was about your age, maybe a few years older."

She shook her head, turned the water on in the sink, and began scrubbing the potatoes.

"Sure you do. They lived on Ash Street a couple of blocks over. The father, I think his name was Lorell. He was disabled in some kind of hunting accident in Canada, soon after he retired from the Air Force." Pek pulled open the veggie drawer in the fridge. "They moved here so his mother could help care for him and look after the boy while his wife, her name escapes me right now, worked."

Candle's brows knitted together, considering her mother's description. "Nope, not a clue."

Pek rolled her eyes and put her hand to her mouth, silent for a moment. "I've got it. Ok, then when you were about thirteen, you and Gabby—you remember Gabby, your best friend?"

"Yes, Mom, of course." Candle turned the water off, examined the potatoes, and put them on the counter.

"Remember how you used to take the long way home, walk by the Zanes' house just to get a look at him driving home from high school?" She yanked out a bag of salad and shook it. "You said to me one day that he was the most gorgeous hunk of male you ever saw or something like that." Her mother laughed.

"Mom, I never said something like that to you. Especially about a boy at that age." She viciously poked holes in the potatoes, then tore off three sheets of aluminum foil and spread them flat on the counter. Sprinkling sea salt, butter, and bacon grease on the sheets, she then wrapped the potatoes.

"Well, maybe I overheard your conversation with Gabby," Pekabo conceded, waving a hand in dismissal, tearing open the bag of salad and pouring it into a cut-glass bowl.

Candle opened the preheated oven, avoiding the whoosh of hot air, and placed the potatoes inside. "That's more likely. You were always listening to my conversations, either on the phone extension or at my bedroom door." She giggled, studying the salad bowl. "You know that's an invasion of privacy, don't you?"

Hands on hips, Pekabo cocked her head. "Of course. How else was I to stay a step ahead of my genius daughter? For your information, miss smarty pants, a mother's right to know trumps a teenage daughter's right to privacy every time." She tossed the salad with more gusto than necessary and put the bowl in the refrigerator.

"Okay, okay, you win, Mom." She snatched the open bag of croutons off the counter and popped two in her mouth. She crunched down hard, began chewing slowly, then stopped and stared.

"Oh, God, Mom. Was he that tall boy with straight black hair and haunting blue-green eyes? His face looked like it had been sculpted by angels. He had one deep dimple on his right cheek." She felt her face flush at the memory. She'd had the worst crush on him.

Her mom burst out laughing, almost dropping the pie pan she'd retrieved from the cupboard. "That would be the one."

"You said that family was strange. Is he still here?"

"Oh, no, honey, he left shortly after you did. Joined

the Air Force or Navy. I forget now. He's a SEAL or in some kind of secret operation. I didn't say strange, just kept to themselves. That never changed."

"He's in Air Force intelligence. Not a Navy SEAL." Hunter walked in the back door. "You're not carrying tales now, are you? Pek?"

"No, of course not, just filling Candle in about the people of our fine town."

"Right. The charcoal will be ready in about twenty. Did you pull the steaks out of the freezer? Or should I?

"They're in the microwave," Pek answered. "Anyway, where was I? Oh, yeah."

"Mom, is Gabby still around?"

"Oh no, she married some big shot she met in Aspen. Jetted all over the world with him. But…" Her mother waved her hand dismissively. "It was a beautiful wedding. Too bad you missed it. Bet her mom could put you in contact."

"No, that's okay…maybe later, after I've settled in."

Hunter smiled as he carried the steaks on a platter out the door. "Glad to have you home," he called over his shoulder. "Hope you're not running from something," he whispered to himself.

"I heard that, Dad. Not running from anything." She leaned over, tugged open the oven door, and checked the potatoes. "Nearly done."

"Good to know. Steaks will be ready in fifteen minutes. Potatoes?"

"It's all handled. Everything will be ready when the steaks are." Pekabo grinned at her husband and blew him a kiss as he went out the door with a plate of steaks. "Anyway, the Zane boy's father passed away about ten years ago. Miacoh, I believe that's the Zane boy's name, was out of the country on assignment. They were able to reach him, and he made it back for the funeral but left the next day."

"Wow, must have been tough on him, not getting to even say goodbye." She shook her head.

"A couple of years later, the mom moved out of town. Rosy, Miacoh's grandmother, was still in good health and stayed in her home. She was in her late eighties then. A couple of weeks ago, she took a turn for the worse. Her daughter-in-law came back, but Rosy passed away. They couldn't reach Miacoh. He was out of the country again."

"Oh dear, he didn't make it back for the funeral?"

"No, the only choice was to have the funeral without him. It was last week. His mother looked terrible. Dark circles showed under her eyes, and her face was pale and drawn. She left town right after the reading of Rosy's will." Pekabo poured the chocolate filling into the pie shell, topped it with meringue, and slid the pie into the top oven.

"Oh, how terrible. From what I remember, he was always with his grandmother. That's going to be bad when he finds out." Candle shook her head, making a clicking sound with her tongue. "Bad."

"That's only half of it. Apparently, Rosy's estate was substantial, and she left it all to Miacoh. Word is that someone finally tracked him down. He is on his way here and should arrive in the next week or so. Last time I talked with Rosy, she was worried about him."

She tilted her head and glanced at her mom. "Guess you always worry when your child…grandchild is in the military."

"No, that wasn't what she was talking about.

Claimed he needed to be back here among his own people. Being such a loner wasn't good for him, she claimed. Never really understood what she meant by 'his own people.' Now, he's really alone." Pekabo sighed and winked at Candle.

Chapter Three

It's Said, You Can Never Go Home. What Do They Know?

Candle woke to Terrabyte whining in her crate. Opening the bedroom window, she breathed in the cool, crisp mountain air. *It was good to be home.* Her mouth watered at the aroma of freshly made blueberry pancakes wafting into her room.

The night before she'd taken a pair of fresh jeans and her favorite deep maroon sweater out of the duffel and hung them on the chair in her room along with underwear and socks. She got dressed and let Terra out of her crate. The puppy thundered down the stairs. "Didn't wait for me," she called out as she hit the landing. Terra ran for the back door.

"Sure we did. Just had to cook a trial run, been a long time since blueberry pancakes been prepared in this kitchen," her father joked, eyes sparkling as he turned a pancake over with the spatula. "Let your pup out and have a seat. Your pancake is just about ready. There are scrambled eggs in the warming dish on the table, bacon on the plate, and OJ in your glass. Do you want coffee?"

"Ohhh, it all smells so wonderful." Inhaling a deep breath, she closed her eyes for a second. "Thanks." She yanked open the door. Terra raced between her legs, nearly tripping her, then bounded out the back door.

She returned from letting the puppy out and kissed

her mom on her cheek as Pekabo carried the pitcher of orange juice to the table. Candle turned and threw an arm around her dad, kissing him too. "No, I think I'll pass on the coffee this morning."

"What's on your agenda today?" her father asked.

"Close on the cabin at nine o'clock this morning. Set up my blow-up bed, spread out the sleeping bag, and arrange Terrabyte's crate and her stuff. Then I hope like hell my belongings arrive soon. Gotta see what condition the cabin is in. I asked the real estate agent to have it cleaned, but…After that, decide what I want to do and start looking for a job. Oh, hit the grocery store as soon as I'm sure I have a working fridge. Find a vehicle too. I only have the rental a couple more days."

"Honey, if you want, we could meet over at your house with a few odds and ends of furniture we have in the garage until your furniture arrives," her mother said. "Oh, and you leave that pup here. She can play in the backyard rather than being cooped up in that little thing you keep her in."

"Mom, she likes her crate, but she'd be happier in the backyard. If you're sure it won't be any trouble, I'll fill her bowls with food, and I just gave her fresh water. That should hold her 'til I get back. As far as the furniture, I may take you up on that. I'll call after I've checked out the cabin."

"If you need funds to hold you over…" Hunter started.

"Oh no, financially, I'm good. I made great money with the agency and saved most of it. Never had much time to spend it." She gave a half-laugh. "If you know someone who'd give me a great deal on a new or slightly used SUV, I'd appreciate it. I love the color copper," she said with a grin.

"Got you covered on that. After you get settled, we'll go over to Bill's place. He still owns the Chrysler, Dodge, Jeep dealership. He'll give you a great deal, but he'll talk your ear off." Hunter chuckled.

"Okay, sounds good. Gotta go." She picked up her dishes, put them in the sink, went out in the backyard, hugged Terrabyte, then waved to her parents as she hurried out the front door.

On her way across town, she noticed a lot of things had changed. The beautiful old courthouse appeared to have gotten a facelift with a fresh coat of paint, sodded courtyard, and potted plants surrounding the building. *Nice.*

A new group of houses sprang up around the old high school, which sported several additions since she'd been here. Still, it seemed to be the cozy community she remembered. She checked her watch. She had just enough time to swing by the cabin, see what shape it was in, and if there was a working fridge. She'd arranged to have the utilities turned on yesterday. That way, she'd have heat, light, and power to install the security system she'd designed from the blueprints provided.

The SUV rolled to a stop in front of the cabin. She got out and walked up the path, then peeked in the front, side, and back windows. The backyard fence had a few cracked pickets, but for now, it looked secure enough to hold Terrabyte. Everything else was perfect. The oak floors had been sanded and sealed recently. The light sand-colored walls looked great, and a refrigerator sat in the corner of the sunny kitchen.

She jiggled the doorknob. It was locked. She chewed on her bottom lip for a moment, then slid a hand in her jeans pocket, fingers closed around a lock pick set. *Nope, I'm not going to do that.*

She returned to her vehicle and pulled up to the stop sign, waiting for a jogger to cross the street. As he crossed in front of her, she did a double take. It was Miacoh. She was positive. He was taller and more muscular than the teenager she remembered, but she'd never forgotten his chiseled face and smooth bronze skin, even with sunglasses covering his beautiful blue-green eyes. Gone was the long, straight, raven-black hair she remembered, replaced by a much shorter haircut. *I liked it long.* She chuckled to herself. *He doesn't care what I like.*

Her heart took a wild jump or two, then she stared at herself in the rearview mirror and said out loud, "What are you doing? You're not some schoolgirl crushing on an older boy. Now stop it. Men are nothing but trouble." She glanced around, making sure no one saw her talking to herself. By the time she pulled away from the stop sign onto Main Street, he was out of sight.

The parking lot in front of the credit union was almost full. She pulled into a parking place, climbed out of the SUV, and strode toward the building. She walked into the lobby. A pleasant young woman sitting in the reception area greeted her.

"Hi, I'm here for a closing on my cabin at nine o'clock." Candle grinned.

"Oh, good morning, we've been expecting you. JoDean will be right with you. There's coffee, hot water for tea, and cups in the waiting area over there. Please feel free to help yourself and have a seat."

"Thanks." She wandered over to the waiting area, poured hot water in a cup, chose an orange spice tea bag, and settled into a chair.

A tall woman with miles of black wavy hair cascading down her back rounded the corner into the waiting area. She smiled widely. "I thought that was you. There couldn't be two Candle Bearclaws in this little town. You moving back?"

She looked up from her magazine and grinned. "JoDean, how have you been?" Candle stood and extended her hand. They had gone to school together but were never close. JoDean had a reputation for making the impossible happen, without explanation. Her piercing dark eyes, olive skin, and Romani blood always made Candle uncomfortable as a teenager. She gave herself a little shake. *How stupid was that?*

"Good. And you?" JoDean motioned for Candle to follow her.

"Can't complain." Candle picked up her cup and strolled after her.

"Come on back. My office is the second door on the right. Is Delta meeting you here with the papers? You're on my schedule to close, but I don't have loan papers."

"Yes, she should be along shortly." Out of habit, she looked over the room, no family photos, or personal touches. Maybe the bank didn't allow those things. She noticed JoDean didn't wear a wedding ring, either. When they were in high school, JoDean was a stunning beauty, boys hanging on her every word. Candle assumed that she'd had her choice of boys or men and would be married with a family.

Now, well, it was none of her business. "I'll be withdrawing the purchase price from my account here, so there are no loan papers. Delta should have the bill of sale and the deed. I preferred to close the deal here, rather than take the check to the real estate office or title company," she said cheerfully.

"Sure, no problem. I can withdraw the funds, notarize the documents, and you can be on your way." JoDean waved her to a set of buff upholstered chairs across the oak desk from where the woman stood behind a rich brown leather high-back chair.

"Wonderful." She settled in the chair farthest from the door, leaving the other one for Delta.

"The cabin is a great buy, nice size for a couple, with lots of acreage to expand the home for a family." JoDean eased into the brown chair.

"Oh, there's just me. Never found anyone willing to put up with me, or had the time to devote to a relationship." She shrugged.

"I know exactly what you mean. But my mom, she kept setting me up with her friends' sons." JoDean laughed and shook her head. "When she finally decided I wasn't in any hurry to marry, she even went so far as to tell me that professional women were having children and raising them on their own. I think she wanted grandbabies more than she wanted me married off. That was the way of her generation. You were only a success when you were married to a rich guy and raising a family."

"Apparently Gabby got the memo. Or so Mom told me." Candle chuckled.

JoDean's voice dropped off, and sadness crossed her dark eyes for a moment, then was gone. "Listen to me, haven't seen you for years, and I prattle on. I'm sure you went through the same thing. What brings you back here?"

"Not really. I didn't see Mom and Dad often. It was

easier that way with my job. It was time for a change, so I left the agency and wanted to settle in a small town. This one fit the bill. Your mom still setting you up?"

"No. Mom passed away two years ago, tomorrow. Cancer."

"Oh, I'm sorry, I didn't know."

"Thanks. I still miss her, but life goes on." JoDean glanced toward the doorway where heels clicking on the hallway's tile floor came closer. JoDean stood.

Candle turned around in her chair just as a heavy-set woman with platinum-blonde hair cut short and a round face breezed through the doorway. "Speak of the devil. Hi Delta." Candle's lips upturned in a mischievous grin.

"You all weren't talking about me, were you?" The real estate agent flashed a friendly smile, and a hint of southern drawl remained though she'd been in Colorado for years. Dressed in black slacks and a royal blue sweater with a black jacket thrown over her arm, she put her briefcase down next to the empty chair, shook JoDean's extended hand, hugged Candle, then eased into a buff-colored chair. "Good morning, everyone." Delta smiled brightly. "It's so good to see you, Candle. Is everything set?"

"It is if the fridge in the cabin works."

"Of course, it works. It's an older model but works well. I checked on it yesterday." Delta picked up her briefcase, set it on the desk, and pulled out a stack of papers.

After Candle looked over the paperwork, she nodded to JoDean. "Go ahead and withdraw the funds in the form of a cashier's check. The documents are all in order." She signed the documents and requested copies of everything. Delta handed her the house keys.

Candle slipped the paperwork into her backpack. "It was nice doing business with you." She grinned at the women and started for the door.

"Hey, how about we get together sometime?" JoDean asked.

"After I get settled and the cabin set up, I'll give you a call."

"I'll hold you to it," JoDean said good-naturedly.

"Do you want me to accompany you to the cabin?" Delta raised a brow inquiringly.

"Nope, I've already checked it out. If there is a problem, I'll call you." She strode out the doors of the credit union. She called her mom to check on Terra and then drove straight to her cabin.

A moving truck pulled up in front of the cabin as she arrived. Breathing a sigh of relief, she exited the SUV.

"Good morning, guys. I'll unlock the front door and let you get to work."

An hour and a half later, the movers pulled the roll door down on the truck and drove away. She perched on the edge of a recliner arranging the components and wiring to her security system on the oak coffee table in front of her, then studied the blueprints she'd marked up.

A few hours later, her stomach rumbled as someone knocked on the door. Extra wiring and parts were scattered all over the floor. She had to pick her way carefully to the door so as not to damage anything. When she opened the door, her mother stood smiling with a few bags of groceries in her hands, and her father had several more.

"Well, can we come in, or are you going to leave us standing here with all this stuff?" Her father jerked his chin toward the inside of the cabin.

"Oh, sorry, come on in. Be careful where you walk. I'm kinda in the middle of something." She grimaced, pushing the door open wider. "Did you bring Terra with you?"

Her father glanced at the floor, set the bags down, and reached for Pek's arm. "I think you need to clear a path before your mother and I try to navigate this minefield. Yes, she's in her crate in the car."

She laughed and turned around, surveying the floor. "Good idea." She grabbed a large box with plastic bubble wrap inside and picked up the pieces of electronics, placing them carefully in a box, making a narrow path through the living room to the kitchen. Returning to her parents in the doorway, she stopped, put the box on the floor, and took a couple of bags from her mom. "Follow me." She led them into the kitchen, put the bags on the counter motioning her father to do the same.

"Some of these items need refrigeration." Her father jerked his chin at the fridge. "It works, right?"

"Yes. Give me a minute. I'm going to run out and get Terra, then check that backyard fence again." Candle hurried out the front door.

"Candle, bring that pup around back. I'll meet you there. I'll watch her and check the fence while you put the groceries away. Probably better get the floor completely cleared, or you'll have teeth marks in your components. Fair enough?" Hunter called after his daughter.

"Sure, Dad." She opened the crate door. Terra bounded into her waiting arms. She hooked the leash to the pup's collar and lowered her to the ground, then walked her around the house to the backyard, handing the leash to her dad. "Make sure she can't get out anywhere before you unleash her. She looks a lot bigger than she is underneath all that fur."

"Do you think I've never cared for a pup?" her dad shot back.

"Well—I wasn't sure."

"I've got this."

Once the groceries were put away, the floor cleared, and the backyard puppy-proofed, she glanced from her mom to her dad. "What would you have done if the fridge here didn't work?"

"Oh, we saw Delta at the post office. She said the refrigerator worked well but warned us that the stove was cantankerous."

"She did? That's okay because I have my own stove." She waved her hand in the direction of the stainless-steel range with a black ceramic top and double oven. "I moved the one that came with the cabin out back. I'll replace the fridge soon, but this will do for now. Don't you think?"

Pek nodded and looked around the kitchen. "You sure got things arranged quickly."

"The moving company's contract required them to put everything away." Candle leaned back against the counter. "They did a good job, though I didn't have very much." She shrugged one shoulder. "Never was home enough and lived in a partially furnished apartment."

Hunter wandered over to where his daughter left the box in a chair out of Terra's reach. He leaned over and picked up what looked like a control panel. "Need some help finishing this up?" He eyed the wiring sticking out of the wall a couple of feet from the door.

"Thanks, but I'm almost finished Let me get that control module wired in, and we can check the circuits to make sure everything works." She picked up the screwdriver and wire crimper, finished the installation, then punched in a code. A quiet beep sounded. She walked over to her computer, tapped on the keys, and the room they were standing in appeared on her computer screen. She switched views from inside to outside. When satisfied they all worked properly, she made some final adjustments. "That's it. The system is up and running."

Her father looked over her shoulder and then around the room. "There must be surveillance cams in here, but I don't see them."

"They're tiny wireless remotes. I put them in the corners up by the ceiling where they would be less conspicuous yet cover the room."

"So, the system is wireless?" Her father nodded approval.

"Yes, except the main control panel down here and a few other things."

"One thing that hasn't changed around here is there is still no serious crime. So why would you—"

"Dad don't worry about it. I sleep better with a security system. Comes from living too long in big cities and—" Her heart pounded. She wiped her sweaty hands on the sides of her jeans as her last assignment came to mind. She closed her eyes and gave her head a little shake. That part of her life was over.

"Hey, Mom, when did you say Miacoh was due back in town?"

"I didn't. He's expected in the next week or so. Why?" Pek narrowed her eyes at her daughter, then laughed. "You interested?"

She blew out a breath and shook her head. "No, I just thought I saw him jogging this morning on my way to the credit union. Probably mistaken."

Hunter sent his wife a warning glance. "Just so you know, your mother and I are going out of town for a few days with friends. We planned the trip before you arrived."

"Oh, Hunter, I thought we could call and cancel since Candle is back."

"Don't be silly, Mom. You and Dad go ahead. I'm not going anywhere. As long as we are on the subject. I came back to Aspen Ridge because I liked the small-town atmosphere. The fact you and Dad are here is an added bonus. Please don't change your way of life or schedule for me."

Hunter smiled. "Nuff said. See ya in a few days." He paused and waggled a finger at her. "Oh, stop by Bill's. He's got a copper SUV on the lot you may be interested in. Low mileage, loaded, one owner, and he said he'd give you a whale of a deal." Hunter winked at his daughter. "Keep in mind he probably can't get rid of it because it's copper rather than dark."

"Will do. I'll drop in tomorrow morning."

Pek suddenly snapped her fingers. "Oh dear, I almost forgot. I brought a cheddar chicken casserole with potato salad for supper tonight and chocolate cake for dessert. You interested?"

"Of course."

"Good. I'll just run out to the car and get the fixings. Start the oven, so we can warm it up a bit. The microwave dries the cheese out too much. I also have paper plates and plastic ware," Pek called over her shoulder as she flew through the front door and across the lawn to her car.

She looked at her dad and said with a cheeky smile,

"Well, I have paper towels for napkins."

Hunter chuckled, then the smile faded. "Candle, why the sudden career change? Did something happen?"

"No, just time to move on," she said in a tone that discouraged any further discussion.

"Good to know." He frowned, letting her know he still wasn't convinced.

Chapter Four

A Figment of Her Imagination, He was Not!

Candle awoke to sunlight streaming through the window bouncing off the crystals she'd hung there last night. Rainbows spun around the room giving the desired effect. She lay still for a moment listening to the rustling leaves outside and the whining, panting puppy at the side of her bed. *It's going to be a fine day.* She reached down and petted the pup.

"I know you have to go, Terrabyte. You were such a good girl to sleep all night. Give me a minute to get dressed, check the backyard, and you can romp outside for a bit." Candle pulled on a pair of black leggings and layered a burgundy zip sweatshirt over a pale pink T-shirt. Then she slid her feet into running shoes and hurried to the back door. The last thing she needed was to clean up a puddle that was her fault.

At four months, it had been a long while since Terra had an accident, Chows were easy to potty train and that was a Godsend since they'd spent their first month together in the car or hotel. It was a good thing Terra liked her kennel, and being a puppy slept quite a bit when Candle had to leave her alone for a few hours during their cross-country trip.

"Come on, girl, you can help me check the yard." She snapped the leash on Terra's harness and sprinted outside. Barely out of the door, Terra squatted. "Good girl." She reached down and patted the pup. "Almost didn't make it, huh? I need to do better." The rest of the yard was secure. She unsnapped the leash and returned to the house, poking around in the kitchen cupboards for something to eat.

The new kettle her mother had bought still sat on the stove. That was a good idea. She'd boil water and fix a cup of French vanilla tea. It was time to wean herself off coffee, a habit that keep her up for days on end while hacking into criminal computer networks in her undercover work.

The stress of trying to appear calm, being someone she wasn't, and the overload of caffeine had left her jittery most of the months prior to her resignation. Now, the craving for caffeine still left her a bit tired, but it was getting better, her nerves were steady, and she was herself, which pleased her to no end.

Terra barked at the back door to be let in. "Gonna have to get you a doggy door." She opened the door and let the bouncing pup in. Terra raced through the kitchen, slid around the corner into the living room, sped into the bedroom, and jumped onto the bed. Lowering her front and sticking her butt in the air, she barked for Candle to come play.

"You need to burn off more of that energy." It took a moment for her to clip the leash onto the wriggling, bouncing puppy, but finally accomplished the task. "Let's see how you do on a three-mile walk around town?" She tore open a bag of puppy treats, stuffed them in her pocket, grabbed her house keys, and flew out the door, puppy in tow.

She jogged for a couple of blocks then slowed to a

power walk, easier on her joints all around. It's said, timing is everything, or not. She glanced down to check on Terrabyte. When she looked back up, she had to make a quick course correction to avoid smacking directly into Miacoh Zane. He zigged smoothly without missing a beat and continued on.

After awkwardly trying to sidestep him, one foot landed on the curb and the other on the street throwing her off balance, she landed on her ass, arms flailing. But she held on to the leash. Terra jumped into her lap and covered her face with puppy kisses then backed away and barked bowing in the play bow position. She felt her face heat up as Miacoh slowed and turned jogging back to her.

"You okay?" He reached down, grasped her forearm, and lifted her to her feet with little effort. Terra bounced circles around them barking and nipping at his shoes.

"I'm fine. Thank you." She brushed the crisp leaves from her leggings and bottom, then in a soft but commanding voice said, "Terrabyte off, leave it."

Miacoh raised an eyebrow and stared from her to the puppy.

Terra stopped in her tracks, looked from her to Miacoh then back to her. Terra's butt hit the ground but stayed only for a couple of seconds. The puppy jumped to the end of the leash and tugged. "Oh, no," Candle gasped, spinning around and almost losing her balance again.

Miacoh caught her arm to steady her. By this time, she could feel her face was flushed from her neck to the tips of her ears.

"I'm so sorry. Terrabyte is just a bit wild from being

cooped up overnight I guess." She deftly removed her arm from his hold.

"That's quite all right. Cute puppy. You called her Terrabyte?" His mouth turned up at the corners in a boyish grin. "You named your dog after computer memory?"

"Well, it's different and she likes it," she said putting her hands on her hips.

As if he couldn't control it, he roared with laughter, then choking back the laughter, he snapped his fingers. "It's Candle, Candle Bearclaw, isn't it?"

"Why yes, it is, Miacoh. It's been a long time." She drew herself up to her full almost six feet. "And just what is so funny?"

Subduing his mirth, he bent over at the waist, drew in a breath then stood staring down at her. "I heard that you were accepted into MIT, a computer science major, then recruited by a government agency and turned hacker. But I didn't believe it. The little girl that wore herself and her friend out walking miles back and forth in front of my family's house." This time he kept a straight face. "Grew up and named her dog Terrabyte. I guess that would mean it's all true. One of the world's best hackers?"

"So, they say," she retorted while trying to tamp down her temper. "Thank you for your assistance. We'll just be on our way now that we've entertained you." As the words came out of her mouth, she regretted them and sighed. "Please, I didn't mean to be so snide. I heard about your father and grandmother. I am sorry for your loss."

"Thank you," he said stiffly.

"Are you living in your grandmother's house?"

"Yes and no. I'm staying there only long enough to settle the estate, sell the house, and move on," he said firmly.

"Are you on leave then? I heard that you joined the military, special forces?"

He shook his head and drew his bottom lip through his teeth. "Boy, word travels fast in this little town. I've been back less than forty-eight hours."

"Same here, but I didn't know I was the talk of the town. I bought the old Hamilton place and plan to settle here."

He raised an eyebrow questioningly. "And give up the glamorous world of espionage?"

She rolled her eyes and huffed out a breath. "Oh, it's anything but, and yes, I resigned, tired of looking over my shoulder, dreading the next assignment, playing the next role. I want a nice quiet life."

"I hear that, but there are too many memories here for me to stay. I left the military after my last assignment. Gonna give the private sector a try."

"Where's your mom? I heard…" She stopped midsentence. "I mean, will she be returning?"

"I don't know. She left before I got here. We never really saw eye to eye when I was younger. Now, well, I guess her message was strong enough."

Uncomfortable with the sadness and pain crossing his face, she said, "Well, I guess Terrabyte—" she paused for a moment then smiled, "—and I have detained you long enough from your run. Maybe we could grab a cup of coffee, tea, or a bite to eat before you leave and finish catching up."

"Yeah, sounds good." He stretched his legs and leaned from side to side before starting off again.

Glancing sideways at her, he smiled again.

"What?" she asked. The look in his eyes was more than remembering the adolescent girl on the sidewalk in front of his family home so long ago. He was looking her up and down as if she was...

He smiled. "Look different than I remember. That's all."

She watched his muscles flex, mesmerized by him as if she was that seventh grader again. Terra yanked on the leash snapping her out of her fog. "Hey, how do I get a hold of you?" she asked.

"I'll find you," he called over his shoulder, giving her one more backward glance before he jogged down the street and turned the corner.

Continuing their walk, she stopped to talk to people she hadn't seen for years while they raked their lawns, washed cars, or just stood soaking in the warm sunshine. Soon the snow would fly, and ski season would begin.

****

Candle was sitting at her kitchen table, contemplating what to do next, when her cell phone buzzed. She looked at the unfamiliar number and slid the lock bar across. "Hello?"

"Candle, it's Bill, I was just wondering if you were going to stop by and check out the SUV I have on the lot. Your father said you might be interested."

"Oh, shit, I'm sorry, I forgot. I'm on my way. Thanks for the call." She rushed out the back door, scooped up Terra, put her in her crate, made sure the pup had food and water, and closed and locked the door. "I'll be back soon."

She set the alarm, ran out the front door, and jumped into the rented SUV. Gunning the engine, she peeled away from the curb. After driving only a few blocks, she glanced in her rearview mirror and saw the red and blue lights. She stared down at her speedometer. "Shit."

She pounded on the steering wheel, pulled to the curb, and took her cell phone out of her pocket, and hit the redial button. When Bill answered, she said, "I'm going to be a bit late." Quickly she disconnected the call and pulled her driver's license and registration out of the glove compartment. She rolled down the window and smiled.

"In a bit of a hurry?" the young deputy asked with a smile, reaching for the documents she held out for him. Color rose in his face as he looked at the license. "Are you Hunter's daughter?"

"None other," she said flippantly before she thought. Again. With a quick change of attitude, she said, "I'm sorry, officer—" She looked at his shirt and noticed the name tag. "—Officer Blake, I wasn't paying attention to my speed. I forgot an appointment, and well, you don't care about that." She grimaced more than smiled at him and sat silently.

"Miss Bearclaw, Chief...uh...I mean Hunter would have my head if I ticketed his daughter on her first day or two here."

"Aww, come on, he'd have your head if you didn't." She laid her head on the steering wheel, wishing the world would simply swallow her up.

The young officer took the insurance and driver's license to the cruiser. After ten minutes of back-and-forth conversation over the radio, he returned. He handed her license and proof of insurance back. "Have a good day and watch your speed. This is a warning." He nodded his head and walked back to the police cruiser.

Ohh…she was going to hear about this probably sooner than later. She tucked the proof of insurance back in the glove box and her license in her wallet, signaled, and slowly pulled away from the curb.

Turning right into the parking lot of Bill's dealership, she parked in front of the showroom door where a copper SUV, freshly washed, shone in the sunshine. She got out of the rental vehicle, walked up to the parked SUV, and looked in the windows. She tried the doors, but they were locked. A beanpole of a man came rushing out. "I'm sorry that vehicle is on hold, could I interest you in one of another color?"

"Not right now. Is Bill around?" She craned her neck as she scanned the parking lot.

"Sure, he's in the office."

"Thanks." She walked by the salesman and into the showroom.

"Well, there she is, all grown up." A man with a receding hairline, middle-aged paunch gone wild, and bright blue eyes strode toward her.

She rolled her eyes and wondered just how many times she would have to endure these types of comments. "Glad to be back." But wanting more and more to get back to her cabin and be left alone. Sighing, she smiled wide. "Bill, I'd know you anywhere. How's Jeanie?"

"Oh, doing well. We are getting ready for a trip to Hawaii for our 45th wedding anniversary. Never been, you know."

"You'll love it." She surveyed the showroom.

"Let me introduce you around. Most of these people knew you long before you left."

"Maybe some other time, Bill. Right now, I'd like to take a look at the vehicle you called my dad about."

Shifting, she peered out the window to the copper SUV.

"Didn't you see it? Parked it right in front of the showroom doors." He whipped his head around as if checking to see if it was still there.

"I did take a quick look at that one, but your salesman indicated it was on hold."

"Yep, for you. Let's get a better look and take her for a test drive." He pulled a set of keys from his pocket and gestured for her to walk ahead of him toward the front exit doors. "It's sat on the lot for better'n a year, special ordered, then the customer's financing fell through. Do you need financing?" Bill's forehead creased, and he squinted his eyes against the sun's glare as he opened the door for her. He slipped his sunglasses down off the top of his head and over his eyes.

"No. The deal will be cash. I get a big discount for that, right?"

"Uh, yes, but even at that, it's pretty pricey." He pushed the key fob, then tossed the keys over the car to her. "We'll talk terms when you return."

She caught the keys with her left hand as she opened the car door with her right. "You're not riding along?"

"No, I have way too much paperwork. It's the end of the month. Just come back to my office if the car works for you, and we'll hammer out the details."

The vehicle more than worked for her. It was loaded with nav and state-of-the-art sound system, push-button folding rear seats, and a rearview camera. The heated seats would be nice with winter coming on, she'd never had that particular option, and the electronic seats were a nice touch. The SUV drove like a dream.

Returning to the dealership, she closed the deal and made arrangements with the car rental company to leave her rental with their satellite office inside Bill's dealership. She drove her new vehicle home. She'd planned to check on the sports car when she returned the rental, but she'd take Terra for a ride to Aspen in the new-to-her SUV tomorrow. They could check on it then.

When Candle unlocked the cabin door and opened it, Terra was all wiggles standing at the front door. "How did you get out of your crate?" She glanced around the room, followed Terra to the back door, and let her out. Terra had chewed a couple of boxes to pieces, but there didn't seem to be any other damage and no accidents.

She checked the door on the crate and nothing seemed amiss. "I'll have to make sure the latch is secure after this," Candle mused. Her cell phone vibrated in her pocket. She yanked it out and had two messages waiting. That was strange, she hadn't heard it ring.

Chapter Five

Halloween and Harvest Preparations—Ready in Time?

The first message was from her mom and dad. They'd be gone a week longer than anticipated but would be back for the Halloween festivities. She touched the screen to play the second message.

"Hi there, Candle, bet you didn't expect to hear from me." There was a breathy laugh, and the message continued. "Heard you're back, oh, you know gossip travels fast in our little town. I've kept the Halloween tradition alive even though you left without a word and never, ok, hardly ever visited or called. So—anyway, I need you to call me back to make arrangements for the Halloween Masquerade Ball in the town hall. Bet you thought you got out of that. No way. It'll be so much fun, just like the old days. Call me." She laughed again, left her number, and ended the message.

Smiling, Candle shook her head. It was good to hear from Gabby. They had a lot of catching up to do. She regretted missing Gabby's wedding but had been on assignment out of the country and didn't get the message or invite until it was over.

She tapped the number into her address book, then touched the phone icon. The phone barely rang once, and Gabby squealed into the phone, "Candle, is it really you?"

"Yes, Gabby, it's really me. I'm so glad you called. Mom said you travel the world with your rich husband. How do you have time to organize, let alone attend the Halloween Ball?" She waved her hands as if talking to someone standing in front of her rather than on the phone.

"A girl has to have her priorities. Besides, I have nothing but time. Ben travels all over the world for business. I used to go with him, but after the kids were born, we made Atlanta our home base. I stay there with the kids, and he comes home as often as possible, which hasn't been much.

"During the summer and school breaks, we used to travel with him. But that will change, the kids are getting to the age they want to spend vacations at home with their friends. Enough about me. Are you back in Aspen Ridge to stay? How can you just leave the glamorous world of a spy?"

"Girl, you've been watching too many James Bond movies." She giggled as she walked to the door to let Terrabyte in. "It's not all it's cracked up to be. But I did get to see the world on their dime. But it was time for a change."

"That's it—Time for a change? That's all you're going to tell me? What about the sexy men in your life? What about clandestine meetings, covert operations, hacking foreign governments?"

"If I told you, I'd have to kill you." There was a long pause on the line. Candle laughed then said, "Only kidding, Gabby. There just isn't anything to tell. I lived the job 24/7, no time for personal life, and the people I worked with, well let's just say, I wasn't interested."

"What about that Zane guy? I heard you ran into him this morning, literally. You going to take up where you left off?"

She felt her face growing hot at just the thought of the incident this morning. "How the hell did you hear about that? Take off where we left off, Gabby we were in seventh grade. I have no intention of walking or standing in front of his house." She giggled. "He didn't know we existed."

"Oh, he knows you exist now," she chirped. "I talked to Mom this morning, and she just happened to drive by you and Zane."

Candle sighed. "Yeah, I'm home less than seventy-two hours, and I've already embarrassed myself. Now let's get back to Halloween. I'll be happy to help. When will you be here?"

"The kids have two weeks off end of October, so we'll be out around the 20th. I've already ordered the decorations and should arrive by the time we get there. The theme this year is Vampires, Werewolves, and Witches Oh My! Would you be interested in being head of the pumpkin carving committee?"

"You have a committee to carve pumpkins?"

"Sure, we are going to have them all over this year. The lights inside are battery-operated, so no fire hazard. I remember your jack-o-lanterns were always the best. I still have a picture of the huge pumpkin you carved out and put little tombstones inside with the names of the City Council on them."

Terra grabbed her squeaky ball and proceeded to run circles around Candle while squeaking her ball. She could barely hear Gabby.

"What the heck is that noise? You don't have any

kids, do you?"

"No, but I do have a puppy." She took the ball out of Terra's mouth and threw it across the room. "Okay. We got a couple of weeks. I gotta go and siphon off some of Terra's energy. Good to hear from you. Talk to you soon." She disconnected the call. Gabby could always talk a blue streak, and apparently, that hadn't changed.

The days grew shorter and colder. Planning for the Halloween Ball took up a lot of her time. Gabby's little girl came down with the flu, so their arrival was delayed. Delta and JoDean coordinated the caterers and created the flyers and posters. She hadn't heard from Miacoh since their unfortunate run-in but heard from others he was still in town. Gabby and her family arrived a week before Halloween relieving Candle so she could concentrate on getting thirty pumpkins carved.

How did I let myself get talked into this? She sat cross-legged in front of the roaring fire in her hearth, carving the tenth pumpkin of the day when someone knocked on the door. Terra ran to the door barking as she got up off the floor, stretched out her legs as one had fallen asleep, and limped to the door. "Leave it, Terra, now sit."

She looked out the side window before opening the door. Her heart skipped a beat as she saw Miacoh standing on the porch at her front door dressed in jeans, a royal blue sweater layered over a light blue shirt, which accented his big blue-green eyes.

She looked down at her pumpkin-stained sweatshirt, sweatpants, and worn-out tennis shoes. When she brushed strands of hair off her face that had come loose from her ponytail, her fingers came away with pumpkin guts.

How did I get that goo in my hair too? She shook her head. *Will I never be presentable when Miacoh appears?* She pushed such thoughts from her mind and opened the door. "Hi, Miacoh, what brings you out here this evening?"

A wicked grin curved one corner of his lips for a moment then disappeared. "Gabby said you needed some help carving the pumpkins, so I thought I'd drop by and help out." He looked past her to the pile of pumpkins in the center of the living room floor. "I think that was an understatement." He chuckled looking her over from head to toe. "Who's winning? From here it looks like the pumpkins."

Opening the door wide, she invited him in. With a sheepish grin, she said, "Yeah, you could say that. Mom and Dad are supposed to stop by later to help me too. But I appreciate your offer." She led him into the kitchen, where she handed him a carving knife and newspaper. "You can spread the newspaper out on the floor and pick your pumpkins."

He glanced at the pumpkins already carved, sitting around the room. "Did you carve all these? They are quite unique." He leaned over to get a closer look at one with a skull carved in profile. "These are great. I fear mine will pale in comparison. I only cut triangle eyes and nose with a toothy grin."

"That works for me. At this point, I don't care if I ever see another pumpkin in my entire life." She paused and reconsidered. "At least until next Halloween."

"If I remember correctly, you always had a thing for Halloween." His lips twitched, and finally, one corner turned up in a lopsided grin as his dimple made an appearance.

She turned her gaze from carving the pumpkin and stared at him. "How would you know that?"

"I think everyone in town knew that. I still remember the one you carved and put gravestones in it with the city council members' names on them. Won first place in the contest, didn't it?"

"Oh geez, everyone seems to remember that one. Come to think of it, that was one of my best." She smiled up at him appreciatively and then returned to carving the pumpkin.

He leaned down, spread the newspapers over the floor, picked a pumpkin from the pile, and settled onto the floor, just as someone else knocked on the door.

Terra raced in through the newly installed doggy door, over the newspapers, pumpkin guts flying, and skidded to a stop in front of the front door, barking and her tail wagging furiously.

"That must be Mom and Dad." Candle shoved up from the floor. She walked to the door and looked down at the puppy, pumpkin seeds and guts stuck to her fur. "Leave it. Sit, Terra." The puppy's butt hit the floor as she opened the door. "Hi, guys, come on in and join the fun." She reached up and hugged them both. "How was your trip?"

"Wonderful, perfect weather and good company," her mom said. "I wasn't ready to come back, but he didn't want to miss the Halloween Ball." Pek winked at her husband.

Her dad reached down and picked up Terra, gave her a quick rub, picked the seeds out of her fur, then put her back on the floor. Glancing around the room, he said, "Looks like you've been busy. Terra been helping you?" Then he looked over at Miacoh rising from the floor.

"Hope we aren't interrupting anything."

"No, sir." Miacoh stepped to her father and extended his hand to grasp her dad's. "Nice to see you again, sir."

"Cut the sir, son, it's Hunter, been a long time since I've seen you. You've filled out a bit." Hunter smiled, slapped Miacoh on the shoulder, and turned back to her.

"Oh, Dad, not interrupting at all. Give me your coats and pick out a pumpkin. I'll get the newspapers and knives and bring them in."

"Don't bother. We aren't going to sit on the floor and carve pumpkins when there is a perfectly good table in there." He looked through the arched doorway into the kitchen.

Her mom set the crock pot on the counter, took the newspapers from Candle, and spread them over the table. "This is much easier for us." She grinned and then nodded toward the stove. "I brought over a pot of chili. Needs a little warming up. Do you have crackers around here?"

"Sure do, in the corner cupboard. But I'd like to get a few more pumpkins down before we eat. Okay? A couple of my committee members bailed at the last moment, and I need to get all these carved and over to town hall by tomorrow. The ball is tomorrow night, you know."

"We're aware. Your father and I look forward to it every year. This year you'll be attending, won't you?" Pek looked over at Miacoh and back to Candle.

Miacoh raised both hands, palms out in surrender. "Hey, don't put me in the middle of this. I got roped into carving pumpkins because I was walking by the town hall and stopped to see what was going on."

"Mom, I haven't decided, but I imagine that if

Gabby has anything to do with it, I'll be there."

Looking thoughtful for a moment, Miacoh returned to the floor and continued carving his pumpkin, ignoring any other glances his way.

"Ok, let's get back to carving. Once we're done, Miacoh, can you help me load the carved ones in my SUV for delivery tomorrow?" Hands on hips, she surveyed the progress so far.

The room was full of pumpkins carved into bats, witches' hats, scarecrows, football helmets, the Bronco's horse head, vampire faces, and normal pumpkin faces with toothy grins. The pile of uncarved pumpkins on the floor grew smaller and smaller.

"I'll do one better than that," Miacoh said with a sly wink. "Let's load them in the bed of my truck. I'll deliver them on my way home tonight. Gabby said they'd be there 'til midnight."

"Good enough."

After carving the last pumpkin, everyone pitched in to load the pumpkins in his pickup while Pekabo set the table and dished out the chili.

"Nice truck." Candle closed the tailgate and strolled back to the house.

"Yeah, I bought it when I returned stateside and left the service. Figured I would settle the estate, buy a fifth wheel, then ramble around for a while."

"Not staying here?" Hunter asked a surprised note in his voice.

"Naw, nothing here for me but painful memories." He cleared his throat and swallowed hard. "Present company excepted. I'll put Gram's house up for sale and let the real estate agent handle it until we have a buyer." He grasped the handle on the screen door and held it open for Candle and her father.

Seated around the kitchen table, Miacoh asked, "Candle, what are your plans, now that you've left the agency?" He slipped a spoonful of chili into his mouth.

"I plan to start up a cyber security business based in Aspen Ridge. Gear it toward local residential and small businesses, get the business on its feet, then expand. Maybe get a few government contracts—that kind of thing." She snickered, crumbling crackers into her chili. "Call it Terrabyte Cyber."

All eyes turned to the fur ball pouncing on the squeaky toy in the living area. Pekabo blew on a spoon of chili and glanced at Candle. "After the pup?"

"Nope, the idea and name came to fruition before I turned in my resignation. On a whim, I named the pup, Terrabyte. Thought it was cute—like her." Smiling at the pup scampering to her with a toy in her mouth, Candle shook her head and pointed back to the living area. "Not until we're done."

Terra barked sharply, shook the toy, and trotted across the room, looking back twice, a disgruntled expression on her little face.

After dinner, Candle gathered the dishes, put them in the sink, ran water, and squirted dish soap. "I'll leave them to soak."

"We gotta get going. Gabby roped us into helping her set up in the morning." Hunter chuckled. "She's so excited you're here to help." He shook his head. "You two were always double trouble."

Candle walked them to the door. "See you tomorrow." She turned and nearly bumped into Miacoh.

"I better head out too. Want to drop off the pumpkins before I go home. Thanks for dinner."

"It's the least that I can do after all your help. Besides, Mom brought the dinner."

He pushed the door open and hesitated for a beat blocking the door as Terrabyte barreled toward them. She bent sweeping the pup up in her arms and straightened, her gaze meeting Miacoh's. He leaned over and brushed his lips gently over hers. Heart thundering, she backed away.

"Sorry, couldn't help myself." He caressed her cheek and walked down the path to his truck.

The butterflies in her stomach did a double rotation as she admired the man. God, he was one sexy package.

A tree branch cracked, breaking the silence. Miacoh hesitated and turned.

She stood on the porch and waved.

Chapter Six

Halloween Ball

Her cell's cheerful ringtone split the silence at half-past five on Friday morning. Candle rolled over, bleary-eyed, focused on the clock first, then located the phone. She reached across the nightstand and grabbed at the phone, shoving it off the back of the nightstand. "Shit." Crawling out of bed, she leaned over the stand and reached for the phone, nearly knocking off the charging station and clock in the process.

"Hello," she said in an irritated voice.

"Well, aren't you the cheerful one," Gabby said in a chipper voice. "I wanted to make sure you had a costume for the party tonight and that you were planning on coming. I asked Miacoh, and he indicated you weren't sure. He definitely won't be going. He mumbled something about only being in town until he got the family home sold and the estate settled.

"Okay, what are you talking about? I caught costume and party, but…Gabby, I'm not even awake. Do you know what time it is?"

"Of course, it's almost six in the morning. Oh gawd, I forgot, you're not a morning person. I thought maybe after all these years you'd come to your senses." Gabby snicked into the phone.

"Hell no, I'm still allergic to mornings, and now

you've woke up Terrabyte and she has to go outside right now. So let me call you back at a more decent hour." She swung her feet onto the floor, grabbed a robe, slippers, and headed for the kitchen, phone to her ear.

"Hey, hold on. I need you to meet me at city hall this morning, we didn't quite get done last night. We still have a few things to do and test all the lights that go in the pumpkins. Please," Gabby wheedled.

"Okay, I gotta let the dog out, and I'll get back to you." This time Candle touched the screen without hesitation ending the call and slid the phone onto the kitchen counter as she peeked out the window to check the backyard. Nothing was lurking in the yard, so she unlocked the dog door, and Terra raced out to the middle of the yard and squatted.

Candle warmed up milk in the microwave and got a hot chocolate packet from the cupboard. She stopped and touched a finger to her lips, remembering the kiss from last night. A delicious warmth curled around her chest and teased the knot forming in her stomach. *This is ridiculous.*

Shaking off the feeling, she fed the puppy and set up baby gates to keep her contained with access to the dog door since it was apparent that she would be at city hall all day. Sipping the hot chocolate, she walked upstairs, searching for the vampire costume and custom-made fangs she'd worn last year.

The garment bag hung in the back of the closet with a giant Halloween pumpkin painted on it. She unzipped it and found the slinky black full-length dress split to her thigh, black over-the-knee boots, and long black velvet cape with red silk lining to be in perfect shape.

Opening her jewelry box, she checked for the fangs,

the black velvet choker with bite marks, and red crystals hanging from delicate silver chains. Everything was there. Gulping down the rest of her hot chocolate, she set the mug on the dresser while she pulled on jeans and a sweatshirt and shoved her feet into running shoes. *No exercise today, at least not the intentional kind.*

A quick decision had her turning into a fast-food place for a breakfast sandwich and orange juice. Taking the only parking place in front of city hall, she smiled wickedly and opened the vehicle door. When she exited the vehicle, Gabby was waiting on the steps to the building, her arms crossed as strands of her long red hair blew across her face in the wind. She tucked the wayward strands back in her braid as Candle climbed the stairs. A pumpkin resided on the end of alternating stairs where Gabby stood.

"You didn't call me back," Gabby said in the hurt voice she'd used as a child.

She stopped next to Gabby and bumped her hip against her best friend's. "I figured in person would be better than a phone call." She raised her arms halfway and let them drop to her sides.

Gabby reached for Candle and hugged her. "I've missed you."

"Me too. Now, where are the lights and batteries?" She popped the last bite of her breakfast sandwich in her mouth. Crumpling up the wrapping, she dropped it in the trash and finished the last sip of orange juice, taking aim and tossing it in the wastebasket too.

Gabby smiled and patted her on the back. "You were never one to show emotions. Follow me." With a sigh, Gabby turned on her heel and hurried into city hall.

A haunted castle greeted her in the space previously

occupied by city hall. Carved pumpkins adorned every table, corner, nook, and cranny. A few jack-o-lanterns hung from the ceiling with clear wires on either side of the door, and a couple of pumpkins adorned the long table set to the left of the stage. Spider webs were everywhere, from the corners and down table legs to the floor.

"Geez, you got enough pumpkins?" She surveyed her work on them.

"Oh, wait 'til you see them all lit up with the lights dimmed. The effect will be dramatic. I did this last year for the kids' school carnival, and it was fantastic." Gabby pointed above center stage. "And I didn't have the lighted crystal skull last year. That'll make it even better. Anyway, if you'll check the lights and place them in the pumpkins, we'll be ready to test the effect, then you can go home and get dressed."

"How do you expect me to get up and put lights in the hanging pumpkins? Fly?"

Gabby pretended to look around then, with a mischievous grin. "Leave your broom at home?" She laughed aloud then added, "Oh, Miacoh is on his way here with a twelve-foot ladder. So do the rest first. He'll be here soon. By the way, I convinced him to join the fun tonight."

She raised an eyebrow and stared at Gabby. "Very funny. I believe you have your magical creatures confused. I'm a vampire. I don't need a broom to fly. But just for the record, I know what you are trying to do, and I want you to stop it. He leaves as soon as he gets his grandmother's estate settled and the house sold. I'm staying here. Our plans don't mix."

"You never know." Gabby rested her hands on her

hips. "He has nowhere else to go. Why not settle here?"

"Because there are too many memories for him here. He wants a fresh start, and I don't blame him."

Her friend tilted her head and winked. "Yes, you would know." She waggled her finger in front of Candle's face. "I'm still going to figure out what you're running from."

Hands in her pockets, she fisted them but kept her voice calm. "Gabby, I told you, I'm not running from anything. I just want a normal life without constant drama and upheaval. Is that too much to ask?"

Gabby's shoulders sagged. "No, it's not. But you and Miacoh are so good together, and he's so all alone now."

"Maybe he likes it that way. Or maybe he has someone waiting for him wherever he called home? Ever think of that?"

"No, he doesn't. I can just tell." Gabby straightened and then flounced off toward the door, just as Miacoh walked through it carrying a tall ladder.

"Who needed this so badly that you had to call me first thing this morning? I have a notion to change my cell phone number." Miacoh glared at Gabby, who stood across the room, an innocent expression pasted on her face. "I don't have a problem helping out with this community event, but I am not at your beck and call. Got that?"

"Yes, sir," Gabby replied unruffled. "Candle needs it to put the lights in the hanging pumpkins and test the light in the crystal skull."

He turned his thunderous look on Candle, carried the ladder over, and set it up under one of the hanging pumpkins.

"Don't glare at me, Miacoh Zane. I had nothing to do with it. She called me at the crack of dawn too, so back it down a notch."

"Okay, if that's all you need from me, I have a meeting with the estate lawyer in a few minutes. See you all tonight." His eyes met Candle's, and at her nod, he smiled and walked toward the door.

"Now, what was that all about?" she wondered out loud. *First, the man is all irate, then he...and they say women are moody.* She finished installing the batteries in the little candle lights, made sure they worked, and finally put each one in a pumpkin. Someone turned off the overhead lights. The lit pumpkins transformed the darkness into a magical Halloween kingdom. The crystal skull's green glow added an eerie feeling to the room. She checked the skull's light and timer. She held the remote that controlled all the candle lights, turning them off and on several times to make sure everything worked correctly. Satisfied, she handed the remote to Gabby.

Brushing the cobwebs and dust out of her hair, she peered at Gabby. "If you're finished with me, I gotta go home and let the puppy out, exercise her, then get ready for the Halloween Ball tonight. You know, I am kind of excited about it. Over the years, I may have forgotten how to have fun."

"That's what I'm here for." A giggle bubbled up through Gabby's throat. "Now get out of here. See ya tonight."

****

Arriving at the cabin, Candle unlocked the door only to be greeted by a wiggling, whining ball of tawny fur. "How did you get out again?" Looking around the room, she saw the baby gate formerly wedged in the doorway between the kitchen and living area now chewed on one side, allowing it to fall over. She shook her head, watched the bright-eyed pup, happy to see her, and swept Terra up into her arms, cuddling her close. No use scolding her now. The deed was done. Crossing to the back door, she surveyed the area for any other damage and found none.

Terra made a mad dash out her dog door for the far corner of the yard, did her business, and stared at Candle. Her duties done, she raced around the yard, waiting for Candle to join her. Then Terra nipped at her pant legs and ran away again. She would surely be glad when this puppy phase was over. All her pants had tiny holes all around the bottom from puppy teeth. Terra grabbed a ball, squeaking it as she raced around the yard, finally bringing it to Candle to throw. After several minutes of playing ball with the pup, she returned to the house to don her costume and get ready to go.

An hour and a half later, Terrabyte rushed into the house and skidded to a stop barking furiously two feet from where Candle stood dressed in her costume. "Hey, it's just me," she laughed as the puppy stood there, head cocked to one side. She scooped the pup up and held her. "See, it's just me, she said soothingly. "Don't you like my costume?" She chuckled again and put Terra in her crate with food, water, and the treasured bully stick. This time making sure the lock was engaged properly and left the radio low.

She arrived at the ball a few minutes early, but it looked like the whole town was in attendance. Fog floated across the floor. Shadows from the lit pumpkins danced on the walls and ceiling as she made her way to where Gabby stood with her family. "Very nice, Gabby.

You did a great job with the decorations. Your costume isn't bad either. You're the good witch in the Wizard of Oz?"

Gabby nodded, dressed in a golden ball gown with glitter in her hair and a crystal wand in her hand. "Thank you. Candle, I'd like you to meet my husband, Ben."

"Oh, let me guess, you're the Wizard of Oz, right?"

"Yes, Gabby's interpretation." Ben laughed, striking a pose in a dark emerald-green suit with sequined lapels and a light green shirt with a black tie.

Gabby linked her arm through her husband's, then patted the top of a little girl's head with fiery red hair curls cascading down her back, dressed as a princess. "This is Natalya, my daughter." Gabby whirled around and grabbed the arm of a little boy as he ran by who looked to be about the same age as the little girl and brought him to her side. "This is my son, Nash. Kids, say hello to Candle. This is the friend I told you about."

Candle's cape swirled around her as she leaned down to shake the children's hands. "Nice to meet you, Natalya and Nash."

Nash narrowed his eyes and looked Candle up and down. He slashed his sword through the air bringing his hand to rest at his hip, and said, "I'm Zorro." He announced, then paused for a beat. "You don't look like a spy. Where's your gun? Are those real fangs?"

"Nash, you know better than that. You're being rude." Gabby shook the little boy's shoulder.

She laughed. "No, it's all right, Gabby." Even in the dim light, Candle watched the crimson color creep up Gabby's neck spreading to her cheeks. "I'm not a spy anymore, so I don't carry a gun. My vampire strength and sharp fangs are enough protection. Don't you think?" She opened her mouth, showing off her pointy fangs.

Nash considered for a moment or two. "Yeah, I guess so." He turned to his mother. "Can I go play now?"

Gabby sighed. "Sure, just don't go out of this room, or you'll sit in a chair the rest of the evening, Zorro. Understood?"

"Aww, mom."

Gabby's stare was unwavering. "Understand?"

"Yes," Nash said, irritably over his shoulder after wriggling out of his mother's hold. Slashing his sword through the air, he sprinted across the floor.

"Sorry about that." Gabby shook her head and looked apologetic.

She adjusted her cape, pushing it behind her shoulders. "Oh, don't worry about it. They look about the same age, around seven years old. Are they twins?"

"Yes, but as different as night and day. Nash doesn't know a stranger. Anyone and anything is fair game to him." She watched her young son join a group of boys over by the refreshments, then looked down at her daughter, still standing beside her. "This one is as shy and quiet as Nash is outgoing and loud." Gabby grinned. "They're quite the handful, and very intelligent. They get that from their father." She smiled up at her husband.

Ben nodded and extended his hand to Candle. "It's a pleasure to finally meet you, Ms. Bearclaw. Gabby's told me you've had quite the interesting life."

"Call me Candle. Between you and me, I believe Gabby embellishes…a lot." She grinned and took his outstretched hand.

Ben's eyes flicked up from her to someone standing behind her. She tensed for a minute then recognized the aftershave and relaxed.

Chapter Seven

Not Only Did Miacoh Make an Appearance but So Did the Green-eyed Monster

Miacoh put his hands lightly on Candle's shoulders. Leaning into her, he whispered, "You're not going to bite me, are you?" Chuckling, he dropped his hands and stepped to her side. "Good evening, Gabby." He turned and nodded to Ben.

"Good evening, Miacoh," Gabby said then stared up at him. "What are you supposed to be?"

"Well, apparently James Bond was in the wrong place at the wrong time and reborn into a vampire. Can't you tell?" He grasped the sides of his black silk cape and raised his arms in Dracula style, showing off a European-cut black suit with a red silk shirt and black ascot.

"Very nice." Candle peered at him appreciatively. "I guess that makes you my date." She laid her hand on his arm and smiled wide, showing off her fangs.

He returned her smile. His set of fangs glinted in the candlelight. He gave a low whistle, admired her clingy black dress, low cut in the front, and slit up the side to her thigh, showing off her long shapely legs.

She did a little twirl to give him the full effect.

Gabby made her introductions again, excused herself, and strode toward the group of boys her son had pinned against the wall with his plastic sword. Her husband and daughter followed close behind.

"I'm glad to see that you made it." She slipped her hand through his bent arm.

"After putting in all that work on the pumpkins, I had to see how they looked, didn't I?" He spread his arms wide as he turned slowly to survey the room. "Very nice costume. I guess all vampires are sexy. Is that right?"

"Of course, how else do you think we get close enough to drink our victim's blood?" she said in her best Transylvania accent. "Of course, I could enthrall you to do my bidding."

"Now that would be interesting. I've been a lot of things but never enthralled. Since I definitely object to allowing anyone to drain my blood unless you are willing to reciprocate." He waggled his eyebrows. "Which we can discuss in a more secluded area."

"Interesting offer. Can I get a rain check?" She sent him a smoldering look then grinned.

"Would you like something else to drink? Maybe a couple of cookies or something more substantial?"

"Actually, something else to drink would be nice, and I'm starved. I haven't eaten much of anything all day."

"So, what you are telling me is no spiked punch?" He raised an eyebrow as one corner of his mouth turned up.

"I don't think the punch is spiked. Too many kids here."

"That's how the punch would get spiked." He nodded to the refreshment table with no one around it and a group of teenagers standing nearby.

"Oh, maybe we better wander over that way ourselves." She sauntered toward the refreshments.

The table next to the beverages held plates of cakes, cookies, several steaming crock pots, and baskets of homemade dinner rolls. They strolled by the beverage table, Miacoh stopped, sniffed, then ladled out two cups of punch and joined her at the food table. They filled their plates and found seats not far from the beverage table. The group of teenagers dressed in goth attire served themselves and moved to the other side of the room.

Little knots of people engaged in friendly conversations covered the area. After they finished eating, they picked up their drinks and wandered from group to group, joining in the conversations. When the band began playing, several people found their way to the seating area arranged at the room's far end. Candle reached for Miacoh's hand and began tugging him toward the dance floor.

"If I remember correctly, you were a pretty good dancer back in the day."

"That was in high school and an extremely long time ago. I think an attempt at dancing with you would be putting your life in peril." He started to pull away.

"I'm willing to risk it. I haven't danced in years either, but I love this song." She took off her cape in a swirl of motion, leaving it in her chair.

Miacoh reluctantly did the same, slipping his arm around her waist and guiding her to the area set up for dancing. The first couple of songs were upbeat. She laughed and smiled as she moved fluidly to the music. Miacoh was a bit rusty, but held his own, enjoying how the slinky dress hugged all her curves.

As they made their way off the dance floor, Candle's parents joined them, engaging in small talk. The minute

Miacoh took his seat, the band started a cover of a slow, well-known romantic song by the king of rock and roll. Her favorite artist. She bounced up and grabbed his hand, dragging him back to the dance floor. When he took her in his arms, she melted against him, resting her cheek on his shoulder, and swaying to the music.

He smiled, inhaling deeply. A warm citrus and floral scent wafted around her. "It's been a long time…" A light tap on the shoulder brought him back to the present. He raised his head and glared at a man. She had a vague recognition of the man dressed as the devil himself.

The man took a step back. "May I have the rest of this dance with your beautiful vampire?"

Candle smiled and batted her long dark eyelashes. "I'm not his vampire."

The devil took her hand. Miacoh tightened his grip on her. "No." He growled and glided her in the opposite direction.

She shoved away and stared at him. "That was rude. I didn't even come to the party with you."

He shrugged, dropped his arms, strode across the floor, picked up his cape, moving slowly to the edge of the dance floor, his gaze never leaving her.

She stood in the middle of the dance floor alone, then stepped toward the man in the devil costume. "Let's dance."

"I didn't mean to cause a problem. I just hadn't had a chance to welcome you home. I'm Craig. I own the hardware store. We had chemistry together in high school."

"I'm sorry, I don't remember you, but it's been a long time since high school. It seems a lot of kids stayed here after high school or returned after college."

He grinned. "Yeah, I think we were mostly ski bums, then parents cut us off, and we discovered it took money to ski. At that point, we got a job to maintain our habits. After college, I came back and worked in the family hardware store. When Dad retired, he sold it to me."

"Sold it to you?" Candle asked incredulously.

"Yeah, he didn't believe in a free ride, and that store was his retirement. So it's all good."

"I left right after high school."

Miacoh frowned as he took another step toward them.

Ignoring Miacoh's advancing toward him, Craig continued. "Everyone knows, you got a full ride to the School of Mines, graduated early, and took up doctoral studies at MIT. After that, a government intelligence agency recruited you. Spent…" He whirled her in the opposite direction, away from Miacoh.

"That sounds about right, give or take. What makes you such an expert on me?"

"Your father was chief of police, and he was proud of your accomplishments, though he wasn't too specific after you left college."

"Thank God for that." The music ended, and she broke his hold. "Thanks for the dance. I'll see ya around." She hurried across the floor, only to be caught in the arms of another young man. This one dressed as a gladiator, but he didn't really have the body to pull it off.

"Hi, I'm Sean. May I have this dance?"

Geez, they're coming out of the woodwork now. She glanced around to see Miacoh glaring at her. Shrugging, she took Sean's hand. "Sure, but only one. I need to leave. I have a puppy waiting at home in her crate and I have no desire to clean up a mess."

Sean laughed and spun her across the dance floor. "Understood, I wanted to meet you and introduce myself. I worked for your father before he retired."

"Oh, my dad mentioned you."

"We sure miss him. His replacement, Roark, is good, but he's not Hunter."

"You'll get used to him. It'll be fine."

"Maybe."

"Tell me about working for my dad."

"He's a helluva guy. Knows this town inside and out. Seems to know what the kids are up to before they do it. Really gets their goat when he's waiting for them before they get into trouble. Which is usually the case, not always, but... Well, there was this time..."

"Oh, really, do tell."

Miacoh tapped Sean on the shoulder. "I believe it's my turn to tempt the vampire."

Sean smiled and nodded. "She's all yours."

"Nice to meet you. See ya around town."

Miacoh held her gently, resisting the urge to pull her tightly against him, making a couple more circuits around the dance floor before the music stopped. She wiggled out of his grasp and turned as JoDean, smelling of gin, took his hand and whisked him back to the floor. She smiled brightly, wrapping her arms around his neck, and resting her head on his shoulder.

He smiled down at her before glancing up at Candle. Hands behind her back, she carefully picked her way through the crowd and eased into a seat beside her mom. Glancing back once, she kept her expression carefully unreadable, but her gaze discreetly followed the couple around the floor.

JoDean curved against him and turned her face up to his with a seductive smile. She traced her lips with the tip of her tongue. "So, enjoying your visit?" Her hand caressed his back as it slid downward, pressing him to her.

He shifted away from her. "Not a visit. It's more business. As soon as Grandmother's estate is settled and her house up for sale, I'm gone."

"Oh, you are selling your grandmother's house? Do you have a real estate agent?"

"Yes. That's all settled." The music stopped. He untangled himself from her. "Nice to meet you again." She reached out to catch his arm, but he slipped out of her reach.

"Likewise, I'm sure we'll run into each other. Maybe dinner?" She stepped forward running her finger down his arm.

"Don't have time. But thanks for the offer." He ambled over toward where Candle sat, leaving JoDean standing on the dance floor alone.

"Where's Dad? Did he leave you all by yourself? Some date he is," Candle teased.

Pekabo laughed. "I'm used to it." She glanced across the room, where Hunter was laughing and talking with a group of men.

Pek glanced up at Miacoh approaching Candle's back. "Looked like you two were getting pretty cozy."

"Oh, Mom, don't make a big deal out of it."

"JoDean sure moved in quick. What happened?"

"I don't know and don't care." Candle kissed her mom on the cheek. "Sorry, but I gotta go. I don't want Terra to have an accident." Turning to leave, she smacked into Miacoh's strong chest.

He looked down at her. "Leaving so soon?" His lips twitched with amusement as she gathered her composure and strode purposely toward the door.

"Yeah, Terrabyte is home alone and seems to have Houdini genes."

"That's too bad, my dance card has space for one more dance." He grinned at her extending his hand.

"I'm sure you'll have no trouble filling it." She glanced across the floor as JoDean wove her way through the crowd, gaze pinned on Miacoh.

He turned and followed her look. *Shit.*

****

Candle drove home and unlocked the door with some trepidation, Did Terra escape again? But there was no fuzzy ball to greet her when she opened the door. Terrabyte was still in the crate, whining and barking like crazy. Setting her backpack and keys on the kitchen table, she leaned over and unlatched the crate. Terra shot out like a rocket and skidded to a halt at the back door. She flipped on the light, checked the backyard, and let Terra out to do her business.

Waiting for Terra to come back inside, she pulled her cell phone out of her backpack. The screen indicated there were two missed calls. Both messages were from the same number, a D.C. number. She tapped the play button. A familiar male voice came on the recording. "I'm sorry to leave a message on your phone like this, but I've tried to reach you at this number twice and your emergency number with no luck. There has been an accident. I need you to call me immediately when you get this message. It's Mark. You know the number."

Chapter Eight

The Accident—Be Careful—Things Are Not Always What They Seem

With a slight tremor in her hand, she took a deep breath and let it out slowly as she scrolled to Mark's number and tapped the send icon. The clock on the wall indicated it was one a.m. The phone call went directly to voice mail. She left a message and disconnected.

There was nothing she could do at this late hour, so she called Terra to her side, and they both padded down the hallway to bed. Tossing and turning for most of the night, she was relieved when her cell phone rang at four a.m. She rolled over and grabbed the phone on the first ring. "Hello."

"Where have you been? I tried to reach you most of the day yesterday," a male answered in a deceptively calm voice.

She knew that voice and something was terribly wrong. "Mark, just tell me what's happened."

"It's Carl. He died yesterday morning in a skiing accident. It was opening day. He somehow lost control and hit a tree on his second run of the day. The crash snapped his neck on impact. He was dead at the scene. I'm so sorry."

"Where was he?"

"On his favorite black diamond run in the Catskills,"

Mark answered flatly.

She bit her bottom lip as one tear rolled down her cheek before she gained control over her emotions. "Oh, Mark, you and I know that's not possible. He was too good a skier for that to happen. Had it been late afternoon after skiing all day, and he was tired—maybe—or the lengthening shadows late in the day— still not likely— but not on his second run in the morning on a run he has skied for years. I'm not buying it, and neither are you."

"Candle, I'm at work, so further discussion of this matter needs to wait until I have more information. But the bottom line is that Carl died in a skiing accident. The funeral and memorial service are Friday next week. I knew you'd want to attend—if at all possible. I assume you will not come alone, so I'll make reservations at a local hotel."

"Who would, oh, never mind, thank you. See you next week." She ended the call and remained seated on the edge of the bed in a haze until Terra began biting her toes and whining to go out. *Why would Mark suggest I not come alone? He knows I don't have anyone that would accompany me. Unless...was he suggesting I bring my father? There is something Mark couldn't tell me. But why would he call me from a line that he couldn't be forthright on?*

With more questions than answers, she pulled her robe over her PJs, wiggled her feet into her slippers, and followed Terra to the door. Turning the floodlights on, she stepped outside to check the yard before allowing her pup to run free. The bitter wind whipped the dry leaves around the yard. She breathed in the moist, fresh air.

A promise of more snow. She glanced at the sky, then watched Terra race around the yard. The season's first snow brought just a skiff of the white stuff a couple of weeks back. Ski resorts were busy making snow in anticipation of the major winter storm forecast later this week. She closed the door and watched through the window for a few minutes as Terra slowed and patrolled the perimeter of the yard.

Bears and raccoons rummaged through her garbage during her first days in the house. The trash can now resided safely in the garage. Deer ate late-blooming flowers from the garden and munched leaves on low-hanging branches of trees in the front yard. Foxes and coyotes loped through in the backyard as if they owned the place.

Then there was that skunk. She'd only seen one but figured where there's one, there's more, and had no desire to clean Terrabyte up after tangling with such a creature. Checking the backyard before letting Terra out was an ounce of prevention to her way of thinking. Still, she looked up the concoction used to clean a dog after a skunk encounter and made a list of ingredients to purchase on her next trip to the store.

Pouring milk into a large mug, she popped it in the microwave, waited, took it out, and poured in hot chocolate mix, stirring carefully. There was no use trying to go back to sleep. Her mind would simply try to solve the puzzle of Carl's death—murder. She blew on the hot chocolate, took a sip, then eased into a kitchen chair.

The quiet shattered with Terrabyte's ferocious barking at the side yard. *Now what?* She stood, removed her weapon from the cupboard drawer nearest the door, and stepped outside just as the front doorbell rang. She looked at her watch. *It's 6:30. Who the hell would be at my door at this time of the morning?*

"Shit." She called Terra to her, walked inside, and closed the door. She set her mug on the counter, leaned over, locked the dog door, and hurried to the front door. The puppy, still barking excitedly, rushed to the front door several seconds ahead of her. She peeked out the side window. Miacoh stood on the porch, hands in his pockets. He stared at the ground. .Dark circles shadowed under his eyes, and and his face lined and weary.

Opening the door, she said, "Well, I didn't expect to see you again." Terra woofed a bit more. She gave her a stern look. "Leave it, Terra, quiet," she commanded. The pup's butt continued to wiggle as it hit the floor, letting out one more woof as if wanting the last word. Turning her attention back to Miacoh, she asked, "What can I do for you?" She had no intention of letting him in her home.

He stepped back, ran his fingers through his thick hair, and brought his eyes up to meet hers. In a deep, smooth voice, he said, "I saw your lights on as I was passing by so…well…I believe I owe you an apology. No excuses, only a promise that it won't happen again."

They stood there for a beat. Then she caved. He looked so miserable. She opened the door wide. "Come in." Closing the door behind him, she gave Terrabyte the release command, and the pup immediately began dancing around and through Miacoh's legs. "Terra…place." She pointed into the living room. The puppy gave her a disgruntled look, then trotted over to her blanket, circled twice, and lay down.

Amazed, Miacoh watched Terra for a moment more, then turned his gaze on Candle. "That's quite a pup you have there, so well-behaved and at such a young age."

"We traveled around for a month or so before

settling here. The pup soaked up training like a little sponge and learned quickly I wouldn't tolerate bad behavior. She is quite intelligent."

"Like her owner." His lips softened into a slight smile as he stood in front of the couch.

She gave him a withering glance. "Have a seat. I'd just fixed a hot chocolate when you came. Would you like a mug?"

"I'd appreciate it." For the first time since he arrived, he took a good hard look at her. Her eyes were red-rimmed. She also appeared pale. "If you don't mind my asking, is everything all right? You look a little—"

"I do mind, and it's none of your business," she snapped, then took a deep breath, letting it out slowly. "I'm sorry. It's been a bad morning, but I'm fine. Just never been a morning person."

"Okay, but if you…well…maybe I best be going, I'll take a rain check on that hot chocolate." He shoved up from the couch and started toward the door.

"That might be best." She paused for a moment or two. "Wait, let me ask you something. You're a good skier, right?"

Taken off guard by her sudden change of subject and demeanor, he waited a beat expecting some kind of trap. Hesitantly, he said, "I used to be, haven't had a lot of time to hone my skills in recent years. Why do you ask?"

She needed confirmation that someone else would think the situation with Carl strange. "If you were told that an expert skier hit a tree on his second run of the day, on a black diamond run he skied for years, would you think that strange?"

"Well, if this person was under duress or not paying attention, I supposed it could happen, but…" He rubbed his chin with his thumb and forefinger, considering, then gave his head a little shake. "If he was an expert skier and knew the slope, I believe it would be doubtful. Is this person a friend of yours?"

"He was."

"Was? He didn't survive the accident?" Miacoh gently put his hand on her arm.

"No, it snapped his neck on impact. He died instantly."

"Oh, I'm so sorry. Did he live around here?"

"No, he was my immediate supervisor at the agency. He taught me…" She felt the tears welling up again. Closing her eyes, she willed them back.

"Is there more to this than you're telling me?"

"Yes—no—" She sighed. "I just don't know. Regardless, I shouldn't be bothering you with it. Would you like that hot chocolate now?"

"Yeah. Why don't you start at the beginning? Maybe I can help you make sense of it."

She shook her head as she walked into the kitchen. She lifted her mug from the counter where she'd left it and took a sip. Cold, she thought and put it back in the microwave while preparing another cup of hot chocolate for Miacoh.

The microwave dinged. She took her mug out and put his in. Sipping her hot chocolate, she debated whether or not to tell him the whole story. Why did she even mention it to him in the first place? She should have just let him leave. But she didn't. Finally, her decision was made. She took Miacoh's drink out of the microwave and padded back to the living room.

She handed him the steaming mug of frothy chocolate and plopped down in the chair across from him. She looked into his haunting blue-green eyes and began. "I'm not sure why I told you about this, but you can't repeat anything that I am about to say. Your word."

He shrugged. "You got it."

She explained how Carl had shown her how to use her computer expertise to hack into foreign government networks. He provided her with alternate identities when necessary and when the last assignment went against every fiber of her being, she resigned from the agency with Carl's blessing. Although, he hinted that her leaving put him in a difficult position. At the time, she thought that was just his way of trying to manipulate her into staying. Now, she wasn't so sure.

At the last statement, Miacoh raised a brow and nodded. "So, you think his death had something to do with your leaving or your last assignment?"

"I don't know."

"Are you in danger then?"

"No, I don't believe so. I left when the assignment started down a dark path. A situation I didn't want to be involved in, and I made that known when I left." She paused for a couple of minutes, taking a long swig from her mug. "Looking back on it, I think that everyone involved knew that was the way my career would end, and it did."

"Any regrets?"

"No, except...No."

"Except what?"

"I can't believe that the agency is just going to sweep this under the rug. Let the cause of death stand as an accident when it could have been murder."

"I think you are getting ahead of yourself. Mark told you he needed more information before discussing this with you further. So maybe—"

"No, what he didn't say spoke volumes." She fisted her hand in her lap.

"No, what I am hearing is that he didn't want you to get involved."

"Without someone having my back," she said emphatically.

"Ok, so what are you going to do?"

She shrugged and flexed her hand again. "I guess, talk to my dad, see if he'll go to the funeral with me."

"At the risk of pissing you off again, I think that is a bad idea. I realize he has a lifetime of law enforcement experience, and he'll want to protect his little girl. But, Candle, you can't put him in that position. There is a reason he retired. He doesn't want to chase the bad guys anymore. Physically he isn't a young man. You have to respect that."

"But—okay— I'll go to the funeral alone, pay my respects, and come back."

"Bullshit. I can see in your eyes, you're lying. What if you are right? And I am not saying you are, but do you want to have an accident like Carl?" Miacoh stared her straight in the eyes, then looked at his watch and frowned. "I've got a meeting in a few minutes with the estate attorney."

He stood and started toward the door. "Let me throw this out for you to consider. I'll go with you to the funeral if you promise that you won't do anything stupid. Let's make arrangements to talk to Mark in a secure location. Then we can decide how to proceed. Fair enough?"

Chapter Nine

When It Rains, It Pours—Bodies

The afternoon was dreary and overcast when Miacoh and Candle stepped off the private plane at Ronald Reagan National Airport. He collected their luggage and strode toward the exit when she put her hand on his arm. Standing just to the left of the door with a group of people was a chauffeur holding a sign with Bearclaw written on it.

He shook his head a little and nodded toward the shuttle to the rental car agencies. "Not that I don't trust your former handler, but I'd rather we had our own car for the duration. A simple dark-colored SUV will work to our advantage and will blend in nicely around here."

"I canceled the hotel reservation as you asked and informed Mark. Where are we staying?"

"Falls Church. I know a guy whose family owns a nice four-star hotel there. It's close enough to Langley and Arlington for our needs but off the beaten path. When we get settled in, you can call Mark."

"I'll just tell him my friend preferred other accommodations. Is there a bar in your friend's hotel?"

"Yes, that would be a good meeting place. We can control the situation. Nice thinking."

"The funeral is the day after tomorrow. I'll see if he'll meet us for drinks tomorrow evening." She smiled at him for the first time since boarding the plane.

He noticed she hadn't liked how he simply took over, but his primary responsibility was to have her back. Reluctantly, she'd agreed to his plan, which was a start.

"Nice smile. Are you okay with the plan?"

"Yes, finding out what we can from Mark, then attending the funeral and flying home the next day is a good idea. Poking around on a subsequent trip probably would net us more information."

"If there is anything to your theory," he added.

She shot him a glance that would wither most men. He let it roll off as they climbed into the shuttle.

The next evening, they met with Mark. His gaze darted around the room as he kept his voice low. "Friends and skiing buddies of Carl managed to get the coroner to go against the powers that be and reclassify Carl's death as suspicious, pending further investigation. Carl's family hired a private investigator." Mark shrugged. "Don't know who, or if I'll be privy to the PI's findings. The PI will probably get stonewalled at every turn. But, if I learn anything, I'll let you know."

Miacoh said nothing, but something didn't sit well with the situation.

It was a sunny start to the day of the funeral, but soon gray clouds gathered, and a cold drizzle began falling.

"Funny, I didn't think much about it when Carl used to joke about not wanting anyone to wear black at his funeral. Now it's just plain eerie." She donned a dark rust-colored pants suit with a cream blouse to honor those wishes. The copper parka she wore to stay warm covered most of her outfit.

He wore a dark suit with a light blue shirt and a long

black duster. While several people and dignitaries wore black to the service, the overwhelming majority did abide by Carl's wishes and chose clothing other than black.

"Carl would have been pleased," Candle whispered to him. He nodded while continuing to observe the crowd.

As the casket lowered into the ground, he took her hand, put it through the crook in his arm, and started toward their rental car when his cell phone rang. He glanced at the caller ID, held up his index finger, and walked a short distance from Candle, still keeping an eye on her.

"Hello?"

"Miacoh, this is Hunter. Sorry to interrupt, but I need you and Candle to catch the first plane back here. The man who took over my position as Chief of Police was found beside his cruiser on a road leading out of town. Miacoh—he was shot to death. Nothing like this has ever happened around here. I could sure use your help."

Miacoh sucked in a breath through his teeth, then averted his eyes from Candle, closed them for a beat then began walking toward her. He blew out a breath and said calmly, "Sure, we'll be on a plane within the hour."

"I thought we were staying the night." Her dark eyes stared questioningly into his. Flipping her long tawny cinnamon-colored hair over her shoulder, she gave him her full attention. "Has something happened?"

"Yes. I'll tell you on the way to the hotel." He held the car door for her, then walked to the driver's side and got in. He touched his cell phone screen, put the phone to his ear, and made arrangements to have a private plane fueled and ready to go in forty-five minutes. He turned in his seat to face her.

"So, tell me already. The suspense is killing me."

"That was your father on the phone." He hurried on before she could ask questions. "Your friends and family are fine, but there's been a shooting. He wants our help. The man that took over for your father as Chief has been shot to death. They found him on the road out of town, lying next to his police cruiser." He wrapped his arms around her in a gentle hug as the color drained from her face.

She rested her cheek against his chest for only a moment, then pushed up. "What happened? Who did it? What do they know?"

"Your dad didn't say, only relayed what happened and asked for our help."

****

The plane ride back was a quiet one except for Candle's murmuring over and over again, "Not in my town. How could this happen in my sleepy little town?" Then she'd shake her head.

Finally, Miacoh moved next to her and put his arm around her, pulling her close. "Candle, it can happen anywhere at any time. You and I know that better than most. Society is so mobile. People move from place to place for a variety of innocent reasons. Then you have those hiding from something or someone, running from the law, or coping with mental problems. No town is exempt, including yours."

"It's your town too," she protested. "I came there for the safe, secure feeling of a small town. Where everyone knows everyone, and nothing bad ever happens."

She turned those big chocolate brown eyes on him,

and he couldn't help himself. He cupped her chin in his hand, leaned over, and brushed his lips gently over hers. As her lips parted, he deepened the kiss—something he'd wanted to do ever since carving pumpkins with her. A bit of turbulence bounced the plane around. He backed off, rubbing his thumb slowly across her cheek before releasing her chin.

He ran the tip of his tongue over his lips and shook his head. "I'm sorry, I shouldn't have done that." Shifting in his seat, he looked away. A few moments later, her eyes bore into the side of his face like a laser beam, and he turned to face her.

She stared at him unblinking. She sighed, tracing her top lip with the tip of her tongue. "No need to apologize. I guess—If I was truthful—Oh, never mind. You'll be leaving soon, so what does it matter?"

When she slowly moistened her lips with her tongue, he shifted uncomfortably, the crotch of his pants tightening. "It was my town a long time ago. I've made it quite clear to everyone that I'm not staying. Much as I wish it were possible, I can't. There are too many ghosts."

"What ghosts?" She lifted her hands up and then dropped them into her lap.

"Things that happened a long time ago, before we moved here and after. You don't really know me." He drew in a long breath and let it out slowly. "There are things in my past that—well, let's just say—were beyond my control and still affect me to this day. Enough said." He ran his fingers through his hair, rubbing at the back of his neck where a tension knot formed. "Whoever is responsible for this heinous act must have been just passing through. I certainly hope no one in our town is capable of such a cold-blooded action."

"Of course, they're not," She raised her head and looked him straight in the eye as if daring him to disagree.

His lips twitched, but he said nothing.

"Dad would have done a thorough background check before hiring him. He indicated his deputies were too green yet to take the job, so they had to post the position and ended up hiring from out of town." She chewed on her bottom lip. "I believe he said the man was from Montana."

"I'm sure he did, but…well, let's wait on that until we hear what your dad has to say and what leads he discovered. I'm sure he's the acting Chief right now if he felt his deputies were too green just a few months ago."

"Oh, Mom will be fit to be tied. She was so excited about having time to travel whenever they wanted. And to have Dad out of the line of danger. This will dump that danger on their doorstep."

"I always wondered what kind of parents named their child Pekabo?"

She giggled, sighed, and shook her head. "I asked grandma the same thing when I was a teenager. I remember her eyes sparkling and saying something like they were hippies or something. Then added they considered themselves free spirits and sunshine, moonflower, or moonbeam just didn't fit her, so they named her Pekabo." She laughed. "And you know, she said it like it made all the sense in the world. I asked Mom why she didn't change it. She just shrugged and smiled, saying she liked it."

"Your parents named you Candle. That's not a common name, especially with the surname of

Bearclaw."

"Oh, Mom is just like her parents, a free spirit and artist. She doesn't like conventional things. As you know, my dad is Cheyenne. He's proud of his heritage. As a bright light in their world, they named me Candle."

"What about you?"

He straightened in his seat rubbing the back of his neck, bending it from side to side. "My name is a family name. My father was Native American too, and my mother looked the part, but Grandma, my dad's mom said she didn't know. Dad met and married her when he was in the Air Force. We only moved here after Dad retired and was disabled in a hunting accident in Canada. Don't know what happened because no one ever talked about it." He shrugged, stood up, smoothed the wrinkles out of his pants, and walked up front to talk to the pilot.

After a short time, he returned. "Adam, our pilot, said we'll be landing at Aspen's airport soon, need to buckle up."

Once on the ground, they hurried to his truck and drove the twenty-five or so miles to the Bearclaw home. Hunter stood watching out the front picture window and moved to open the door when they pulled up.

Candle rushed up the sidewalk, throwing her arms around her dad. "I know it's a terrible thing to say, but I'm so glad it wasn't you." She released her father and bent down to Terrabyte, wiggling, barking, and running around her legs. "Sit." The pup's butt hit the ground. She ruffled Terrabyte's fur then picked her up. The puppy had spent a few days with her parents while she attended the funeral.

Hunter raised an eyebrow and looked at his daughter. "Years with the agency didn't squelch your tendency to let inappropriate things you're thinking just pop right out of your mouth?"

She covered her mouth. "Well, it did until now."

"Thank you for coming so quickly." He grasped Miacoh's offered hand. "It's been chaos around here since it happened."

"Who found him? Had he reported any trouble to dispatch?" Candle glanced expectantly at her father.

"He was making his rounds out to the county line. Chief radioed in that there was a disabled pickup by the side of the road, the hood open with two men bent under the hood. He pulled alongside to offer assistance. They declined, indicating it was handled and were almost ready to leave. When he returned to the radio, he reported the status, gave his location as a couple of miles from the county line, and that he'd be turning around there."

"So he continued on patrol after stopping at the pickup truck?" Miacoh asked.

"Appears so. That was the last anyone heard from him. After about an hour, he hadn't returned or reported in. Deputy Blake traced the route he believed Roark had taken. About an eighth of a mile from the county line, he found the cruiser, lights flashing, with Roark's body lying beside it in a pool of blood. Keys still in the ignition, but he'd turned the engine off. The dash camera was on but displayed only shadows or backs of individuals. You can hear Roark say something about changing his mind and then the sounds of two shots. Someone lured Roark out of range of the camera and shot him in the head at point-blank range. Pitkin County Sheriff's Department and the crime lab are working on the tire tracks we found beside the cruiser, but it's a long shot."

"What about those two guys at the pickup? Anyone talk to them?" she interjected.

"Nope. Haven't found them. The Montana plate that Roark called in was stolen," Hunter said grimly. "The description of a Chevy pickup crew cab, dark blue, went out in a BOLO. Nothing has turned up so far."

"Did someone radio him back and tell him the plates were stolen?" Miacoh wanted to know.

"Not at the time. The report came in later. Those plates didn't belong to the truck. That's when Blake felt something was wrong and went looking for Roark." Hunter took his hat off, rubbed the top of his head, then slid his hat back on.

"What can we do for you? Appears you have all the bases covered." His attention riveted on Hunter with an occasional glance toward Candle.

"Let's everyone have a seat. Pek, could you get us coffee?" Hunter turned toward his daughter. "Hot chocolate or tea also?"

"Yes, tea, please. I swore off coffee for a while," Candle confirmed. "Started making me jittery."

"Sure thing. I'll throw together some finger sandwiches and chips to hold off the hunger until dinner. The lasagna has another hour before it's done." Pekabo hurried into the open-concept kitchen.

She opened a cupboard that held several boxes of herbal tea, picked out the orange spice, set mugs on the table, poured three cups of coffee, and refilled the coffee maker. Out of the refrigerator, she grabbed meat, cheese, spicy mustard, and mayo, then took bread from a drawer. "Coffee is ready. Tea will be a minute if someone wants to come get them."

"I'm on my way." Candle padded to the kitchen. She

took her mug out of the micro and unwrapped two tea bags dipping them in the steaming water. Reaching above the cupboard, she pulled down a tray and carefully placed the mugs on it next to the plate of sandwiches.

When she picked up the tray, the cups rattled against each other. She set the tray down again. "Guess this day has caught up with me." She blew out a breath and picked up the tray again. This time she carried it out to the living room where Hunter and Miacoh had their heads together deep in conversation.

Setting the tray on the coffee table, she plopped down on the couch, snagged a sandwich, and took a bite. "Yum. This hits the spot."

Her dad took a mug and leaned back in his chair. "I think reaching out to your contacts might at least rule out what is not going on here." He reached over and picked up a sandwich.

"I'll get right on it." Miacoh took his phone out of his pocket and walked toward the door.

She picked up a mug and wrapped her hands around it glancing expectantly at her father. "What'd I miss?"

"Nothing. I decided to take Miacoh up on his offer. Do you still have access codes for the traffic cams?"

"I don't know, but I can get them."

He eyed his daughter speculatively, narrowing his eyes. "This has to be done through the legal channels."

"Aww, you're no fun." She grinned in an attempt to lighten the mood. "I'll just go get my computer from the car." The door banged shut as she sprinted out. A few minutes later, laptop in hand, she skirted around Miacoh standing just outside the door phone to his ear.

Hunter's phone rang. He picked it up off the end table next to his chair and checked the caller ID. "Talk to me." Silent for a couple of beats, he listened to the voice on the other end nodding his head once. "I understand. Well, at least we know it wasn't any locals. So, what do you think we are looking at?" Again, he listened intently. "That is not what I wanted to hear." Hunter touched the screen with a heavy sigh, ending the call and turning his eyes on Candle.

Chapter Ten

The Worst Part is the Waiting

The front door swung open and Miacoh strode in, tucking his phone into his jacket pocket. "What?" His eyes met Candle's and then shifted to her father, who rose from the chair.

With a grim expression, Hunter met his gaze. "The plates and the truck belong to Billy Duckett, a survivalist that lives off the grid in Northern Montana. But the plates don't belong to the Chevy truck but to another truck that is still on Billy's property. Appears the plates were switched deliberately. Plus, the registration decal tag belongs to a different vehicle entirely."

Miacoh shook his head as his forehead creased. "But they all belonged to the same person?"

She handed Miacoh a cup of steaming brew and motioned him to the couch. He sipped the coffee and eased down on the couch, then fidgeted unable to settle down.

Hunter nodded. "Yes. Except for the decal. It belonged to someone who applied for a replacement due to the first being lost. And before you ask, Billy Ducket is ice fishing somewhere in Canada, according to neighbors. Been gone a couple of weeks."

"Think he is one of the guys in the pickup?" Miacoh took another drink from his coffee and shoved up from the couch to stand in front of the fireplace.

"Doubt it. Neighbors say Old Billy goes ice fishing every year about this time. Usually gone a couple of months or so. Got relatives in Canada."

"So, it's probably safe to assume the truck was also stolen. Billy just hasn't missed it yet." Candle nibbled on a sandwich and took a sip of her tea.

"Yeah, we've hit a dead-end for tonight. Pitkin County Sheriff's office has issued an APB for the truck." Her dad raked his fingers over the top of his head and slapped his cap back on his head.

"But given the circumstances, it'll be found abandoned somewhere by morning." Miacoh rubbed his hands together next to the fire.

"So, our best bet is to use traffic cams to locate the truck before it arrived here. Are we sure this is the right avenue to pursue, or are we just chasing our tails?" Candle finished the last of her sandwich, picked up her plate, and slid it into the dishwasher. Returning to settle onto the couch with the laptop, she tapped several keys then waited.

"It's all we got right now. Nothing in Roark's background is suspicious. No enemies that we know about, still looking into that. Let's face it. This town has very little crime, no violent crime in the last thirty years. Now we have an officer of the law shot in cold blood." Hunter stood, paced the room's length, then paused at the large picture window.

She rubbed her eyes with her thumb and index finger, still waiting for the results of a search of traffic cams. Glancing at the screen, she straightened. "Well, well, well, what do we have here?"

Miacoh returned to the couch and leaned over

Candle's shoulder, staring at the computer screen. "What you got?"

She pointed to the original file, then pulled up another file, then another. "That truck was spotted in the parking lot of a building supply center in Colorado Springs and two in Denver the same day Roark ran into them. The video only captured the back of the individuals, but if we can get surveillance video from the stores, maybe we can get a facial shot."

Hunter strode over, put his hands on the back of the couch, watching the video on the computer. "Is this footage legally obtained?"

"Yes, Dad, I still have a few friends in the agency. But to get the surveillance from the stores, it's up to you to go through official channels." She blinked, stretched her arms above her head, and yawned wide.

"I'm going to hand this info off to the Pitkin County Sheriff's office. At present, they are better equipped to handle it than we are. You two look like you could use some sleep. Both of you have been very helpful. Thank you." He hugged his daughter then held her at arm's length. "Sorry to dump this in your lap right after you return home."

"They're not the only ones in need of sleep." Pekabo joined the group wiping her hands on a towel. "I supposed you'll be reporting to the office bright and early tomorrow morning?"

"I'm afraid so. Don't have a choice. I'll be acting Chief until this is solved or we find another candidate for the position." He wrapped his arm around his wife's waist, pulling her close and kissing the top of her head. "It won't be long, I promise."

"Yeah, that's what you said three years ago. I

understand, but I don't have to like it." Pekabo snapped the hand towel at him playfully. "The lasagna is ready. I can fix a couple of to-go containers for you two."

"Perfect." Candle powered down her laptop

"On that note, I'm going to take Candle and Terra home, then head home myself. I'll check in with you in the morning. If there are any new developments, you know how to reach us," Miacoh said as he scooped up a sleeping bundle of fur and watched Candle close her laptop and return it to the case.

****

On the way to Candle's cabin, they discussed the unfinished business with Carl's death and decided that could wait. She would call Mark in the morning, apprise him of their decision, and give him a glimmer of what was happening in Aspen Ridge. Miacoh brought his truck to a stop in front of the cabin and cut the engine.

Slipping his arm around her, he leaned toward her. She looked up at him questioningly and saw desire smoldering in his eyes. Her heart leapt in anticipation as her lips parted. Softly she felt his breath on her face, then the caress of his mouth on hers. His kiss sent the pit of her stomach into a wild swirl as she closed her eyes, caught up in the moment.

A wet nose on her face and a fuzzy paw on her arm broke the spell. From the backside of the console, Terrabyte looked from one to the other and whined. Miacoh smiled then brushed his lips over hers once more. Their eyes locked on each other as he drew away and gently caressed her cheek with the palm of his hand.

"I guess our chaperon decided it was time for you to go in," he murmured, chuckling softly.

"So, it would seem." She slowly turned to open the

truck door. The last thing she wanted was for Terra to have an accident in Miacoh's immaculate truck. She handed him his share of the lasagna care package and stepped out of the truck. "At least we won't go hungry. Mom's lasagna is to die for." As soon as the words were out, she covered her mouth.

"Yeah, there's been enough bodies for the time being." He snickered.

"Couldn't let it pass." No sooner did she put Terra down on the ground, than the pup rushed to the end of the leash and squatted, then pranced down the path to the cabin ahead of them. She unlocked the front door, let Terra in, and turned to Miacoh. "Do you want to come in?"

He paused for a moment, got out of the truck, then sighed. "No, I'm afraid if I do, I won't want to leave, so better all around if I go on home."

Standing on tiptoe, she touched her lips to his and he returned her kiss with smoldering heat.Pulling her against him he trailed kisses down her neck to the hollow of her throat. He paused for a moment, then continued kissing and tasting her as far as her low-cut sweater allowed. She arched against him, feeling his arousal, and urging him on. It had been too long since she allowed herself to care about someone. God help her. She cared about this man.

"I think we better go inside," she breathed, pulse racing and moisture gathering between her legs.

"Not—a—good—idea." He backed away. His eyes held hers for another moment, then his gaze dropped from her eyes to her shoulders and lower. He shook his head and kissed her lips softly. "Not tonight."

Her face heated as anger pulsed through her tired

brain, then she opened her mouth. "Bullshit." Once again, her thinking versus saying filter failed. The scowl on Miacoh's face was black as the night. She winced. *Okay, here it comes. I deserve it.*

Surprisingly, he looked to the sky for a beat, drew in a breath, blew it out hard, and returned her stare. "I'll pick you up in the morning. We'll go for a drive and stop somewhere for breakfast. There are some things we need to discuss before engaging in a physical relationship." Terrabyte barked in the backyard. He stepped to the side where he could see her and said, "Yes, Terra, you can come too."

"Like what?" she said irritably, watching his movements. Her anger melted like butter at his demeanor with her pup. Staying mad at him was impossible, even in her aroused but not to be sated state. *At least he wasn't in any better condition.* Her lips twitched to keep from smiling.

"I can't stay in Aspen Ridge, and this is your home." He turned his back to her and trudged down the path to his truck. He got in and slammed the door. "Shit."

She stood on the porch as his truck peeled out and sped down the street. *What the hell was the deal with that man?* She shrugged, stepped into her cabin, and shut the door.

****

Still dark outside, the waning moonlight filtered through her window as her eyes popped open. She lay still listening to an owl hooting in a tree, and the rustle of bushes as a deer or moose crossed the property behind her lot. At least she hoped it wasn't a wolf or coyote. Terra snored quietly, occasionally making soft woofing sounds, feet brushing the wall as the pup chased squirrels in her dreams.

She sighed, already tired just thinking about the recent events shaping her life. Rolling to her side, she stared out the window. *Am I better off now than at the agency where my assignments consumed me, free from any emotional ties? Didn't I leave there seeking a better, more fulfilling life? Is this it?* She didn't know.

What she did know is that Miacoh was an infuriating man, and he'd be back today to taunt her again. At that thought, she swung her legs over the edge of the bed and nudged Terra awake at the side of her bed. She stepped over the pup. Terra blinked up at her, then got up and stretched.

Bending from side to side, arm raised over her head, she worked out the kinks a night of tossing and turning caused. Terra whined, bolted to the back door, and danced around in a circle. "Okay, okay, I'm coming." Sliding her feet into her slippers, she sprinted to the door. Flicking the flood lights on, she surveyed the backyard then opened the dog door.

In the bedroom, dressed in jeans and a shaded red sweater, she pulled on knee-high black boots, gathered her long cinnamon hair into a ponytail, and tied it with a matching red ribbon. Surveying herself in the mirror, she smiled, then sashayed down the hall to the kitchen and put on a pot of coffee for Miacoh's arrival.

For herself, she fixed a cup of hot chocolate sprinkled with tiny marshmallows and sat at the kitchen table. She took a sip as the sun peeked over the mountains spreading orange across the horizon, then pulled out her cell phone. *No messages or missed calls were reflected on the screen. Maybe that was a good thing.* She touched speed dial #2 and waited.

Pekabo answered quietly on the first ring. "Good morning, you're up early."

"I could say the same thing about you." She smiled. Mom was always perky in the morning. "Any news?"

"No, your father is still asleep. He was up most of the night working with a deputy from the Pitkin County Sheriff to access the surveillance tapes. Finally, he came to bed in the wee hours of the morning. I turned the alarm off and sneaked out of the room."

"Oh, Mom, he's going to be furious."

"I know, but he needs rest. Candle, I'm worried. He retired for a reason. Now he's right back in the thick of things." Pekabo paused for a minute. "That job is going to kill him."

"Does he have serious health problems?"

"Candle, he's 65 years old, spent most of his life in law enforcement. What do you think?"

"What can I do?"

"Ride the council members' collective asses until they find another replacement." Her mother's voice rose, then quieted again.

"Sooner is better."

"Okay, I'll see what I can do." She paused. "Hmmm, is Gabby still here?"

"I think her plane leaves tomorrow or the day after. She delayed leaving, hoping to see you. Why?"

Chewing on her bottom lip, she devised a plan. "She knows this town much better than I do. Enlisting her help in this situation could make a big difference. I'll give her a call."

"You do that. Dad or I will let you know of any new developments in the case." Pekabo ended the call.

As she scrolled through her address book for

Gabby's number, a truck rumbled up the street. Terra rushed to the door, tail wagging. She located the number and tapped the screen waiting for Gabby to answer. After several rings, the call went to voice mail.

"Gabby, I need your expertise in an important matter. Can we get together for dinner tonight? Call me. Please." She disconnected the call and walked to the door, opening it to a surprised Miacoh with his hand raised to knock.

"Good morning, Miacoh," she said cheerfully pushing the door open for him to enter.

"Good morning to you." He wrapped his arm around her waist, brushed his lips over hers, lingering only a moment. He strode past her into the living room and ruffled Terrabyte's fur as she bounced around his feet.

"Don't pay attention to her until she settles and sits."

He grinned. "Your rules, not mine." He waved his hand dismissively.

Narrowing her eyes, she scowled at him. "It's important that rules are consistent. She doesn't get attention until she sits politely. A well-trained dog is a joy to have around."

"All right, I'll try to remember, but she is just so damn cute."

"Be that as it may…" She picked up her chirping phone and held one index finger up to him. "Gabby. Thanks for calling back."

"Sure, what's up?"

"I don't want to get into it over the phone, but are you free for dinner tonight?"

"Let me check, just a minute." She paused, murmuring to someone. "Yes, Ben's still here. He'll watch the kids."

"How's around seven at Angus Steak House?" Candle suggested.

"Works for me, sure you can't give me a hint what this is about?"

"Not really, but it concerns my dad."

"Okay then, see you tonight."

She tapped the screen again and turned to Miacoh, who returned with a mug of steaming coffee from the kitchen. She brought him up to speed regarding her mom's worry, the Chief of Police position, and the council members.

"So Gabby is hopefully my ace in the hole."

He took a sip of the coffee and closed his eyes. "You make great coffee." He opened his eyes and winked at her. "Bringing Gabby in is a great idea. Anything new on the case?"

"No, but Mom thinks they have access to the surveillance tapes. Dad is still asleep, and that's a whole 'nother can of worms."

Eyebrows raised, he nodded. "You and Terrabyte ready to go?"

"Almost." She picked up her hot chocolate, put it in the microwave, and grabbed the leash. "Okay, we are ready to go." She grabbed her warm to-go mug out of the microwave.

They drove the mountain roads for most of the morning, enjoying the scenery and discussing the local case and the situation with Carl. Miacoh stopped the truck at a trailhead. Candle hopped out as he released Terra from her harness in the backseat. During the few-mile hike into the forest, the stress of the morning ebbed away.

Returning to the truck, she paused. "I'm famished.

Is lunch on the schedule soon?"

"Yep, about fifteen minutes. Can you wait that long?"

"I don't know, could be touch and go, but I'll try."

"Well, if worse comes to worse, I bet Terra will share the kibble you brought for her." He chuckled.

"Oh, very funny. Besides, she's already eaten it all." She turned back around in her seat after checking on Terrabyte.

Deciding to broach the subject of last night, she studied him. "So, do you have something to tell me?"

"After lunch," he said curtly. "I have something I need you to read. I'll hand it to you after lunch and you can read it before we take off again. Only, I don't want you to discuss it until we are in the truck."

Chapter Eleven

Black Bear Inn, Good Food and Secrets Revealed—
Almost

A few minutes later, Miacoh took his foot off the
gas. The truck coasted to a stop in front of the Black Bear
Inn. A large sign in the window read, "Home Cooking
At Its Best. Pies Baked Fresh Every Day."

"I didn't even know about this place. Is it good?"
She licked her lips. "I love homemade pies." She turned
in her seat. "Terra, you stay here. Miacoh, crack a couple
of windows. It's a cool day so the pup will stay
comfortable in her crate in the vehicle."

"It's been here for years. I came here as a little boy
with my parents, before Dad's disability got so bad he
wasn't mobile. It's owned and operated by relatives on
my dad's and grandmother's side."

He held the door to the restaurant open for Candle
as a bell clanged above the door. A statuesque woman
with bronze skin and long flowing black hair came
around from the cashier's counter and greeted them.

"Two for lunch?" She stared at Miacoh for a beat.

"Yes, could we have that booth over in the corner?
Is Mac or his son, Jacob, around?" He tightened his grip
around Candle's waist.

Recognition lit the woman's face. She smiled wide.
"Miacoh, is that you?"

"Yes, Coco, it's me. This is my friend Candle. I've bragged about the wonderful food here, so she's going to check it out," he laughed easily.

Coco cocked her head to the side and stared for a second. "Candle, that's an unusual name. You from around here?"

"Not far. She's Chief Bearclaw's daughter from Aspen Ridge. I mean Chief of…"

"I know what you meant. He was good to Rosy and Graham, you too when you were a little boy."

Candle pointed to herself. "Standing right here capable of talking for myself," she said in a hushed tone.

"Hey, Jacob, you'll never guess who's here," Coco called out, pushing a strand of hair over her shoulder.

A tall, heavy-set man with black hair, graying at the temples, stepped out of the kitchen. "Miacoh, they finally found you, but not in time for Rosy's funeral." The man shook his head sadly. "When did you get back?"

"I've been back a couple of months." Miacoh stepped forward and grasped the man's shoulder. "Mac, it's good to see ya."

"And you just now getting around to stopping by?" He jerked his head toward Candle. "Who's this ravishing beauty?"

"I've been busy taking care of the estate business. This is the first chance I've had to get away."

Coco interrupted. "Candle is Chief Bearclaw's daughter."

"Welcome, Candle. Take her to your favorite booth, Coh. It's on the house."

"No, it's not or we'll leave." Miacoh fisted his hands at his hips. "This is your livelihood, Mac."

"We'll see. Just get your asses over there and decide what you want." He waved the spatula he was holding above his head as he skirted the counter, returning to the kitchen.

Candle watched Mac cross the floor, then turned to Miacoh. "That is one big man."

He grinned. "Hence the name Mac, like a Mack truck." He let his hand slide to the small of Candle's back and guided her to the booth.

"Oh, that makes sense." She slipped into the booth. He slid in beside her and she picked up the menu. "Everything sounds so good. I think a ribeye, baked potato, and wheat rolls will do it." She licked her lips and pointed to the cherry pie a la mode. "I want one for now and one piece to take home to freeze for later."

"That's my favorite too. We'll just order a whole pie, eat our pieces here, and take the rest home. Work for you?"

"Oh, yes. I might even share another piece with you later. If you behave."

"Well, there went that offer. Behaving is not in my genetic makeup."

The waitress returned to the table and took their orders. "The man speaks the truth, but he can't help it." She winked at Candle.

She savored each bite of her steak as Miacoh did the same. After finishing her steak, she saved four little bites for Terra and wrapped them in the napkin.

After clearing the table, Coco brought out the whole pie and two plates with ice cream. She served each person one piece of pie, then snapped a top on the pie tin. "It should freeze nicely in this container." She tapped a finger on top of the lid.

"Wow, that's great, thank you." She picked up her fork and slid a bite into her mouth. She closed her eyes. "Mmmmm."

Miacoh reached into his jacket, pulled out an envelope with his name scrawled across the front, and handed it to her. "This is a letter from my grandmother. It is self-explanatory. After you've read it, we'll discuss anything you want to know in the car. Not here."

Mac stopped by the table. "Still keeping secrets, boy? How was everything?"

"Yes, I am. Everything was excellent. Now, the bill?"

"Well—see—there's a problem with that. Coco's pen quit working, and there isn't another one in the place. Sorry, it's on the house, with one stipulation."

Eyes narrowed, Miacoh stared at the older man. "What would that be?"

"You have to come back here at least once a month while you're staying in Aspen Ridge. Bring Candle along. Fair enough?"

"I can do that, but I won't be there much longer. Got a couple of things to wrap up with my grandmother's estate then I'm gone. I will stop by before I leave."

"Good. But I think you should stay."

"You and lots of others. But I can't." He stood, reaching for his wallet.

"That is hogwash, and you know it. You're afraid to face your demons." Mac shoved his meaty hand on his hips. "Maybe this pretty lady could help."

"Not an option. I don't remember you facing yours." He pulled a twenty-dollar bill from his wallet, palming the bill. "It's been great seeing you. Tell the family I said hi."

"I didn't have any to face. You were the lucky one. But now the tide is turning."

"Exactly." He turned to Candle and offered his hand. "Are you ready to go?"

She sat wide-eyed in the booth, knuckles turning white from her grip on the letter. She heard him call her name in a faraway fog. Breath whooshed out of her as she shook her head. *Wow, how long was I holding that?*

"W…What?" She looked at his outstretched hand and reached for it. "Uh, yes, I guess I'm ready to go." Getting to her feet, she hoped her legs would hold her. Candle's gaze met Miacoh's as she waved the letter and blurted out. "These things don't exist."

"I'm sure I don't know what you mean. The letter is genuine, written by my grandmother's hand." Lips pulled taut, he forced a smile, which faded quickly as he said firmly, "Let's go." He slid an arm around her waist, negotiating the dinner crowd that had wandered in while they ate.

Mac raised a brow and shot Miacoh a knowing look. "I hope you know what you're doing, bro."

"Me too. I've flown by the seat of my pants most of my life, and I'm still alive. Why change now?" The corners of Miacoh's lips turned up in a cocky grin. He stopped at the cashier counter on the way out. Tucked the twenty in Coco's hand, and folded her fingers over it, giving her a sly wink. "See ya around."

Candle barely got into the truck, and Miacoh closed her door when her cell phone rang. "Hello."

"An agent from Homeland Security is making inquiries about you. Candle, what are you mixed up in now?" Mark's voice boomed through the phone's speaker.

Miacoh took the leash from her and clipped it on Terrabyte, allowing Candle privacy for her phone call. She took a deep breath to settle herself and mouthed the words thank you as he closed the door and sprinted toward the trees, with Terra leading the way.

"First of all, Mark, I'm not your concern anymore. Remember, I resigned. I have no idea why Homeland Security would be looking for me. I haven't had time to address the subject we discussed last time we met." She calmly shoved the letter topic to the back of her mind. She'd deal with it later.

"The only thing I could get out of him was that his business with you had something to do with a traffic cam you accessed recently. Ring a bell?" Mark narrowed his eyes.

She blew out a breath. "Oh, that. I had permission. The reason I left after the funeral so abruptly was an emergency at home. The man who took my father's place as Chief of Police in our little town was gunned down on the side of the road. Keep in mind my hometown has never had a violent crime committed within its boundaries in the thirty-five years Dad was Chief."

She paused for a moment. "Okay, there was that time that Darla hit Joey over the head with a cast-iron frying pan. Knocked him out cold. But he deserved it. No charges were filed." She waved her hands in a dismissive gesture and continued. "The only clues we had on the new Chief's murder was a truck with a stolen license plate and two men that he stopped to see if they needed assistance before his death.

"When he left the men, he was alive and well. An hour later, he was dead. A long story short, I used the traffic cams to see if I could track down the truck before its arrival here. And I did. They stopped at home improvement centers in Denver and Colorado Springs. My dad, who is now acting Chief of Police, turned the info over to Pitkin County Sheriff's Department. Hopefully, we'll get surveillance tapes of the men's faces and what they were buying."

"Was that surveillance obtained?" Mark asked.

"I don't know. Dad was up most of the night and was sleeping when I called this morning. Since then, I've been out of town, and cell service is spotty. I'm surprised you reached me."

"You might want to check your messages. This morning, there was a computer glitch with your personnel file, but it's fixed now, so tread lightly and call me if you need me. I suspect Homeland Security will be in touch soon."

"Thanks, Mark." She tapped the screen ending the call, then cut her gaze to Miacoh returning from walking Terra. "Homeland Security is looking for me," she said in a voice filled with amazement. "Has something to do with the video cams I hacked last night, with permission. So don't get your hackles up."

She filled him in on what Mark told her then checked her messages before Miacoh pulled away from the Black Bear Inn. He just started to ease the truck out of the parking area and onto the road when she dug her fingers into his leg and said, "Shit, I've got 25 messages." She turned to him, holding out her phone.

He put the truck in reverse and returned to the parking lot. "You better listen to the messages, so you're prepared when we get back to town."

She listened to her messages. "Mom, Dad, and Gabby called. The rest are from Agent Patel and Gomez of Homeland Security."

He cocked his head toward her. "Trouble?"

Chapter Twelve

An Unexpected Twist

"Can't tell from the messages. They're pretty generic. I'll wait until we reach Aspen Ridge to return Homeland Security's phone calls. My guess—they probably already contacted Dad. I want to hear what his thoughts were before jumping into this apparent hornet's nest I seem to have created." She winced and turned to watch out the window.

While keeping his eyes on the road, Miacoh jostled Candle's arm when they reached the outskirts of town. "Why so quiet?"

"Just trying to figure out why all the attention to my traffic cam search, it was a sanctioned search. I turned the information obtained over to law enforcement in a murder investigation. So, what does Homeland Security want with me?"

Cracking his neck side to side, then rolling his shoulders, he stole a glance at her. "Candle, you're not that naive. You know as well as I do where this is leading. The occupants of the truck are not ordinary citizens. As suspected from the onset, with wrong plates and fraudulent registration decals, the truck was possibly stolen or borrowed from a survivalist who does his best to live off the grid. It adds up to a terrorist situation. The Chief was in the wrong place at the wrong time. What do you think?"

"But they didn't kill him when he stopped to offer help. They had to know he called it in. Why wait?" She reached into the back seat to pet a restless Terrabyte. "We're almost home, girl. Then you can run wild in the backyard."

"Because he had called it in. They also knew he cleared the call before he left the scene. At that point, the individuals were in the clear. They must have had something in that truck that worried them. What if he'd seen it and driven off, calling in reinforcements? So they tracked him down after they got the truck running or finished whatever they were doing. He recognizes them. They wait for him to get out of the truck, clear the dash camera, and shoot him. I don't believe he ever saw it coming. Why would he? Aspen Ridge is a nice quiet place. Nothing bad happens."

"'Til now." She shook her head slowly. "This is as bad as it can get. This town will never be the same. Shattered their sense of safety and security."

"Yeah, but with your dad at the helm again, they'll get through it."

"That's the problem. It's only temporary. He deserves retirement. The town will do anything to keep him in office now. An old man is not what they need. Like my dad said, that job is for a younger man. His reflexes are not as good as they used to be. The fact he thinks like that could get him killed."

"True. Then you need to get Gabby on it. Do you know what qualifications you want in the candidates?"

"Sort of, but Dad can help on that end, and we could use your input as well. Can you join Gabby and me for dinner tonight?"

He looked at his watch. "First, you better call her, and let her know you could be delayed."

"There's no way they could be on the ground yet unless this all went down last night before we left this morning."

"Better be prepared. Call your dad, see what he knows, then call Gabby," he advised.

"Okay." She pulled her phone out of her backpack then turned to look at him. "You didn't answer my question."

"You're trying to keep me here," he accused.

"No, I am trying to make sure my father is around to enjoy his retirement," she shot back.

"Touché. I'll join you and Gabby for dinner. Keep in mind, when all this is done, I will be on my way."

Not if I have anything to say about it. The corners of her mouth turned up in a slight smile as she touched the speed dial for her dad.

"Where the hell have you been?" Hunter said, forgoing the pleasantries of greeting. "There are agents from Homeland Security looking for you. I thought you said you had permission."

"I did. Calm down, Dad. Miacoh and I left early this morning for a ride and lunch. He took me to a place called Black Bear Inn. The food was good, but their pies are fantastic. I have part of one I'd be willing to share. Do you know a man named Mac? He sure seemed to know you, and so did the waitress there, Coco."

"Yes, I know him. He is part of Miacoh's...You're stalling. What's going on?"

"We believe the truck and its occupants may be the cause of Homeland becoming involved. There is no other explanation. I spoke to my former handler, and they wouldn't tell him anything either. I will call the agents right now, but I wanted to see if you knew anything before opening that can of worms. Did you hear from the sheriff's office? Were they able to obtain the surveillance from the building centers?"

"Why would Homeland Security be interested in a small-town murder? Even if it was an officer of the law?" Hunter asked.

"Miacoh has an idea, but we don't know for sure. We're going to stop by my cabin to run a check on my computer. Then we'll be over. If Homeland swarms the town, give me a call, would you?"

Miacoh shifted his eyes to her. "Weren't we headed for your parents' place? That changed?" He rubbed the back of his neck and blew out a breath. "You need to let me in on these changes, especially if I'm the one driving." He pulled a U-turn and headed in the opposite direction.

Her eyes rounded as he executed the U-turn. Terra went tumbling end over end in the back seat, only her seatbelt stopping her from crashing into the door at the opposite side of the seat. "I think that was illegal."

"Oops. Seriously, we need to get a handle on this situation, or it'll be the least of our problems." He screeched to a stop as the traffic light turned from yellow to red, waited for the light to turn green, then eased across the intersection. "What time is dinner with Gabby?"

"If you are right, there has to be more to it than the truck spotted in home improvements places. I want to track back a couple of weeks and see if we can spot them anywhere else. We're missing something. Somewhere that would bring Homeland's attention front and center.

Gabby is meeting us at seven."

"You have permission to hack into those networks again?" He raised an eyebrow quizzically.

She chewed on her bottom lip while twisting a strand of hair around her finger. "Well, permission wasn't exactly rescinded from last night, as far as I know."

"Great," he muttered, then drove right by the cabin and doubled back.

"What are you doing?" She twisted in her seat as they passed the cabin.

"Making sure nothing seems out of place—suspicious." He brought the truck to a stop in front of the cabin.

She paused a moment surveying the area then put a hand on Miacoh's arm. "Before we dive into this hornets' nest, I need some answers."

"It can wait."

"No, it can't. Expect me to believe you're a creature of myths and legends, a werewolf."

"In a manner of speaking. It's all in the genes. Either you're cursed with the wolf gene or you're not. It seems to skip generations. In our family, I suspect my father's hunting accident occurred while he was in wolf form. However, my parents avoided the subject like the plague and never answered my questions. When we were alone, Grams alluded to things changing as I got older, and I should be prepared. I could have the gene. But Mom would interrupt and say the old woman was making up stories for attention. My father died and the secret died with him. Until… That's enough info for one night, we gotta take care of the immediate situation. My history can wait."

"You're right. It's going to take me time to wrap my head around werewolves are real." She shook her index finger at him. "But don't you think we are done with the subject." She pushed open the door, stepped out of the truck, opened the truck's back door, clipped the leash on Terrabyte, and lowered her to the ground. They raced to the backyard gate. She unlocked and opened the latch. Terra raced forward, bounding across the yard, checking the backyard's boundaries. Miacoh's cell phone rang. Tapping the screen, he put the cell to his ear and walked back toward the truck.

After his call, she remained outside the gate, watching Terrabyte. He walked up behind her, brushed her hair from her neck, and breathed a kiss there. She flinched.

He backed away. "Are you going to go inside or just stand here?" He impatiently tapped his boot on the ground.

Without a word, she turned on her heel, marched to the front door, unlocked it, and deactivated the alarm. Sprinting straight to the computer, she switched it on. The machine whirred to life. He watched over her shoulder as she tapped the computer keys. Several files scrolled across her computer screen until one centered on the screen blinking "access granted."

"I'm in." She pumped her fist in the air. A few more keystrokes and she sat back, watching the screen intently. She highlighted a location and sucked in a breath. "Oh shit, oh my God, Miacoh, look at this."

A picture of the suspect's truck appeared on the screen next to the Pueblo Chemical Army Depot sign. The vehicle rolled to a stop. Two men dressed in jeans and safety yellow-colored sweatshirts with hard hats stepped out. One of them had paperwork attached to a clipboard. The other man waved to a woman across the screen, who promptly disappeared off camera.

"What are they doing there?" Her forehead creased.

"I don't know. The individuals appear to be contractors. There is active mustard gas from WWII stored at the depot, which is in the process of being destroyed. Bet that's why Homeland is calling you." He pumped his fist triumphantly.

She exited out of the files and program as her phone rang. She looked at the screen, then up at him and said, "Guess who? Right on time." She touched the screen to connect the call. "Candle Bearclaw."

"Ms. Bearclaw, you are a tough person to track down. We'll have agents in your location within the hour. Please wait where you are until one of them makes contact."

"Well, everyone might be better off if you tread lightly around here."

"—A threat, Ms. Bearclaw?"

"Oh, no, the townspeople are already edgy. Understand there hasn't been a violent crime in this town in over thirty-five years, probably more. They don't take kindly to strangers invading their town."

"Go on."

"As you already know, I was an employee of the government. Last night I was authorized to do some investigative work regarding the murder of the town's newly appointed Chief of Police. A position previously held by Hunter Bearclaw, my father, for those thirty-five years. Who, by the way, is now acting Chief of Police. So, in the interest of everyone's time, I think it would be better for me to meet your agents at my dad's house. That way, we can clear the air and move forward in the investigation. Have you been in contact with the Pitkin County Sheriff's Department? They were in the process of obtaining surveillance video that might be of interest to you."

"So, this breach of security is supposedly condoned by your agency? In connection with the death of Chief Roark Westin? Is that correct?"

"Yes, but you already know that. So, what is this really about?"

"The agents will meet you at Chief Bearclaw's residence in fifty minutes."

The call was disconnected. She took the phone from her ear and stared at it. "That was plain rude." She paused for a couple of beats. "I'll get Terra, and let's go to Dad's house and fill him in before the suits get there." She tucked the computer in her backpack and walked to the back door.

"You got it."

Fidgeting in her seat, she checked the side mirror for any signs of being followed. "I didn't realize how much I distrusted government entities and their agents."

"Not distrust. Experience and knowledge of how they operate. In this case, I wouldn't worry about it. I doubt they are lying in wait. My sources indicate that Homeland only put the pieces together early this morning. When you accessed the traffic videos again and backtracked, that's when it all clicked, but they already had agents in the air."

"Your sources?" She raised an eyebrow turning her attention to him.

"Of course. You don't think I'm going to let either of us walk into this blind. Always be prepared for the unexpected." He turned right a couple of blocks before the Bearclaw home, drove down a few more blocks, and circled.

"Don't see anything out of the ordinary." He pulled up in front of her parents' house. Her dad stood in the doorway as she jumped out of the truck. Miacoh opened the back door and released Terra. She bolted down the sidewalk and he sprinted after her leash in hand.

A slight smile crossed her lips. "That's why you clip the leash on her before you release the seatbelt." She smirked.

Hunter, jaw clenched, ushered the group into the house without a word and closed the door. "You going to tell me what the hell is going on?" were the first words out of his mouth as he turned, glancing out the window before his gaze landed on her.

Pekabo stood in the doorway to the kitchen, dark circles under her eyes, her mouth set in a thin line, gaze darting from her husband to Candle, over to Miacoh, and back to Hunter. "Coffee, anyone?"

Candle shook her head. Hunter and Miacoh nodded in unison. "Yes, please."

"Let's all sit down, and I'll fill you in." Candle motioned to the chairs.

She relayed the events of the morning as they happened. "So, the agents should be here within the next thirty minutes. The best way to handle this is to try and give them the full picture. Have you heard from Pitkin County? Did they get the surveillance video?"

Pekabo carried a tray with mugs of steaming coffee into the living room, setting it on the coffee table in front of the group. She picked up a purple paw print mug with small marshmallows melting into the frothy liquid, handing it to Candle. "I made this for you." She quickly headed for the kitchen, then returned shortly, sipping on a mug, and eased down on the couch next to Candle.

"Thank you, hon." Hunter smiled at his wife, picked up a mug off the tray, blew on the hot liquid, and took a careful sip. "The good news. Yes, we have pictures of their faces, somewhat obscured. But I bet Homeland can run facial rec on them, get IDs, though the sheriff's department was working on that last I checked."

"Heck, Dad, I can do that." She set her mug down and reached into her backpack.

"How about we wait for the agents? Need to calm the powers that be and get them working with us, rather than ready to pounce on us. Now may I continue?" Hunter frowned at his daughter.

She nodded, zipping her backpack, reaching for her mug, and taking a sip. She licked frothy marshmallows from her upper lip.

"The bad news is what they purchased. The man with stringy blond hair bought a large number of nails and fertilizer. The other one appears to have dark hair, cut short. He picked up ball bearings, wires, and tubing. They purchased this stuff in large quantities at several stores. In Colorado Springs, they walked over separately to a discount store next to the home improvement store and bought vinegar, peroxide, sugar, and eight car batteries.

"Who the heck needs eight car batteries?" She pulled her bottom lip through her teeth.

"Shit. Those are an excellent source of sulfuric acid." Miacoh let out a low whistle.

She wiped her sweaty hands on her jeans staring at Miacoh, who took a swig of his coffee.

Her eyes rounded as the color drained out of her face.

Miacoh put a hand on her arm. "Candle, you okay?"

"We are dealing with—terrorists, aren't we?" She paused before the word terrorists slipped off her tongue. Heat now coloring her cheeks. "I left that world behind, only to have them show up in my backyard. Some coincidence." She fisted her hands in her pockets.

Nodding solemnly, Miacoh confirmed her statement and said, "It's believed to be exactly that, a coincidence. There are many potential targets up and down the Front Range. What better place to lie low and gather supplies than near a quiet little town next to a playground of the rich and famous?"

"How long have you suspected this?"

"Since I took that phone call at your house. At this point, we need to back off and let the feds take over. These may be very nasty people."

"Ya think? Your sources have ID'd the men in the truck?" Hunter rubbed at the back of his neck.

"Not yet, but they're close. The surveillance video was kinda intercepted," Miacoh said matter of factly.

Pekabo let Terrabyte in through the back door. The pup streaked through the living room, barking just as the doorbell rang.

Candle shoved up from the couch. "Here we go. Let me answer the door." She put her hand in front of her dad's chest and shot Miacoh a warning glance as he stood up.

"You can handle the situation, but you're not answering my door alone." Her father pushed aside her restraining arm.

Hunter looked out the peephole then opened the

door. "What can I do for you?"

One man dressed in a dark, pinstriped suit, and the other a woman dressed in a black and white suit stood on the porch with badges flipped open. "We are looking for Candle Bearclaw and Miacoh Zane."

"May I?" Miacoh stepped in front of Hunter. He reached for one of the badges and pressed a number on his phone. "Yeah, I have Agent Jedediah Adams, and," he leaned forward to get a better look at the female's badge and ID. "Caitlin Rossy standing in front of me. Can I get a description and confirmation of assignment?"

He held the phone away from his ear so Candle could hear. The voice on the other end said, "Jed is five feet ten inches tall, stocky build, light brown hair and hazel eyes, distinct scar over his right eyebrow. Never smiles." There was a little snort from the man on the phone. "Caitlin has auburn hair, cut short, five-foot seven-inches tall, athletic build, and bright blue eyes. Computer status has them enroute to your location. Confirm this matches the individuals standing in front of you."

"Affirmative. Thanks."

He put the phone back to his ear. "Hey, Miacoh, Caitlin can kick your ass with both hands tied behind her back, so don't test her," the voice on the other end of the phone added, laughing.

"Highly doubtful but copy that." Miacoh ended the call and stepped aside.

"Come in." Hunter held the door open. He pointed to his daughter. "This is Candle Bearclaw. Miacoh is the one that confirmed your identities. Can I get either of you a cup of coffee?"

"No thanks." Agent Adams eyed the crease in

Candle's jeans at her right ankle. He nodded to Caitlin.

"Would you like to sit down? We'll share the information we have obtained. A deputy from Pitkin County should be here shortly." Hunter returned to his chair and motioned that the agents should have a seat on the couch across from him. Candle and Miacoh sat on the loveseat at Hunter's left, nearest the door. Once seated, Agent Adams took out a pen and a flip-type notebook. Caitlin slid an electronic tablet out of her inside jacket pocket.

Hunter tossed a file on the table between them. "This is the case file of our murdered Chief of Police, Roark Westin. He replaced me when I retired a few months back. I hope you understand that our top priority is to catch and bring to justice his killers. We intend to use any resource available to us."

"Understood. But if we're dealing with terrorists, national security takes precedent over your murder investigation. Withholding information or interfering in our investigation will not be tolerated. Do all of you understand? That includes Ms. Bearclaw. We know your reputation with the CIA and…"

"Hold on there, anything I've done regarding this case is with permission. I'm willing to share what we've learned. Coordinating our efforts will work better than threats. As you know, I am or was very good at my job."

"Now who's throwing around threats?" Agent Rossy slid to the edge of her seat, eyes narrowed.

"No one. I was merely offering my services to your agency should you need them. In return, we—" Candle took a moment to glance at her father and Miacoh then continued, "—expect to be included in your investigation as it pertains to ours. Currently, I believe we have a jump on your investigation, quite by accident."

Hunter and Miacoh nodded in agreement. She shifted in her seat, waiting for confirmation from either of the agents.

Agent Adams cleared his throat. "Unfortunately, we aren't authorized at present to share our information."

"Ok, then we don't have anything to add to your investigation until such time you obtain authorization. If you want, I'll contact my sources and obtain that authorization for you." Hunter smiled and snatched the file from the table.

"That won't be necessary. We're going to step outside for a moment." Caitlin gave her partner a little shove toward the door.

"Sure. Would you like that coffee now?" Hunter asked.

The agents nodded in agreement, then walked outside and closed the door behind them.

Pekabo stood up from her corner of the couch. "I'll put on a couple pots of coffee. Would anyone like something else to drink besides Candle?" Her lips twitched as she looked at the door the agents exited then glanced back toward her husband. "Should I fix a light meal?"

"That would be a good idea. We're going to be here for a while." Hunter kissed his wife. "I don't know what I did to deserve you, but I'm thankful."

"Aww, you sweet-talker." Pekabo kissed her husband on the lips.

"Geesh. Get a room." Candle covered her eyes then giggled.

"Got one right down the hall." Her mother pointed

and snickered.

Shaking her head, Candle stood, reaching for Terra's leash. "I'm going to take her for a walk. I don't want her outside alone right now. Be back in a minute. Mom, you need any help in the kitchen?"

"Not right now, dear." Pekabo sauntered toward the kitchen. "Hunter, just so you know, you owe me big time for this." She winked at him before disappearing into the kitchen.

"So, what's new."

She headed out the back door. "Oh, Mom, don't fix anything for Miacoh and me. We have a dinner meeting in town at seven this evening."

Pekabo whirled around to face her daughter, raised an eyebrow, and grinned.

"Aww, mom, not that kind of meeting. It's a business meeting." She shut the door behind her.

****

Miacoh stood up and stretched his arms above his head. "I don't want to tell you how to do your job, but I think we're better off letting Homeland take the lead. It won't be long before the FBI is involved if they aren't already. I'm sure Candle will be able to keep us in the loop. And my sources are usually a couple of steps ahead of the Feds too."

"I couldn't agree more." Hunter pushed up from his chair and stared down the hallway. "I'll be back shortly."

Miacoh paced around the living room. The doorbell rang again. He glanced out the window and saw a Pitkin County Sheriff's cruiser parked behind his truck and the black SUV parked in front of the house. Opening the door, he smiled at the deputy as the agents glared at him, moving off the porch toward their SUV.

"Come on in," Miacoh waved them through the door.

"I can't. We're short-staffed today. I got to get back." The deputy handed Miacoh a large brown bi-fold file folder and asked that he sign for it. "If you have any questions, contact Commander Williams. He's heading up this investigation." The deputy handed him the commander's card.

He closed the door as Hunter walked into the living room. Miacoh waved the folder. "The sheriff's office just delivered this. The agents saw the deputy pull up, but they didn't intercept him for some reason. Do you want to review the contents before they come back?"

"It's probably the surveillance records, which I imagine Homeland already has, but let's take it into the kitchen and have a look."

He slit the red tape with his pocketknife then unwrapped the string from the back of the file. He started to slide the papers out onto the kitchen table. He stopped and sucked in a breath. "Uh, Hunter the surveillance records are here, but...look at this."

Chapter Thirteen

Life Goes On With a Bit of a Cat and Mouse Game

Miacoh held up an 8x10 photograph marked on the back "Chief Bearclaw only—original." Candle and Terra came in the back door and looked at the pictures.

"Who're those men in the picture with Councilwoman Wright?" Candle looked at Miacoh as the scorn on his face darkened to thundercloud level as he shuffled through the other pictures.

"It looks like our esteemed councilwoman has a connection to our two persons of interest." He tossed pictures of the two men inside the home improvement center, next to the image of Mrs. Wright. Then pulled out his phone and flashed photos of two men and a woman then scrolled to an encrypted email that stated, "facial recognition matched your men at the building centers to Adrian Murphy and David Smith (which may be aliases, still checking). In other photos attached is their sometime associate Erin O'Shea, an Irish citizen in the United States on a student visa. My sources say her file with Homeland and NSA has been corrupted. They are working on that now."

Candle and her dad compared the photograph with the pictures on Miacoh's phone.

"When did you get these," Hunter asked.

"Just a few minutes ago," Miacoh said. "I believe

that Erin O'Shay is the woman in the pictures at the Pueblo Chemical Army Depot."

The front door slammed, and footsteps sounded on the tile floor of the entryway. Hunter shoved the pictures and file in a kitchen drawer. Miacoh cleared the screen of his phone. Terra intercepted the agents, snuffling at their feet and barking.

"Leave it, Terrabyte. Sit." Candle ordered, sprinting in from the kitchen and ignoring the strange looks from Agents Rossy and Adams.

Terra's butt immediately hit the floor, and her big brown eyes looked at Candle. She pointed to Terra's pink paw-printed blanket in the corner of the tiled kitchen floor. "Place." Terra ambled over to the blanket and lay down. Head resting on her paws, she looked up to Candle, who tossed a treat directly between her paws. Terra gobbled it up.

Hunter and Miacoh joined Candle and the agents in the living room. Negotiations were back and forth as to who would provide what. If they agreed to a joint investigation, who would be lead?

Finally, it was decided that Hunter would retain the lead on the murder investigation. Homeland or the FBI would maintain lead on the terrorist aspect of the case. All information is to be shared among the law enforcement entities involved. Miacoh raised a brow and glanced in Hunter's direction, who shook his head slightly. Miacoh stood. "Candle and I have a meeting in town in an hour, so we are going to leave the exchange of information to you enforcement types." He turned to Candle and asked, "Is Terrabyte coming with us?"

"Yes, I'll go get her. She'll go to sleep in the truck and be fine." She rose from the couch, grabbed her unzipped backpack and Terra's leash. She walked into the kitchen and kissed her mom on the cheek. "See ya tomorrow."

Out of sight of the living room but in plain view of her daughter, Pekabo opened a drawer, drew out the pictures and file, slid the items into Candle's backpack, and zipped it up. She returned to the living room, planted a kiss on her dad's cheek, and followed Miacoh to the front door.

Once in the truck, she said, "Mom put that photo of the suspects and councilwoman in my backpack. What do you want to do with it?"

"I don't know what your dad has in mind. I'm a little surprised she gave it to you. Must have wanted it out of the house. We'll talk to Hunter about it tomorrow. For now, I think we'll leave it at your place, in the safe."

She stiffened. "What makes you think I have a safe?"

"Because it's in your nature. Trust no one. So, it stands to reason you would have a safe for any documents you don't want compromised or items of value. Am I right?" Miacoh asked.

Shrugging her shoulders, she grinned sheepishly. "You'd be correct."

He snorted a laugh and pulled into the parking lot of Angus Steak House.

"There's Gabby's Beemer over there. Park behind it." She unfastened her seatbelt and turned around in the seat to make sure Terra had food and water in her travel bowls. "We'll be back in a little while. You stay." She ruffled Terrabyte's fur affectionately.

Gabby already had a booth in the back. Menus and drinks were on the table. She smiled and stood when they approached. "It's about time you guys got here. Now, what's all the mystery about?"

She gave Gabby a quick hug and slid into the booth. "Thanks for coming. I need your help. With dad acting as interim Chief again, the council isn't going to be in any hurry to hire or even look for a replacement. Especially given the circumstances and the ongoing investigation."

"No kidding," Gabby said.

"But, Gabby, Dad isn't in the mindset to be Chief anymore. He believes his reflexes are slow. That kind of thinking could get him killed. I need you to light a fire under the council and get a search going for a replacement. I know we should still have the finalists from the last search. It hasn't been that long ago."

"Sounds like you are on top of the situation. What do you need me for?" Gabby cocked her head to one side.

"I don't have any influence with the council. They can't figure out why I gave up the glamorous spy job to live and work in a small town."

"I understand that. Why did you?" She smiled mischievously.

"Don't go there. As I said, it was time for a change. Now, will you help me or not?"

"It'll be an uphill battle until this case is solved. Would you want the position of Chief if your predecessor was recently murdered in the line of duty and no suspects were apprehended?" Gabby shook her head as the waitress passed. "Let's order and resume this discussion after dinner." She raised her eyebrows and nodded toward the rapidly filling up dining room.

Over rib-eye steak, baked potatoes, and green salad with ranch dressing, they talked over changes in Aspen

Ridge and its citizens since the murder. When the Chocolate Mousse dessert came, they kicked around making the residents feel safe and secure again. Then they formulated a plan to make sure the council listed the job and interviewed the candidates in a timely fashion.

Miacoh and Candle fielded questions from the residents dining in the steak house regarding the case. Upmost in the townspeople's minds were suspects. They assured individuals it didn't appear that the perpetrators were local or still around. Indicating there were persons of interest that they were not at liberty to discuss—hoping to ease the residents' minds.

"Well, this evening didn't go as planned." Candle stretched her arms over her head.

Miacoh nodded. "But the people seemed more reassured after voicing their concerns."

Gabby covered a yawn with the back of her hand. "I have an early flight tomorrow back to Atlanta. Ben and the kids flew back this morning. School tomorrow. I'll do what I can from Atlanta and have a full report for you when I return with my family the Monday before Thanksgiving." She picked up her purse and reached for the check.

Miacoh swept the check off the table. Candle waggled her finger in front of Gabby shaking her head. "Nice try, but this was at our request."

"Okay." Gabby started toward the door then abruptly turned around nearly causing them to run into her. "Let me just say this. The best candidate for Chief of Police is standing right beside you." She poked her finger in Miacoh's chest.

He frowned and opened his mouth to speak.

Gabby held up her finger and shook her head. "No,

no, don't say a word. I know you're not staying. You've made that abundantly clear. But—I'm just saying." She spun around on her heel and sashayed out the door, looking over her shoulder once to wink at Candle.

"What was that all about?" Miacoh grumbled, his frown deepening into a thunderous scowl.

"I'm sure I have no idea." Her brow creased as she watched Gabby pull out of the parking lot and speed down the road, red taillights bouncing in the dark.

Wrapping his arm around her waist, he nudged her hair away from her ear with his cheek and whispered, "How about I take you home and build a nice fire in your fireplace? I put a nice bottle of wine in your refrigerator earlier today. When Coco bagged the pie at the restaurant, she included a box of homemade peanut butter cookies. We could relax and enjoy cookies and wine by firelight." He gave her a little squeeze and pulled her closer to him.

"Is this a come-on?" She leaned into him.

"If you want it to be. I'm tired of everyone yammering at us and would like a nice quiet end to the evening with you." He brushed his lips lightly over hers.

She closed her eyes and let warm feelings wash over her. She knew it wasn't wise to become involved with a man who'd made his intentions very clear. But she couldn't help but hope he would change his mind. *They could battle his demons together if he would only talk about them with me.* The family secret his grandmother wrote about in her letter didn't bother her as much as she thought it would.

She turned to face him and wound her arms around his neck. Her lips still warm and moist from his kiss, she raised her mouth to his and returned his kiss with reckless abandon. Heart pounding in her chest, knees weak, her emotions whirled and skidded to a stop as she made a decision. She wanted this man, and she was going to have him. Slowly she eased away and opened her eyes to see him gazing into hers. What was that she saw in his eyes?

"I accept your offer," she said quietly.

Effortlessly, he swept her off her feet and carried her to the truck. He braced her against his chest as he dug in his jeans pocket for the key and unlocked the truck. Sliding her into the passenger seat, he kissed the tip of her nose and closed the door.

By the time he reached the driver's side of the truck, Terra had woken up, her paws on the console and tail wagging. She gently pushed the pup to the back seat and rubbed her belly for a couple of minutes. The pup yawned and went back to sleep.

As they approached the cabin, she wiped her damp palms on her jeans and blew out a breath. Nothing seemed amiss. The porch light on a timer shone brightly. Opening the truck door, she turned to see Miacoh holding the drowsy pup and walking around to her side. He carried Terrabyte into the cabin and placed her on the pink blanket. She promptly bounced off the blanket and skidded to a halt at the door whining.

"I'll let her out while you start a fire." She reached for his arm and leaned against him as she stood on tiptoe to kiss him gently. "Then we can take up where we left off."

"Deal." He bent down to crumple the newspaper next to the logs and kindling on the hearth.

****

A few minutes later, Miacoh stood brushing his

hands against each other to get the pine bark off and watched the orange flames lick at the edges of the kindling. In the kitchen, he pulled the bottle of wine out of the refrigerator, popped the cork, and left it on the table to breathe.

The first cupboard he opened had an assortment of tumblers. On the top shelf, crystal wine glasses sparkled. He took two and poured the rich red liquid into the glasses. He swirled the wine and breathed in the fruity scent with just a hint of spice. Closing his eyes, he took a sip. "Nice." Next, he warmed the cookies up on a plate in the microwave, took them out, and set them next to Candle's wine glass. Footsteps on the back porch turned his attention toward the door. The wind howled around the corners of the cabin.

The back door flew open with a burst of face-tingling cold. Candle and Terra rushed into the warm kitchen. Candle slammed the door behind them.

"Whew, it feels like a storm is brewing out there." She shrugged out of her coat and stepped into his waiting arms.

"I'll warm you up." He smiled seductively, wrapping his arms around her and drawing her to him.

He rested his cheek against the top of her head for a moment. "Better?" The cheery fire reflected in their wine glasses.

"Much." She glanced around the room. "Perfect ambiance. You must have had lots of practice then, leaving a trail of broken hearts behind."

"Not as much as you think." He chuckled. "Like you, my job left little time for social endeavors. Women are looking for stability in a relationship. I couldn't give 'em that."

Easing down on the couch, he patted the seat beside him. "Don't want to mislead…" Terra barreled toward the couch and jumped. Front paws on his chest, she licked his face then curled up in a little ball beside him with her head resting on his leg and her rear to Candle.

"Well, I guess I see where I rate." She took a seat next to Terra. "It's probably for the best. You'll be gone soon." A little sigh escaped her lips. "Terra, you know you're not allowed on the furniture." She gave her pup a little shove. The dog snuggled closer to him.

"You're right." He picked up his wine glass and took a sip. The prospect of leaving town was becoming less and less attractive. *Maybe I could…* Taking a deep breath, he blew it out slowly, took another sip of wine, and leaned against the couch, his arm slung over the back, resting across Candle's shoulders.

The pup raised her head, her big brown eyes switching from Candle to him and back. She shifted then panting jumped down off the couch.

"I knew it wouldn't be long. She gets too warm on the furniture. Besides, she really isn't allowed up here." She waited a beat. "Good dog." She reached down and scratched behind the pup's ears who then trotted off and plopped down on the cool tile floor of the kitchen.

Feet tucked up beneath her, she rested her head on his shoulder. They relaxed and enjoyed the wine in companionable silence while the flames raced up the aspen logs turning the wood to glowing embers.

He glanced at his watch. *Where had the time gone? It was nearly one in the morning.* "I'd better be going. It was nice to relax without interruption."

"It was." Lifting her head off his shoulder, she straightened, yawned, and got to her feet. "Wow, how'd it get so late?" She picked up the empty wine glasses and started toward the kitchen. "Hey, why don't you crash on my sofa?"

"What will your neighbors think if my car is parked here all night?"

"Does it matter? It's past midnight now. If they want to talk, they are already doing it." She snorted. "Or—" Standing on tiptoe, she wrapped her arms around his neck and slipped her fingers through the soft hair at the back of his neck. He tugged her closer, tipped her head back, and cupped her chin tenderly in his hand. He took her mouth with his.

Her lips parted as his tongue slipped inside, caressing, teasing, tasting, and enjoying her flavor. His fingers caressed a trail down her neck across her shoulders, finally feathering the side of her firm breast. He reached for the bottom of her sweater and paused his gaze, searching hers as if asking permission.

She gave a slight nod. He pulled the garment up over her head, displaying a lacy barely-there bra against her smooth bronze skin. Fingering the lacy material, he flipped open the clasp spilling her soft chilled mounds into his warm hands.

"Oh my God. That feels good," she murmured, arching against him.

"It's going to get a lot better," he whispered, unbuttoning the top button of her jeans, massaging her lower stomach, and slipping his hand inside her lacy red panties. "Are you sure about this?"

"Never been more positive," she said breathlessly.

"We need to get this off." He lifted her, and she wiggled her hips out of the jeans. To her surprise, he eased her down on the cool countertop, positioning himself between her legs. His fingers teased at the crotch of her panties then slipped under the band to where she was already hot and wet.

A growing bulge beneath the zipper of his jeans ached for release. He started to adjust himself when her hand slid over his stopping him.

"Let me do that." She fumbled with the button on his jeans for just a minute then it released. She pulled the zipper down slowly, leaned forward, and shoved the jeans over his hips. With the palm of her hand, she massaged his bulge.

Her fingers grasped the waistband of his briefs, she tugged them down. Curling her foot between his legs, she pushed the offending material down his thighs. Her hand wrapped around his length, her fingers lightly caressing him. She thrilled at his response. Built for a woman's pleasure, she had no doubt.

Yanking his shirt over his head, he brushed her hand away, then caught her nipple in his mouth. He sucked for a long moment, then licked his way over to the other breast swirling his tongue around the nipple until it was a hard little berry. Her breath hitched. She arched toward his mouth, moaning softly, inching her center closer to him, spreading her legs wider to wrap them around his hips. He grasped the crotch of her panties and ripped them away.

"You're going to pay for those." She giggled.

"Gladly." Sliding his hands under her cute little ass, he lifted her off the counter and slid inside her, pinning her back against the wall. Locking her ankles around his waist, she spread wider wiggling to get the friction needed at her center as he thrust into her deeper and deeper.

Groaning, he moved inside her until he felt her muscles tighten around him. Waves of ecstasy throbbed through her as she pushed hard against him. Riding her out until the last bit of control snapped, he shoved up in her until his pulsing stopped and slid to the floor with her. Rolling to his side, he cushioned her against his body. Hair damp with sweat, he brushed a strand away from her face and kissed her, running his tongue softly around her lips.

Exhausted, he helped her to her feet, swept her into his arms, and carried her down the hall to the bedroom. They collapsed atop the king-size bed. They rolled up in the quilted comforter and drifted off into the sleep of sated lovers.

****

Sunlight streamed in the bedroom window when Candle felt a cold nose on her hand and heard a muffled woof. She ruffled the pup's fur, then leaned over the edge of the bed to see that Terrabyte had a brightly colored sock in her mouth, butt up in the air, tail wiggling excitedly. "Oh, no, Terra. Drop it." She remembered all the clothes they'd left on the kitchen floor last night and groaned, flopping back onto the bed.

"What's wrong?" Miacoh mumbled sleepily, wrapping an arm around her and pulling her closer.

Trying in vain to wrestle out of his grasp, she pointed. "Terrabyte has one of my new red and white striped socks in her mouth. Heaven only knows where the rest of our clothes are that we left on the floor last night."

Unconcerned, he nibbled on her ear, then kissed his way down her neck while his fingers gently teased between her legs. "How about a repeat performance?"

Silent for a beat, she pressed against him and stretched up and brushed her lips across his slowly, deliberately. The house phone on her nightstand rang.

"Shit." She rolled over and took the phone out of its cradle. "Hello."

"Where have you been? I've been trying to call you all morning on your cell."

"Mom? Has something happened?" She sat up in bed and swung her feet to the floor.

"No. Not exactly. Your father thought you'd be over early this morning, so he set up a meeting with the councilwoman in the picture. He went alone because I couldn't reach you. He just called and said she canceled the meeting at the last minute. He's on his way back. Thought maybe you'd want to be here when he returned."

"Mom, we agreed to let him handle this, so unless I hear from him. I'll be over later."

"I called Miacoh's cell phone, but he didn't answer either. Do you know if he got home safe?"

"I'm sure he did. Don't bother Miacoh. You know he can handle himself."

Her mom sighed. "Ok, see ya later."

Candle surged to her feet. "I'm going to take a shower."

Miacoh reached for her hand but missed. "I had other things in mind," He sat up and swung his legs over the side of the bed.

"Not in the mood, now." Not bothering to put on a robe, she strode across the floor naked and into the bathroom, leaving the door ajar.

After a big jaw-popping yawn, he stood and padded silently across the floor. "I'm going to let Terra out. But

I'll be back."

She turned on the shower, adjusted the temperature, and stepped into the water spray. She heard the bathroom door creak open farther, and close softly then Miacoh pushed aside the shower curtain. Still naked, his massive shoulders filled the shower doorway. His raised brows asked, and her nod answered as he stepped inside. His arms snaked around her slick, wet body, hands massaged her breasts, as his arousal slid between her legs and steam wafted through the room.

****

Candle quickly dressed in jeans, a worn School of Mines T-shirt over a pink stretch tank top, slid her feet into slippers, let Terrabyte in from the backyard, and opened the dog door.

She got mugs out of the cupboard, put the coffee on, and surveyed the kitchen. An open bottle of wine and two wine glasses with red wine still in them sat on the kitchen counter. What a waste of a nice wine, she thought. Clothes lay in piles all over the floor.

Breathing a sigh of relief, she picked up the piles from last night. Everything appeared to be unscathed except for her brand new socks and Miacoh's sweater, which currently resided on Terrabyte's blanket. After finding little damage on the sweater, she laid his clothes across the chair back.

She tossed her garments in the clothes basket for wash day. The aroma of freshly brewed coffee filled the kitchen. Miacoh's heavy footsteps sounded down the hall before she saw him saunter naked into the kitchen and pick up his clothes from the chair.

"I guess I left these here last night." He grinned, pulling on his black silk briefs and then the jeans. When he picked up his sweater, he shook it out and held it up for Candle's inspection. "I think this one has seen better days. I'm not sure I agree with Terra's modifications. No fashion sense." Shaking his head, he poked his finger through several tiny holes. He balled up the sweater and tossed it toward the pup's area. "Someone might as well get use out of it." He chuckled.

"Could be a little chilly outside this morning without a shirt," she mused as the corners of her mouth turned up.

Walking over to her, he put his hands on her waist and pulled her against him kissing her tenderly. When he released her, he leaned his backside against the counter, one hand in his pocket, his bare feet crossed at the ankles, and watched her scramble eggs in a pan. "I always have a change of clothes in my truck. I'll get a shirt from there for the drive home."

"You could make yourself useful and get down glasses and plates." She pointed to the upper corner cupboard. "The silverware is in the second drawer next to the door."

He got down glasses and plates then pulled open the silverware drawer. "Do you always keep your weapon with the silverware?" he asked raising a brow.

"Only when the silverware drawer is near the back door," she quipped back at him, taking the eggs from the stove and dividing them between the two plates. "The orange juice is in the refrigerator, mind putting it on the table?"

"Nope." Inside the fridge, he spied the orange juice, a jar of strawberry jelly and grabbed both then set them on the table. Four pieces of toast popped up.He added butter, put the bread on the table, and eased into a chair.

After breakfast, Miacoh helped clear the table, dried the dishes that Candle washed, and put everything away. "I'm going to head home, change, then check messages, and things like that. Any plans for today?" He paused before walking out the door.

"Not that I know of, I have to go over to my parents' house and see what set my mother off this morning." She shook her head.

"Probably making up for all those years you had them on permanent ignore," Miacoh snorted before closing the door.

"I didn't have them on ignore. It was just safer for them. They understood. I called home once in a while," she said to an empty room. "And made Christmas a couple of times." She sat down at the computer and touched the power button. She tapped in the access code given to her recently and tried the NSA's files on Erin. After a few minutes, she was in. The file appeared to be damaged by a virus attack. Hmmm, on one file, seems odd, she thought. Her phone rang as she was about to run it through one of her many repair programs.

Chapter Fourteen

Holiday Planning vs. Homeland Security—A Bad Mix

Candle checked caller ID as her cell phone rang. "Hi, Gabby. Back safe and sound? How was your trip?"

"Oh, the trip was fine, the twins bamboozled their dad into letting them stay home from school an extra day." She blew out a breath. "But other than that, smooth sailing. I'm going through the applications of the finalists for the Chief job and there weren't many with good people skills and law enforcement expertise. Roark was it, which explains why he got the job hands down."

"I guess we need to post the job again, huh?" Her heart tripped with anxiety. The last thing she wanted to do right now was deal with helping to locate a pool of good candidates. But on the flip side, she didn't want to see her father do the job any longer than necessary.

"That might work if they haven't heard what happened to the last one. I gotta tell ya, that is going to make this a real challenge." Gabby paused for a beat then continued. "But that's not the reason I called. Remember years ago, when our families would get together for the holidays? It was such fun."

Candle's mind drifted back to a time when card tables sat in the front room of her family's home, giving them extra space to accommodate their guests. The fire crackled merrily with the adults' table closest to the stone hearth and the kids' table pushed up next to it. Board games spread all over the couch and floor while they decided which game to play first. There was good-natured bantering, Gabby's dad's bad jokes, but everyone always laughed. It was a great time among good friends.

"Candle? "Gabby raised her voice a bit.

Gabby's voice yanked her back to the present. "What…uh…yes, on Thanksgiving, we'd get up early, go skiing, come back to eat, and play board games while football blared on the TV with no one watching. But your dad always cheated." Candle laughed.

Gabby giggled into the phone. "That's because he thought your dad needed to be taken down a notch or two. Good times. Anyway, I wondered if we could do it again. There'll be a few more people, but I think your mom and dad would love it. I know my mom and dad would. Ben and the twins—really have no choice." Gabby chortled. "It's two weeks to Thanksgiving. Plenty of time to pull it together. Don't you think?"

"Sure, I'll run it by Mom and Dad. Dad will fuss he has too much to do with this murder investigation. But a day off would do him a world of good. Mom's worried about him being back on the job. You know what happened?" Candle proceeded to tell her about the phone call this morning and the worry in her mother's voice.

"That's so unlike free spirit Pekabo," Gabby said gravely.

"I know. An old fashion Thanksgiving celebration will be good for everyone." She was already excited at the prospect and raring to get the preparations underway.

"I think Miacoh will benefit from it too," Gabby

added.

"Oh, so that's what this is about." Candle glared at the phone. "Don't play matchmaker. We're not in seventh grade anymore." She tried to keep the irritation out of her voice, but the last thing she needed was Gabby's interference.

"I know, but really, I thought the get-together would be good for everyone, considering the situation. And…"

"Gabby, I know that tone. What else are you cooking up?"

"In recent years, Aspen Ridge's Maintenance Department has strung the lights on that big old Blue Spruce in the center of town, you know at the pavilion. That's it. Thus far, no decorations. No events—nothing."

"Oh, that's so sad. The town used to celebrate the lighting of that tree. Everyone came out no matter what the weather. There were carolers, school bands, choirs, contests, then everyone moved over to the church and had a potluck and chewed over the events of the past year," Candle said wistfully. "That was so fun and heart-warming. No matter where I was on Christmas, I always remembered the celebrations here. It made my Christmas. The town doesn't celebrate like that anymore?"

"Nope, haven't for years. I think revitalizing the celebration would be good for the town's morale. Get everyone together. It'll be a lot of work. Need to find or buy new decorations for Main Street lampposts, decorations, and new lights for the tree. Bright, colorful posters announcing the celebration and potluck. We need someone from the church to coordinate the potluck. What was that lady's name that always coordinated the food?"

"Martha Moranti. She's getting up there in years, Mom says, but has a passel of daughters active in that church. Maybe they could help. I'll check with her." She paused for a moment. "But as far as new decorations for Main Street, the street department would have to put them up and that could be costly. And new decorations and lights for the tree. I'm not sure the town can or will spring for it."

"Oh, they will, after the generous anonymous donation made to the Christmas Tree Lighting Fund." Gabby giggled mysteriously. "What's the use of being rich if you can't enjoy spreading the money around? That's my husband's motto and the only reason I married him." She continued to giggle. "Not really. He's a great guy. Besides, it would be so much more fun for the twins."

"If Dad is on board, he has some influence. After all, he is the Chief of Police. I'll talk with him about it this evening when I go over there. It'll be nice to talk about anything but the murder. I think once Mom and Dad think about it, they'll be on board."

"Good. I'm going to try to come out early for Christmas to help, leave the kids with Ben for a week or so, then they can come after school is out."

"But doesn't Ben travel a lot?"

"Yes, but not during the holidays. Family is significant to him. In fact, he's the one that suggested the Christmas thing. I always tell him how it used to be every year at Christmas. He thinks there should be more towns with that type of community." A loud crash and then screaming came through Gabby's side of the receiver. "I gotta go. Kids are fighting. Talk to you next week. Be sure and include Miacoh in all this."

"He's not going to stay, Gabby. Too many bad memories here for him." She sighed.

"Never underestimate the Christmas Spirit. Things will work out. I can feel it," Gabby said cheerfully.

"Ok, Miss Glass is Always Half Full." Her lips twitched. No wonder Gabby was her best friend.

"Nope, that has changed since you left. The glass is always full. Bye."

She ended the call and stood for a while, staring at her phone. Excited by the prospect of a Thanksgiving get-together with Gabby's family and her own. The holidays were always the roughest away from family and friends. She was usually in some foreign country, holed up in a hotel, hacking a system to get intel, hoping to get out of the country without being caught. Except for the last assignment, hacking was only a small part of it, implanting a virus created by her for destruction and playing the role of… Well, that was over. Or was it?

****

After finishing the shopping, she put everything away and straightened up the cabin. Finally, it was time to head over to her parents' house. Anxious to discuss the holiday plans with them, she walked to the back door and opened it. "Terrabyte, time to go." Candle shut the door and waited. Terra raced in through the dog door, tore through the cabin, and skidded to a stop at the front door. Candle closed and locked the dog door, secured the back door, and set the alarm before exiting the front door with Terra in tow.

When she arrived, there were two black SUV's and a Pitkin County Sheriff's cruiser parked in front of her parents' house. The happy song she'd hummed on her way over faded from her mind. Cheerful thoughts of holiday preparations disappeared, replaced with a cloud of foreboding. She shook herself, pasted a smile on her face as she clipped Terrabyte's leash on her harness, then lifted her from the back seat. When Terra's feet hit the ground, the pup immediately started barking and pulling on the leash toward the front door. She stood her ground until the puppy stopped pulling and turned its attention to her.

Her mother opened the door before she knocked. The dark circles under Pekabo's eyes remained, maybe worse than yesterday.

Wrapping an arm around her mother's shoulders, Candle whispered, "What is going on? Have these people set up command in your house?"

Pekabo gave her a wan smile. "It sure feels like it. Didn't leave until late last night and were here about dawn this morning. I don't know what's going on. I've decided that if I'm going to survive this, I have to go about my business and let them do theirs. It can't be all-consuming like it is for your father. I don't know how much more…"

"Mom, this will all be over soon. I know why they spend so much time here. It's your cooking. You're providing most meals, aren't you?" At that thought, the muscle in her jaw quivered. She didn't like these people taking advantage of her mother's good nature. She hadn't seen her mother at the easel in several days. The last time she'd been here, the dabs of paint on the pallet that her mother used were dried up with the brush still sitting there. Not in the cleaning solution. She'd meant to mention, but…

Her mom grimaced. "I can't very well feed your father in front of them? Can I? And keep your voice down, they'll hear you." She nodded toward her guests as they stood in the entryway.

"Sure you can. The agency gives allowances for food, etc., when on assignment. It's time they used it to get their own meals. There's a fine cafe right down the road." Candle crossed her arms across her chest and stared into the living room.

"Oh, I couldn't do that. Anyway, come see the new painting I've started." Pekabo smiled and grasped her daughter's hand, dragging her through the living room to the studio in the back of the house. Lifting the cover, she sucked in a breath as big brown eyes stared at her from various shades of golden fur, a flower garden in the background with mountains reaching for the sky.

Relieved she hadn't mentioned the dried paint, she gushed, "Mom this is beautiful. I bet that garden looks just like yours did this summer. Huh? But Terra wasn't here then."

"Honey, it's called imagination. I see her in my mind running near the garden, and that's the result."

"If she'd been here in the summer, you wouldn't have a garden." Candle laughed. "She'd romp through it, destroying it. That reminds me, we need to fence your flower and vegetable garden for next year if you are going to let her run free out back. She is still a puppy and prone to puppy destruction. I can get a pen for her if you like."

Pek fisted her hands on her hips and frowned at Candle. "Absolutely not. I'll not have Terra in jail while she's here. You were very destructive as a child, taking things apart and not always putting them back together—at first. Of course, that changed. At any rate, we didn't jail you."

She held her hands up in the air in surrender. "I only meant if she is an inconvenience…" At her mother's continued storm cloud looks, she stopped, changing the subject.

"I talked to Gabby today before I came over. She wants to celebrate Thanksgiving with both our families together like we used to. As I remember her parents' house is quite a bit smaller than ours, do you think we could fit about ten to twelve people in here for dinner? Since we'd like to have it here, everyone will bring something, and you don't have to fix any food unless you want. Gabby's talking to her parents today and will let me know this evening if they agree."

"Of course, they'll agree," Pekabo said fiercely. "I'll call Rita right now and make sure."

"Mom, let Gabby handle it."

"Rita will think it will be too much for Hunter and me right now. Nothing could be farther from the truth. Thanksgiving, like it used to be, will be good for us. Take our mind off this terrible business for a while."

"Ok, you know Rita and Matt better than I do, but Gabby…"

"Gabby will be fine. Rita and I can work out the details. It'll be easier than going through Gabby. She still tries to be in the middle of everything." A giggle bubbled up from her mom's throat. "Just like when she was a little girl. Who all are you counting on being here?"

As she talked, Candle ticked off the fingers of both hands. "Gabby's family, four, plus her brother and parents, that's another three, our family makes three more, and Miacoh."

Pek's eyes lit up and her lips curved into a wide smile. "Miacoh?"

She sucked in a breath, then just sighed. "Now don't start. We're taking it one day at a time. He can't stay here."

"Sure he can. Miacoh needs to buck up. Everyone has skeletons in their family closet. Some more than others. But with good friends, they get over it, he will too. Thelba Rice called me just before you came over and asked if Miacoh was having trouble with his truck. It was parked at your place all night."

Another sigh escaped her lips as she rolled her eyes. "No, Mom, his truck is just fine."

Her mother smiled wide.

Hunter walked through the doorway. His usually sparkling eyes seemed dull, and his lips set in a thin line. He forced a smile. "There you are. I'd like you to join us in the living room. Miacoh should be here shortly." Hunter swung an arm around Candle's shoulders and kissed her on the cheek.

"Ok, but...Mom, Gabby has some great plans for Christmas too. Maybe Rita can fill you in when you call her."

Pekabo took her cell phone out of her pocket. "I'm calling her right now. By the way, I want to include Jedediah and Caitlin in the dinner count if they can't go home for Thanksgiving."

She did another eye roll and turned her attention to her dad. "Did you get much sleep?"

"Enough," he answered evasively. "Jed had the pickup the men were driving taken to Colorado Bureau of Investigation's lab in Arvada. They found traces of C-4 in the bed and what appeared to be blood splatter on the right front headlight. Found out this morning, it's Roark's blood type, so..."

"That could tie the men to Roark's death. Any closer to locating them?"

"Not yet. Looks like they disappeared into thin air. And the girl…"

"I know, her Homeland files for her student visa were corrupted, NSA's too, but I'm working on that, as we speak."

Hunter quirked a salt-and-pepper eyebrow. "Do I want to know how?"

She licked her lips and rolled her tense shoulders. "Probably not. I'd rather you not say anything to the agents yet, either. Don't want to cause problems if I can reconstruct the info and their techs can't. I believe the suspects are lying low until time to execute whatever they are planning. Do we know if they are members of a faction or working alone?"

Her mind slowly sifted through recent terrorist cases she'd been involved in. A case in Great Britain where a terrorist attack used PE-4 in the streets of London popped up first. Stateside, nothing came to mind, but that wasn't her area of expertise.

"None of them have a record or are on any watch list. But they are mercenary types, have nice bank accounts, and have no permanent address. Move around a lot." Hunter took his baseball cap off and scratched his head. He replaced the cap with a tug. "Which means they are good at flying under the radar or haven't been involved in any illegal activities on US soil." She followed her dad back to the living room. Scattered over all the horizontal surfaces were charts, maps, and files. Laptops set atop the clutter.

She stared from her dad to both agents and the sheriff's deputy. She fisted her hand on her hips and drew herself up to her full height, narrowing her eyes. "Did any of you happen to notice this is a home, not a command center? It's not open 24/7. The food is provided by my mother, who has worked herself to the bone. Not to mention my dad, who…"

Hunter's eyes flew wide open. "Candle, that's enough. It's my home, and we need to solve this murder, so everyone in town can get on with their lives, rather than hole up inside their homes in fear." The dark expression was one that she knew well after crossing her dad on his turf.

She looked around the room, noting the sheepish expressions on the agents' faces. The deputy seemed oblivious as he pushed the front door open and walked out, talking on his cell phone.

"Dad, we'll discuss this later. But they will clear out of here by six tonight because you and Mom are going out to dinner with me."

Miacoh strode in the front door as the deputy walked out. He stood in the middle of the floor surveying the situation. "With us," he corrected firmly.

"Nice to see you, Miacoh." A smug expression spread over her face.

"Right back at ya. Now, what did I miss?" He shifted his eyes from the mess to Hunter.

Hunter repeated what he told Candle. The agents added their input while picking up the maps and folding them into a neat pile. The deputy returned, indicating he had to leave but would be in touch.

Miacoh put his hand on Hunter's shoulder and nudged him into the kitchen. He poured a cup of coffee and turned to Hunter. "Any word on the councilwoman? I stopped by the building center parking lot on my way here and checked around. The spot where that picture was taken is almost beside the cart corral."

Hunter scrubbed his hand over his face. "So, it could have been just an innocent exchange as she put her cart away, which is what I'm hoping. That woman would talk the ear of anyone who would listen. The weird thing is there appear to be gaps in the surveillance video around the time the picture was lifted from the video."

"Homeland aware?"

"Yes, but I've requested they let me handle her until there is more proof she is involved."

"Could be a malfunction."

"I hope so."

Candle leaned against the door frame into the kitchen. "I'm going to run home and change clothes. I'm not really dressed to go out to dinner. Besides, I want to pick up my computer. Don't like being without my laptop. I'll meet you back here then we'll go to dinner."

Chapter Fifteen

What the Heck Happened, Holiday Plans and Dinner Discussions

When she drove up the circle driveway, a chill shot up her spine, and a strange feeling came over her, almost like someone was watching. Reaching under the seat of her SUV, she pulled out her handgun. She checked the weapon to make sure it was loaded, chambered a round, and tucked it in the back waistband of her jeans, covering it with her shirt and jacket. She backed out and then drove the entire driveway more slowly, checking the perimeter. Nothing.

The cell phone alarm app hadn't chirped to alert her of a breach, but she checked her outside surveillance cameras, then the ones inside her home anyway. Again nothing. She shrugged off the feeling and stepped out of her SUV. Drawing her gun, she flicked off the safety and turned on the laser. It didn't hurt to be safe rather than sorry.

Peeking in the window, she saw the alarm keypad was still set and secure. Then she walked around the house, entered through the back door, closed, relocked it, and deactivated the alarm. Nothing was out of place. Part of her wished she'd brought Terrabyte along.

Though still young, the pup's tracking ability was well-developed. Terra would know if someone were in or around the cabin since they left. Her back to the wall, she moved carefully through each room, nothing. When she was sure the house was clear, she sat down at the computer, laying the gun next to it.

Warning windows popped up everywhere on the screen. Someone had tried to hack into her system but hadn't gotten very far. Closing out the windows one at a time she found a message planted just under the first layer of security.

It must have set off the warnings. Her throat went dry as she read the message. "Poking around where you don't belong is dangerous business. Carl's death was unfortunate but an accident. Leave it be or pay the consequences."

Fingers poised over the keyboard. She started to X out of the message but stopped. If this was a disintegrating message, she would have no proof it ever existed. Taking out her cell phone, she took a picture of the screen. The handle on the front door jiggled.

She grabbed her gun and jumped up, making her way to the front bay window. Miacoh's truck had parked behind hers. She blew out a breath as she padded silently to the door and checked the peephole.

He pounded on the door. "Candle, are you in there? Are you all right? It's Miacoh. Open the door." He stepped back a couple of feet from the door, his hand behind his back, holding a gun she'd bet.

She opened the door. "What are you doing here?" She glanced around behind him.

He flicked the safety on and tucked the gun back into his waistband. "I don't know. Just a feeling after you left that something wasn't right. Rather than ignore it, Terra and I drove out here to check. Besides, there's no need to take two vehicles to dinner." He looked back at the truck, where Terra was scratching at the windows and barking loudly.

She glared at Miacoh. "You should've transported her in her crate." She rushed to the truck, opened the door, and snapped on Terra's leash. She picked the puppy up out of the vehicle and hugged her before setting her down on the ground. "You tear up the interior of Miacoh's truck and he won't let you ride in it anymore."

She examined the interior of the truck. "No damage. As you can see, I'm fine. But I'd like you to take a look at this." She led him into the house and pointed to the computer screen.

He read the message on the screen, then looked at Candle. "Did they hack your computer?"

"No, I have several layers of security. It got caught in the first layer. But the person knew their way around a computer." She frowned. "Funny thing is. My computer wasn't connected to the internet. I purposely disconnected it and unplugged it."

"Was the alarm tripped?"

"No. I don't see how anyone could get in. But contrary to all appearances, someone got to my computer."

"Surveillance cameras show anything?"

"Unfortunately, there seems to be an intermittent software glitch I haven't figured out yet. I'll scrub it and reload the program."

He frowned for a moment, staring at the computer screen over her shoulder. "Do you want me to call your parents and tell them to go on ahead without us?"

"No. Tell them we'll meet them at the restaurant. I'll send that message to Mark, then shut down my computer and take it with me. The home security system wasn't tampered with. I want to reload and check the surveillance before we leave. Make sure it's working. Should only take a minute." She took a screenshot and sent it off to her handler then cleared the screen, rebooted the computer, and made adjustments to the code as the program loaded. Exterior shots of her cabin popped up. She rotated through them then switched to the interior view.

Miacoh leaned over her shoulder. "Looks like they're working correctly. You appear to have a blind spot in one area."

She nodded absently and pulled out her cell phone. After she tapped an icon on her phone, she entered a series of numbers and letters, and the same view popped up on her phone. "Yep, seems to be working right now. I'll reset it and we'll go. I think events over the past couple of months are wearing on me. My imagination is working overtime."

"Okay. But you're not sleeping alone any time soon."

Her brows flew up and her eyes rounded. "Say what?"

"Boy, that came out wrong." He chuckled, his cheeks flushed. "I meant I don't want you spending time alone at night until we have all this sorted out. So, either I'll stay out here at the cabin with you, or you can stay in my grandmother's house with me. Separate rooms, of course." He winked at her.

"I'll think about it and let you know." She smiled and started to the back door to let Terra out. "You know Thelba Rice called mom to see if you were having vehicle trouble because your truck was parked in front of my cabin all night."

He grinned. "Some things never change. Still…" Grabbing her arm, he took a step toward her. His mouth set in a thin line, his facial expression thunderous, but he loosened his grip when she gave him a hard stare. "This isn't up for discussion."

"Let go of me, or you'll be cleaning up the puddle." She glanced at the wriggling puppy.

He released her, the corner of his mouth twitching. "I don't do puddles. But you aren't staying alone."

"Understood." She turned the doorknob.

With every fiber of her being, she wanted to rail against his demanding demeanor. But the reasonable side of her knew he was right. At the agency, she learned to pick her battles.This was no different and a skirmish she wasn't going to win.

She shrugged, turned on the flood light, checked the backyard, and let Terrabyte outside. The pup raced around the perimeter of the yard, skidded to a stop on the far side of the yard, sniffed, and let out a low growl.

In a flash, Miacoh sprinted out the door and over to where the pup stood. He vaulted the fence with ease and disappeared. A few minutes later he returned.

Still standing in the doorway, Candle shouted, "Leave it."

"Nothing here." He ambled back to the porch.

Terra thundered through the door and raced to the front door. Her whole body wiggled impatiently in the entryway. She stood looking at Terra until her butt hit the ground. "I don't want to leave her here by herself. I'll grab her crate. We take my SUV. I'll put her crate in the back. We can return later and pick up your truck."

"Probably better to have a strange vehicle sitting out

front anyway." He picked up the crate and walked toward the door.

After Candle set the alarm, they trooped out to the SUV and got inside. Miacoh slung the crate in the back and seat belted it in. She coaxed Terrabyte in with a chew bone, closed the door, and slid into the passenger seat tossing him the keys. On the way to dinner, she filled him in on Gabby's plans for Thanksgiving, leaving the Christmas plans for another time.

"Will you come to Thanksgiving dinner with all of us? Should be a lot of fun."

"You know, I'd like that. Besides, how else will I be able to keep an eye on you?"

The standoff passed, and she decided to broach the subject again. "About that. Miacoh, I've been taking care of myself since I left home. And in some pretty dangerous situations, I might add. I don't need a bodyguard."

"I know that, but humor me, your dad will sleep much better knowing you are not alone out there at night."

Candle shifted in her seat and studied him. Gabby's words floated through her mind. Now that she'd had time to think about it, Miacoh would make a good chief.

He glanced at her for a moment, a quizzical expression on his face. She didn't look away.

In her professional life, she'd always chosen her battles carefully and avoided situations that could have cataclysmic results. While this one was fraught with land mines, she had to at least mention it for the good of all involved though he wouldn't see it that way.

She took a deep breath. "My dad would sleep better if you applied for the Chief of Police position."

His head swung around, he hit the brakes and stared at her for a beat, then he returned his attention to the road. "What…where'd that come from?"

"Oh, come on, you know everyone's been thinking about it. I'm the only one brave enough to bring it up."

"That's unfair, Candle, and you know it." The muscle in his jaw twitched.

"What I know is that you don't want to face your demons, so you use them as an excuse to keep people at arm's length, never settling down. You can't live like that forever." She turned away from him, watching out the window but still able to see his reflection in the glass.

The corners of his mouth turned up in a sly grin. "I don't believe you were at arm's length last night."

She whipped her head around to face him so fast she nearly gave herself whiplash. "That's not what I meant, and you know it. I read your grandmother's letter. That's quite a family legacy. Let's talk about it, so you can deal with it once and for all."

"If it was only that easy. You don't understand. But since we are here, let's go into the restaurant and table this discussion for now."

"Okay, just answer me one thing. During your time in the special forces, did you ever experience any of what your grandmother described?"

His eyes met and held hers as he paused for a couple of seconds. "Yes, I did. The heightened abilities of strength, hearing, smell, and sight came in handy during my assignments. The shifting not so much. I kept that under wraps. Our team's assignment completion record was one of the best."

Her eyes widened as a rush of adrenalin tingled through her body and her pulse quickened. "Can you still—shift?"

"Yes. But the longer I'm away from my people, the less desire I have to shift. It's a pack thing and in the genes. Or so my grandmother believed. She also claimed the ability to shift skipped my father's generation, but as I said before, I don't think that was true. I believe the accident that injured him happened while he was in wolf form.

"I've no proof. Mom would shush Dad any time he seemed ready to open up to me rendering the topic taboo at home. Grandmother didn't—never mind we've been over this. We need to go." He pointed across the parking lot where Hunter and Pekabo stepped out of their car. Pekabo immediately spotted them and waved enthusiastically.

"This conversation is not over, not by a long shot." She shook her head slowly and stepped out of the truck, grinning at her parents.

Chapter Sixteen

Dinner Uninterrupted—It was Good While it Lasted

"Sorry we're late." She hugged her parents and followed them to the restaurant entrance.

Her dad stopped short and turned to her. "Did something happen?"

She shrugged. "Had a last-minute computer SNAFU."

Her father raised an eyebrow questioningly.

She'd never been able to lie to her dad. "Well… someone tried to hack my computer at the cabin. Didn't get through, nor did they get in—but Terra thought someone was outside."

"And you're just now telling me? You should have reported—"

"Dad…it's okay. Everything is fine. I deal with this type of stuff all the time. Besides Miacoh checked it out and found nothing."

"Not in my town you don't."

"Men." She huffed out a breath. "Miacoh is going to be staying with me at the cabin as security, just to be sure." She glared at her dad. "Satisfied?"

Another couple walked up behind them. "We'll see." Her dad yanked open the carved wooden door to the restaurant, held it open for Candle and her mother, and let Miacoh catch the edge of the door and follow them in.

"Welcome to El Toro's, Chief, it's good to see you. Pekabo, how's the painting coming? Usual table?" The waiter motioned to a square wooden table in the far corner of the room.

"Yes, thank you, Tom. How's the family?" Hunter clapped the waiter on the shoulder. Then he slipped his arm around Pekabo's waist and followed Tom.

"Good. Cindy starts school next year and she's more than ready. Only missed the cut-off this year for kindergarten by sixty days." Tom shrugged. "Pam takes her to preschool three days a week. The other two mornings Cindy stands in the window and watches the other kids walk down the street to school." He moved the table away from the wall and pulled out Pekabo's chair.

"That's tough." Pekabo rested her hand on his arm for a beat. "Our Candle was the same way. It gave her an advantage in school. Your daughter will be the same." She eased into the chair. Hunter scooted around behind the table.

Some things never change. Dad always liked the table where he could see everyone and had his back to the wall. She smiled. *They deserve a relaxing retirement.* She vowed to make sure they got one. Miacoh held out the chair for Candle, then took a seat next to her.

El Toro was the best Mexican restaurant in town. Once they placed their orders, between waitress visits, Hunter quietly recounted the discussions and decisions made regarding the local case after Candle and Miacoh left. Pekabo said the council was actively seeking candidates for the Chief's position. Especially after Homeland indicated it could be several months before their case was strong enough to make any arrests.

"But they have Roark's blood on the front headlight of their truck. Why isn't that enough to bring them in?" Candle stared at her father.

Hunter shrugged. "In my book, it is, but we don't have the DNA test back, only that the blood type was his, a common blood type. That makes a difference. And we don't have the murder weapon. We know it was a .45 caliber used at close range, but no matches in the database. Homeland won't even let me tell the townspeople we have persons of interest, and they're not local, which would go a long way to putting their minds at ease. Pitkin County is supportive but claims their hands are tied. It's the feds' investigation." He paused as the waiter made his way to their table.

The waiter brought out enchilada plates with rice and refried beans for Candle and her mom. Miacoh had an empanada plate with queso dip and rice, while Hunter had chile rellenos. A ceramic dish with warm tortillas was placed in the center of the table. "Will there be anything else?" the waiter asked.

"Don't think so. Everything looks wonderful," Pekabo said.

"The wine." Hunter reached for a tortilla, rolled it up, and took a bite washing it down with a sip of water.

"I'll have it right out." The waiter hurried away.

Using his fork, Hunter cut into the chile rellenos and continued, "I imagine that Homeland is afraid if they pick them up too soon then have to release them, they'll go underground and never be found again. If we are dealing with organized terrorists, rather than just homegrown dissidents."

"Or something else entirely," Candle added hopefully. "There's something not quite right about this whole scenario."

Her dad narrowed his eyes. "You got a better idea?"

"Not yet, but I'm working on it," she shot back.

"Then may I finish?" He paused for a beat.

She nodded and took a sip of her water.

"On the flip side of that, if they are planning something, it might be better to flush them out, throw charges at them, and see what sticks. If the DNA is a match, I'm sure the DA will issue a warrant for the men's arrest, but the woman wasn't involved, that we know of. No reason to pick her up." He paused as the waiter returned and placed a bottle of wine in the center of the table and opened it.

"Will that be all?" the waiter asked.

Candle glanced around the table at the nodding heads. "Yes. Thank you."

Her dad poured the wine but hesitated at Miacoh's glass. "Wine?"

"Yes." Miacoh shot him a questioning look.

"Are you driving home?"

"Of course. One glass with the meal will not cause a problem," Miacoh said testily.

Hunter poured the wine and chuckled. "Just giving you a hard time, son."

Miacoh shook his head. "Damned if you do, and damned if you don't.

"Do they know the whereabouts of the men?" Candle inquired.

"If they do, they're not telling us," Hunter said disgustedly. "Our next move should be to contact Bess before they get wind of her. I want to rule out her involvement. I'll set another appointment with her tomorrow morning. Will you two be able to attend?"

"I don't think a formal appointment is the way to handle this. I am not questioning your abilities, sir, but in my experience, catching them off guard is the best way to find out what you want to know."

"Dad, I have to agree with Miacoh."

Hunter scratched his chin, then lifted his water glass, taking a long drink. He set the glass down and looked at Miacoh. "We put a discrete tail on her until the time is right, then walk up to her and start a conversation eventually leading to the men and the picture?" He pursed his lips and nodded slowly.

"Dad, I see you do that all the time. That's why you are so successful and well respected as Chief." Candle eyed her dad. "This is no different, except you have to be sneaky since there are other agencies involved."

"We aren't talking shop tonight. Remember?" Pekabo pursed her lips. "But I've something to add then I'd like to change the subject to Thanksgiving and Christmas celebrations."

"Sure, Mom. Did you get a chance to talk to Rita?"

Pekabo smiled, nodding. "Yes, we had a nice conversation. Thanksgiving is a go, and we are working on Christmas. I want to tell you all about it, but first I'd like to talk about Bess."

"Sorry to interrupt." Candle shifted in her seat to face her mother. "Go ahead."

"She visits the beauty shop every Tuesday at nine a.m. sharp. I could stop in and make an appointment about the time she's finished, which should be around ten-thirty. Then when we walk out of the shop, Hunter here could join us and talk about council business, then Candle could wander by, bring up the topic of people in parking lots, maybe being rude or nice and see if she volunteers anything."

"Wow, Mom, that's a great plan. Don't you think, Dad?"

"I don't like your mother involved in this." Hunter's forehead creased in a frown.

Pekabo's shoulders stiffened. "Well, I don't like you being Chief of Police again either, but we all gotta pitch in to get through this." She narrowed her eyes at her husband, then glanced at Candle and back to Hunter.

The table was silent for a few minutes as Hunter and Pekabo glared at each other. The waiter stopped by to refill coffee cups and offer a dessert menu.

Candle took the dessert menu. "I want something decadent and chocolate, with lots of calories." She licked her lips, perusing the menu. "Anyone else interested?" She waved the menu in the air, brought it back down, and studied it again. "I'm going to get this fudge lava cake with chocolate chips. Add extra fudge sauce."

"You will be sick tonight if you eat all that." Her mother reached for the menu. "Let me see that."

"I don't care. It's been a rough day, and I want to discuss holiday celebration plans. Thanksgiving is only a few days away." She made eye contact with each party at the table. "Okay?"

Hunter tilted his head to the side, raising his eyebrow. "Anything I should know?"

"Nope." Candle peered over the menu at her dad just before her mom snatched the menu. "So, what do you think the chances are of us getting the town to provide labor to put up new Christmas decorations? Gabby's going to purchase the decorations."

Her dad's head jerked up. "Why?"

"Gabby said the town quit decorating for Christmas

a few years back, except for the shops that do window displays and the big tree in the town square. She claims last year half the bulbs were burnt out on the tree. We'd like to revive the holiday traditions, including putting up working lights and decorations on the huge evergreen in the town square."

Her dad rubbed his chin with his thumb and forefinger. "Hadn't thought about it, but she's right. Town went through a tight budget spell. I'd finally put my foot down and insisted the town was getting too big for one part-time deputy and me. It became a pissing match and the council let everyone know they had to cut the Christmas lights and decoration budget to pay for two more police cruisers and find money for salaries for two full-time deputies."

"I see. So now—"

"I don't see a problem getting the town to provide the manpower to put up the decorations. That particular storm blew itself out quite a while ago." He shrugged. "No one brought up the subject of Christmas decorations after that. Leave it to Gabby to bring it up again." He chuckled. "This town needs you two."

Candle's cell phone chirped. She checked the caller ID. "Shit. Excuse me, I gotta take this. I'll be back in a minute."

Miacoh took the opportunity to discuss the housing market in Aspen Ridge. "Do you two know anyone interested in buying a property? Grandmother's estate is almost settled, and the house will be transferred to my name. I want to put it on the market."

Pekabo knew of some young families that were outgrowing their current residence. Hunter didn't think the house would be on the market very long.

"Are you sure you want to sell it? It's a nice house." Pekabo glanced at him.

"Yes, it is, but way too big for one, even if I was looking to stay here. Which I'm not," Miacoh said firmly.

"Son, what do you have against our town?" Hunter wanted to know.

"Too many ghosts." Miacoh's tone meant the subject was closed.

Hunter raised an eyebrow. "You'll have to deal with those ghosts one day."

"So I've been told." The words came out harsher than intended. "I didn't mean it like it sounded. I'm just not ready to dredge all that up."

The waitress stopped by the table and took the dessert orders. Miacoh ordered the fudge cake for Candle and more coffee for himself. Hunter ordered strawberry cheesecake, and Pekabo chose the same chocolate lava cake as her daughter, minus the extra fudge.

Candle strode back to the table and stuffed her phone in her jacket pocket. "I'm sorry to cut this short, but I need to take care of something. The high-speed internet service at my cabin is required."

"That's too bad. We just ordered you the fudge cake," her mother said. "Guess it'll just have to go to waste."

She paused, glanced at her watch, then fingered the phone in her pocket. "Oh, well…What the hell, a few more minutes won't make that much difference. If it does, I'll deal with it." Candle straightened her shoulders and sent Miacoh a covert look.

After finishing dessert, they said their goodbyes in the parking lot. Candle and Miacoh climbed into her

SUV and waved as her parents drove toward home.

"Now, back to the tabled discussion." Candle shifted in her seat to face him.

"Not much more to tell. Our family history died with Dad and Grandmother." He shook his head sadly.

"What happens if you shift unintentionally?"

"Never going to happen. I have full control. And before you ask, a full moon makes me restless, but otherwise has no effect whatsoever."

"Okay. What are the odds you could pass that gene onto the next generation?"

"Not sure. But probably pretty good. I'll be upfront if it happens. You worried about it?" he teased, sending her a sideways glance.

"Of course not." She sniffed and turned to study the landscape whizzing by the window. "You're leaving town."

"So, what about the phone call?"

She sighed. "It was Mark. They traced the attempt to Falls Church but couldn't pin it down. He wants me to see if the hacker left any trace on my computer that could help them. Did the hacker create a back door to use later? That kind of thing. Mark was emphatic that my involvement be limited. I'm all for that. When we get to my place, I'll fire up the laptop and see what I can find. Limiting any kind of deep dive into the attempted hack is going to make finding anything more difficult, if not impossible, even for me."

****

The soft glow of the porch light welcomed them as he slowed the SUV in a cursory pass around the cabin. Parking in back, he hopped out and opened Candle's door.

"And they say chivalry is dead." She giggled ambling around to the back of the vehicle. She flipped open the back door and unlatched the crate. Terra bounded out of the crate.

He snapped on the leash before the pup was able to reach the ground and handed the leash to Candle. "I want to check the perimeter of the house before we go in. Wait here?"

"No. We'll go with you. Always like to make sure the backyard is secure with no unwelcome visitors before letting Terrabyte loose." She pulled out her phone, tapped an icon, entered a password, and checked her surveillance system moving the screen so he could see. One blank frame scrolled past.

"Looks like you may need to adjust the one camera on the outside corner. It's not recording."

As they passed by the front window, she peeked in. The solid blue light on the alarm shone brightly indicating it was armed and hadn't been breached.

He stood behind her. "It didn't show a breach last time you were here either. But…"

"I don't think anyone was inside. Somehow, they activated my computer remotely."

"Without it turned on, or plugged in?"

"Yeah. It has a large-capacity backup battery. Mark thinks I may have left it connected via the Ethernet wire. I don't remember unplugging that."

He nodded and reached for her hand. "You don't use Wi-Fi?"

"Sometimes on my tablet or phone. As far as the computer, having it hardwired should make it more secure."

Passing the corner where the camera needed to be

adjusted, he flicked his flashlight on and directed the beam at the camera. Two wires stuck out at odd angles.

"Hey, I connected those myself." Candle stared at the damage as Terra pounced on something below the camera, stopped, picked it up in her mouth, and began crunching. Candle knelt and grabbed the pup's muzzle. "Drop it." She forced open Terra's mouth and cleared it with her finger. A small plastic object dropped to the ground.

He brought the beam down to the ground. A mangled wire nut lay in the dirt a few inches from another one not quite so mangled. "There's the answer to your blank frame." He bent down and plucked both from the ground.

He reached behind his back and drew his gun, holding the flashlight below the weapon. "Bet these didn't just fall off."

She shook her head. "I made sure all connections were tight and tested the circuits after dad and I finished installing the outside system."

They completed the perimeter search, released Terra, and strolled to the back door. She unlocked it and the system began beeping. After disarming the alarm, she flicked on the lights. He searched the house while she stood at the back door keeping an eye on Terra.

"All clear."

"There's a ladder in the garage, next to the bucket of tools I used to install everything." She opened a kitchen drawer and pulled out a bag of wire nuts. "Need to fix that tonight."

"On it." He holstered the gun and opened the interior door to the garage. "Tomorrow we might want to clear out this space so you can park inside. Don't know what's going on around here, but it appears someone is messing with you."

Her eyebrows squished together, she tilted her head and chewed on her bottom lip. "I don't have any idea why. I turned in my work computer and never stored any work documents on my personal laptop. Then there's the issue of knowing my whereabouts."

"You've used your personal computer to investigate this murder." He raised his hands, palms up, and shrugged. "Could be related."

"True, but...it doesn't feel like...I gotta call Mark anyway."

"He's your or was your handler. Right?"

She nodded.

"Didn't you close the book on your spy life?"

"Yes, but with Carl's death so soon after I left—I can't help but wonder if it had something to do with me."

"Or the assignment you refused to continue."

"I wasn't in deep enough to warrant this much attention. Again, my work computer and all files pertaining to that are at the agency."

"Possibly someone doesn't know that?" He hauled the ladder into the cabin and carried it to the back door. The pup came racing in the dog door, collided with his leg, and looked up growling and barking at the ladder.

"Terrabyte." Candle squealed, grabbing hold of the ladder to steady it as he widened his stance in an attempt to keep his balance and control the ladder.

"I've got it."

She released the ladder and snatched Terra off the floor. "It's all right, girl. She's never seen a ladder before. She was in her crate while I used it outside." She grinned sheepishly. "So, this sort of thing didn't happen." Leaning into the garage, she grabbed the bucket and closed the door.

"No harm done." He carried the ladder outside and kicked the door closed with his foot. Leaning the ladder against the cabin, he took out his gun and flashlight again. Directing the beam to the ground he searched for footprints, tire tracks, and signs that someone had been around. A few nights had been below freezing, so the ground was firm leaving no trace. The only thing he found was scuff marks leading toward the woods behind her cabin. They appeared to stop a couple of places along the outside of the fence where pickets had been replaced recently. *Probably her dad or her, yet they continued a few yards on into the woods and then disappeared entirely. Huh?*

After one more circuit around the cabin grounds, he climbed the ladder and repaired the wiring, tucked the wires behind the camera, and tie-wrapped them in place out of sight. He checked the other cameras, both vehicles, and returned to the cabin.

"All fixed. Want to try the system again?"

"Already did. Watched you check the other cameras, your truck, and my SUV before you came in." She laughed. "Talked to Mark, he claimed to be able to access my computer via the Ethernet without a problem. Like the perpetrators, he couldn't get past the first layer. He offered to send me a scrambler to plug into, but I'll get my own. That way I know it's not been tampered with in the event there is a mole in the agency."

"So, you refused his offer. Pricy stuff on your own."

"I didn't say that. Only I won't use his. It might come in useful later. What he doesn't know… Besides, I already ordered the scrambler I want. It'll be here late tomorrow. Money isn't a problem, especially where my security is concerned. I worked so much with the agency I didn't have time to spend my paychecks."

"Know that feeling." He shoved his hands in his jeans pockets and yawned. "It's late, we both could use some shut-eye."

Chapter Seventeen

Holiday Lighting and Unexpected Estate Complications

Days flew by without any further intrusions. As the holidays approached, the fact a couple of snowstorms failed to show any footprints around the cabin eased Miacoh's mind and confirmed no one but the birds were nosing around the cabin, at least not physically. Cyberspace was Candle's area of expertise. She was confident the countermeasures she'd installed would prevent a repeat attempt on her computer. *Good enough for me.*

The two women dynamos, Candle and Gabby were busy holiday planning. With Hunter's help, they'd convinced the town to supply the manpower to put up the Christmas decorations and the town council to okay a holiday festival in conjunction with the tree lighting ceremony.

Candle and Gabby were still sifting through the vetted applications for Chief. *The girls were forces to be reckoned with.* He smiled. *Just like their high school days.*

Meanwhile, he concentrated on tying up the estate's loose ends. There seemed to always be one more thing the lawyer missed like the discovery of a safe deposit box in his grandmother's maiden name in a neighboring town. At Candle's suggestion, he'd had the bank run an inquiry under his grandmother's maiden name. He'd driven to Snow Mass, Colorado, and closed the box this morning surprised to find an envelope with his mother's name scrawled across it in his grandmother's handwriting.

A call to his attorney advised him to open the manila envelope in front of a bank employee, verify the contents, and add it to the estate closing statement. A sealed letter was enclosed. He left it that way. The bank employee certified the several thousand dollars in cash inside the main envelope and he tucked the envelope in his jacket. Inside his truck, he pulled out his phone and dialed the last number he had for his mother. She answered on the third ring.

"Hello?"

"Mom. It's Miacoh."

There was a long pause. "Yes, what do you want?"

Nice way to greet your son. He shook off the temptation to hang up and concentrated on keeping his voice neutral. "I'm closing out the estate and ran across a safe deposit box in Snow Mass. Do you know anything about that?"

"No. Your grandmother was secretive about her personal affairs and finances."

He ran his fingers around the underneath of the steering wheel, feeling the ridges and valleys. "She left an envelope with your name on it in the box."

"I don't need anything from her."

"Mom, there's several thousand dollars here. I can't close the estate without you signing off as receiving it." *While the last statement wasn't exactly true, it might convince her to…to what…what am I expecting?*

Another prolonged silence.

"You and I are all that's left of our family. Maybe you could come pick this up and we could talk?"

"I'll think about it," she finally said.

"Okay. I'll be in Aspen Ridge through the first of the year or until the house sells. Let me know."

"I'll be in touch." She disconnected the call.

He drove to his grandmother's house and put the envelope in the safe. *Why didn't Grams leave it in the safe in the first place?* He closed the door, spun the dial, and replaced the floorboards sliding the throw rug over them.

Sprinting downstairs, he grabbed his coat off the newel post and reached for the doorknob as someone knocked.

"Miacoh are you here?" She knocked on the door again.

When he yanked the door open, Candle stood fist in the air posed in front of the open door. She pulled her fist back. Gabby popped her head around from behind Candle and snickered.

"Do you know how close you came to having her knock on your face?" Gabby covered her mouth in a futile effort to stem the giggles.

Candle snorted and grabbed his hand before he had a chance to answer. "Come on, they're going to test the town's Christmas lights at dusk. Hurry."

Pulling his hand away slowly, he picked up the coat he'd dropped and shrugged into it. When did the Christmas decorations go up? *Have I been too preoccupied to notice?* "Wait a minute, ladies, I need to set the alarm and lock the door."

At the tone of his voice, Candle hesitated and peered

into his eyes for a beat. She tugged on his arm again. "We left the decorations at the town warehouse with a request and instructions a couple of weeks ago. Since I didn't hear anything, when Gabby arrived, we were headed back to town hall to…"

He pushed the situation with his mom to the back of his mind and grinned at the women. "Let me guess. Corner your dad or better yet a poor unsuspecting town council person—"

"We would never do that—well not exactly. We went through the proper channels," she protested. "Anyway, as we stood in front of town hall—"

"My phone rang." Gabby finished for her. "It was the city manager reporting the decorations were done and would be tested at dusk. Including the huge tree in town square."

"And you two didn't notice the decorations were up?" He eyed Candle suspiciously.

"I did. But they were only installed last week. I checked, and the wiring wasn't connected." Candle finished for her friend. "Anyway, come with us." She stopped dead in her tracks searching his face. "Unless you have something more pressing."

He sighed not wanting to dampen their spirits nor air his family situation. "Nothing that can't wait."

They clambered into his truck and drove down Main Street which was lit up like he remembered as a child. Only the new LED lights were much brighter. He parked at the town square. As they crossed the square, the dry grass crunched beneath their feet, and the towering evergreen came to light with multi-colored lights that pulsed to the Christmas carols playing through the sound system.

Gabby and Candle clapped their hands their eyes shining bright under the colored lights. They high fived each other as gales of laughter surrounded him. "We did it," the women chorused together.

"And right on schedule, the day before Thanksgiving." Candle added. "We couldn't have asked for better timing."

It is growing harder and harder to think of leaving this town...or Candle.

Chapter Eighteen

Thanksgiving Festivities—A Reason to Eat, Drink and Be Merry, While Cheering for Your Favorite Football Team—Or Not!

A few days later, Miacoh, Terrabyte, and Candle arrived at her parents' house, with six homemade pumpkin pies in hand. The home was a beehive of activity. Pekabo put a twenty-four-pound turkey in the oven. A large bone-in ham sat on the counter next to a pan of her secret family glaze.

Pekabo smiled broadly, throwing an arm around her daughter, and kissing her on the cheek. "It's been a great morning so far. Gabby's family's plane landed early. Matt went to pick them up. This morning, Rita dropped by with a big bowl of warm cranberry sauce, wanting to put it in those Thanksgiving molds I have. I already had the molds on the counter. She took care of that and went back home to finish up the candied sweet potatoes and green bean casserole. As soon as Ben and the kids arrive, the whole family will be over."

"You sound excited, Mom."

"Oh, I am. It's been a long time, and we used to have such fun." A rose flush crept across Pekabo's cheeks, and she grimaced. "I invited Caitlin and Jed. They are under orders to stay in Aspen Ridge. No one should be alone at Thanksgiving."

"It's your house and decision. But absolutely no business discussions," Candle said firmly.

"Of course." Pek sent a warning glance to her husband. "Candle, would you run upstairs and bring the board games down? I think they are still in your closet on the top shelf."

"Miacoh, I set up the game tables in the living room, but I think the folding chairs are also in Candle's closet. Would you be a dear and bring them down for me?"

"Sure." Miacoh bounded up the stairs after Candle. Silently he padded across her room, stepped inside the closet, and grabbed her waist. He ducked the blows she tried to send his way and lifted her to the bottom rung of the ladder, turning her around to face him. Brushing wayward strands of hair out of her face, he pressed his lips to hers in a slow, sensual kiss. His tongue traced the soft fullness of her lips, then slipped inside her parted lips.

The touch of his lips on hers delivered a shock wave through her entire body as his tongue sent shivers of desire racing through her. She melted into him and wrapped her arms around him like velvet chains. Her heart beat in rhythm with his, while what felt like butterfly wings fluttered inside her stomach. The whole sensation was making her weak.

He nibbled his way down her neck and kissed the pulsing hollow at the base of her throat. Heavy footsteps echoed across the bedroom floor.

Standing in the closet doorway, her dad cleared his throat. "Your mom wanted to know what was taking so long. I don't suppose you want me to tell her the truth."

Miacoh battled his way out of the sexual haze and sighed. "Sir, it's no secret how I feel about your daughter. It's a problem with genes and geography."

"Son, I strongly suggest that you work on both later. Right now, Pekabo wants to check the games and Candle to set the table." Hunter turned, chuckling, and walked out of the room. "Gabby and her family are just walking up to the door," he called up to them from midway down the stairs.

Miacoh helped Candle off the ladder, brushed his lips lightly over her still moist lips, then took the boxes of games from her. He liked the rosy color that had bloomed in her cheeks. He carried the boxes downstairs and put them on the coffee table as the doorbell rang. Candle rushed to the door and flung it open.

"So glad you could all make it." She hugged each person in turn, though the twins tried to wiggle away.

Pekabo glanced at her husband as he walked into the kitchen. Then she did a double take. "You look like the cat that ate the canary."

"And it was delicious." He put his arms around his wife's waist and breathed a lingering kiss against her neck. "You smell good enough to eat." Hunter winked at Pekabo.

"Hunter, not in front of company," she squeaked, watching Gabby smile standing in the kitchen doorway with her parents right behind her. The twins burst through, looking for Terrabyte.

"Why? We're married," he said nonchalantly, sauntering across the floor to greet his guests. "Terra's out in the backyard."

Everyone licked their lips at the roasted turkey aroma, scent of pumpkin pies, and Rita's freshly baked rolls wafting through the room.

Before the kids could bolt out the door, Gabby

grabbed them by the back of their shirts and whirled them around to face her. "First you ask Candle for permission to play with her puppy. Then if it's all right, put your coats back on before you go outside."

"Sure, Terra would love someone to play with. Don't get too rough 'cause she will get really rough and mouthy. Don't let her do that. Understand?"

The twins nodded their heads in unison.

She scooped up a couple of Terra's squeaky balls off the floor and tossed them to Nash and Natalya. "She loves to play ball."

Caitlin and Jed arrived a few minutes later, with two bottles each of red Pinot Noir and white Riesling wine. Miacoh told them to take a seat anywhere or come into the kitchen, where everyone gathered. The agents followed him into the kitchen, where he set the wine on the counter.

The Bearclaws' large oak table had seen little use over the years since Candle's departure. Now it was set with rosebud china and Pekabo's mother's silver place settings. She'd polished silverware the day she'd learned the big Thanksgiving dinner would be at their house, like years long past.

"Everyone, take a seat at the table. Dinner is ready. Let's eat while it's hot," Pekabo said as Hunter carried out the turkey on a colorful platter. Candle brought the cranberry molds to the table along with rolls tucked carefully in a wicker basket. Miacoh set the green bean casserole and sliced ham plate on the table. Hunter, of course, carved the turkey.

The holiday to be thankful brought a welcome reprieve from sorting out the sins of man. It was good to see and visit with their good friends, plan the next town celebration, and get together for Christmas.

Candle enjoyed watching her mom and dad smile and laugh as they reveled in the company of friends. She'd loved the time spent with Gabby reminiscing. While in the back of her mind mulling over the phone call from Mark. However, she was unable to provide much help regarding the attempted hack of her computer and hoped that was the end of it.

Chapter Nineteen

The Search For Answers, Nets Unwelcome Results

The drive to her cabin was a quiet one. Both Miacoh and Candle were lost in their thoughts and exhausted from telling stories to Ben about their escapades as children right through their teenage years. This included a few stories about Gabby that Ben hadn't heard.

Including, much to her chagrin, her several-year, not-so-secret crush on Miacoh. He was the only one that was oblivious. There were enough embarrassing moments to last a lifetime.

Ben enjoyed them all. "I'm looking forward to Christmas and more stories." Laughter rang throughout the Bearclaws' house for most of the evening.

Terrabyte was sound asleep in the back seat of the truck, completely worn out from playing with Gabby's twins. Finally, the pup had to seek refuge in the house at Candle's feet.

"Miacoh, at the risk of sounding stupid, what did you mean when you told my father it wasn't a secret how you felt about me? You made it quite clear that our relationship could never be anything but a fun fling for us."

Keeping his eyes on the road, he shrugged.

"I agreed, knowing you would leave as soon as you wrapped up the estate and sold the house. But—what you said to my dad—well, it just doesn't..." She turned to look out the window, not wanting to see his face.

"Things change, Candle. I tried like hell to keep you out of my heart. But I just couldn't do it. I thought if we engaged in a sexual relationship, we would tire of each other, and that would be that. It didn't work. Only made things worse, and instead of moving on when I knew I should, I moved all right, straight into your bed and into your life. This was the best Thanksgiving I've ever had."

She turned in her seat to look at him. "But you had to stay to settle the estate and sell the house."

He shook his head. "Yes and no. Though inconvenient, I could have settled everything via mail and e-mail, with one final appearance to close everything. I nearly left without saying goodbye when I couldn't shake my feelings for you. But I just couldn't do it. Now, I'm going to end up hurting everyone I care about when I leave." His grip on the steering wheel was so tight his knuckles started to turn white.

"You don't have to leave. We'll deal with your problem together. My folks will understand." She tilted her head to one side and winced. "Okay, Dad might take a while, but..."

"No, no, you don't understand. Hunter knows. He helped me through a rough patch around the time I turned eighteen. He helped me learn to control the wolf."

"What? My dad helped you control your werewolf and didn't freak out?"

"Everyone has secrets, even Hunter. Still, my anger colored everything. At his suggestion, I joined the military. The discipline was good for me. I learned to keep moving. Destroy what got in my way. Never depend on or trust anyone but myself. Well, that's not exactly true. My unit was tight. And now…"

She sucked in a breath and compartmentalized that tidbit until she could corner her dad. "You have to learn a new way of life. We take it one day at a time with family and friends who care about you and have your back." She shifted in her seat to reach her backpack and get the cabin keys. "At this moment, you have no choice. Dad is depending on you to help solve this murder. His officers aren't worth anything. And he has trust issues with the feds, I can see it."

"No, that's not fair. His officers are inexperienced. With time and training and they'll do a good job. And everyone has trust issues with the feds these days. Though, Caitlin and Jed seem all right."

He slowed the truck in front of her cabin, checked the area, drove into the circular driveway, and cut the engine. He leaned across the console and slid his arm around her, pulling her close. "I can't make any promises about us. But you have my word. I'll stay until this case has concluded."

"And you won't leave without saying goodbye?"

"Agreed. Let's go inside. I'm beat." He opened the back truck door, leashed a sleeping Terra, picked her up, and set her on the ground. The pup promptly lay down and yawned. "Me too, girl, now let's get up and walk into the cabin." He nudged her butt with his foot. Terra gave him a crusty look, stretched, and got to her feet, slowly following him up the path.

She picked up her computer, sprinted through the cold air to the front door, unlocked it, shoved the door open, and turned off the alarm. Miacoh and Terrabyte trudged in behind her. She closed the door and turned on the light, checking the supply of firewood inside.

"Miacoh, would you mind starting a fire? I need to talk to you about the update I got from Mark.

"Good news?" He yawned, crumpling newspaper into little balls and tossing them into the fireplace.

She plugged in her laptop, flipping open the screen. "They were able to trace the hacker, but the bad news is that it went back to our satellite office in Falls Church. He wanted me to see if I could trace it to the exact station. But the signal bounced around too much to get an exact location. The hacker is good, I'll give him that. But my security held, he or she couldn't install a backdoor. By now, I'm betting that computer is long gone. Anyway, I can use my laptop and my software on our other case without fear of compromising the case."

"So, it wasn't a local threat."

"No, we don't think so. They've also started an official investigation into Carl's death. After further investigation, a second opinion by an independent medical examiner ruled his death a homicide." She booted up the computer and entered the login and password given to her for Homeland Security's database. Giving a silent cheer when it still worked, she opened the file containing the code she was working on.

"That's going to be an ugly can of worms." He built a tepee of kindling inside a framework of bigger logs. Striking the match against the stone fireplace, he lit several newspaper edges then tossed the match in the middle. Flames blackened the newspaper and raced up several sides of the kindling. "Your name involved?"

"Unfortunately, yes. It's because I questioned the circumstances surrounding Carl's death that a second opinion was requested. But now that higher-ups share my opinion, the hacker will have other targets. At least that's Mark's opinion."

"So, you've made powerful enemies in high places." He fanned the flames with a newspaper. "Not good."

"Yes, but no more than before. Anyway, I left that can of worms with Mark. Switched my attention to trying to open Erin's file." With a few keystrokes, she watched the fruit of her efforts, hoping her program would be able to repair Erin's Homeland Securities file. Only time would tell. They needed to find out which college she attended and talk to her.

After an hour or so, the screen blinked a couple of times, brought up Erin's file, and it opened. Candle squealed, jumped up from the chair, and did a pirouette on one foot while pumping her fist. Plopping back in the chair, she moved the mouse to student history and clicked.

"What's wrong?" He hurried to her side.

"I fixed it, well, mostly." She scrolled down to the school attended and major. "Oh shit. Miacoh, do you see this?"

He leaned over her shoulder and stared at the screen. "Yes, she's a chemical engineering major at the School of Mines in Boulder." He whistled. "That's not good."

"No, not good at all. But we need to verify this information before we notify anyone. I'll call the school tomorrow. Then we can tell Dad and Homeland Security. That will also give their techs time to discover the file is partially available if they are still working on it. Don't want to step on any toes." She smiled wide, pumping her fist in the air again.

"I'm going to bed. Tomorrow will be a long day. I can tell," he mumbled trudging toward the bedroom.

"I'll be right behind you. I want to withdraw my

program without a trace leaving the file intact." She stretched her arms above her head and yawned. "Only a few more minutes." A short while later, she padded into the bedroom, undressed, and climbed into bed. A moment later she let out a blood-curdling scream.

Terra bounced out of bed racing around the dark room, nose in the air sniffing and barking.

Candle flew out of bed, grabbed her weapon, flipped on the light, and muffled another scream as the large bronze wolf blinked its blue-green eyes, shimmered, and transformed into Miacoh.

"Holy shit." Her heart still pounding in her chest, still gasping for breath, she returned her weapon to the nightstand and braced both hands on the stand. "I could have shot you."

He jumped out of bed and shook his head. "That hasn't happened since I was a teenager. Sorry, Candle." Slowly, he walked around the bed and gathered her into his arms.

Terra trotted over to him and sniffed then returned to Candle's side. Apparently satisfied there was no intruder, the pup went to her bed.

Candle pushed her fists against his muscular chest. "You could have warned me."

"About something that hasn't occurred in over twenty-five years? Must have let my guard down after we discussed my heritage. It's the only explanation. You're only one of a handful of people that know my secret and none I share a bed with."

"Will it happen again?"

"Hell, if I'd know... It better not. I've kept a tight rein on the wolf all these years." He released her, shoved his fingers through his hair, and paced the room. "It has to be a momentary lapse because I let you in."

Heartbeat nearly back to normal and nerves not so much on edge, she snickered. "Guess the wolf is out of the bed."

"Oh, that's so bad." He chuckled and glanced at the wall clock. "We better try to get a few hours of sleep. Best be on our toes when the feds come calling." Crawling into bed, he patted the sheets beside him.

She puffed out her cheeks and let out a breath. "True. No more surprises?"

"I'll do my best."

Chapter Twenty

A Rude Awakening to the Morning After

It was still dark outside when Candle's cell phone rang. Blurry-eyed, she reached for the cell on the nightstand and nearly brushed it onto the floor. "Hello?" she answered sleepily.

"We got trouble," Caitlin said.

"How did you get my cell number?" she asked annoyed.

"Your father gave it to us. We called him first. Pek answered and told us to call you."

Slightly more awake now, the memories of Miacoh's transformation surfaced first, then her breakthrough last night seeping into her sleep-deprived brain. "Did you verify the information?"

"What information? I haven't even told you about the trouble yet," Caitlin demanded suspiciously.

"Oh shit." She blew out a breath. "I figured the trouble was information related, and you have to verify before acting on it, right? Or bringing us into the loop. If it was a physical threat…"

"Okay. Okay. Our techs were able to clean up Erin's corrupted file partially. She is a chemical engineering major at the School of Mines. Our people are verifying that as we speak." Caitlin tapped something on the phone's receiver.

She glanced at the clock. Not if it's before six in the morning, the telephone system is switched off until then or was. "What are our options?"

"As soon as we get confirmation from our emergency contact at the school we will pick her up."

"How well do you know the area?"

"Well enough," Caitlin said smugly. "We'll keep you in the loop." She disconnected the call.

She sat up and looked over at Miacoh shaking her head, lips pursed. "They'll never set eyes on Erin."

"You okay about last night?"

"Do I have a choice?" she shot back, then reconsidered. "Yes, I believe I am. Not saying it wasn't a shock. But let's concentrate on what we got going on now."

"What do you want to do?"

"Eat breakfast," she said cheerfully.

"You're going to let them fall flat on their faces, aren't you?" His lips twitched to keep from grinning.

"Who, me?" She held her hand to her heart and blinked innocently at him. "After thinking about it as I closed down the computer last night, Erin's probably not there. Given her background, if they're planning something big, she would be an intricate part."

The carpet was warm on her bare feet as she padded across the bedroom floor, stepped into the bathroom, and locked the door. She still wasn't sure about last night. *However, I'm not going to let him know that. He's got enough on his plate*. Wanting to clear her head, she figured avoiding intimate contact with him would be the best way. The minute he got close, wrapped those strong, sinewy arms around her, brushed his full lips on hers... She shook her head vehemently. *That's enough. Get a*

grip, woman, or I'll be spread eagle on the bed before I even get my shower taken. Shit.
****

Lying there listening to Candle lock the door, he glanced down at Terrabyte whining impatiently on his side of the bed to be let outside. "Well, I guess it's you and me, girl." He pulled on his jeans, leaving the top button unbuttoned. He walked to the back door, checked the yard, and opened the dog door. Terra raced out, squatted, and glared back at him. *Can't make any of the women in my life happy this morning.* He grunted and put on the coffee as his phone rang. Racing back to the bedroom, he picked up his phone off the floor.

"What ya got?" He listened for several minutes. "Thanks, I owe ya."

Standing next to the bed, he listened to see if water was still running in the shower. Taking a small leather case out of his pocket, he ambled to the bathroom door. He opened the case, pulled out a shiny silver pick, stuck it in the keyhole, wiggled it, and pushed the door open. He unzipped his jeans, let them pool at his feet on the floor, and closed the bathroom door.
****

Miacoh sat at the kitchen table drinking his coffee as Candle put two heaping plates of scrambled eggs, biscuits, hash browns, and bacon on the table. A pitcher of orange juice sat in the center of the table, along with two juice glasses. She picked up a steaming mug of hot chocolate from the counter nearest the stove and took a sip. He got up, poured another cup of coffee, and rinsed out the pot.

Holding the pot over the sink, he turned toward Candle. "Do you want me to make another pot?"

"No, we need to meet Mom and Dad at the salon to talk with Bess."

He grabbed the sponge wand and washed and dried the glass container. Putting it back on the coffee maker, he ensured the power was off. "Candle, I got some disturbing news this morning."

She sat down and forked up a bite of scrambled egg. "About what?" She put the egg in her mouth and chewed slowly, giving him her full attention.

"On a hunch, I had an associate check out Roark's wife. They've been separated for a couple of years, and never divorced. They have one young son."

She raised an eyebrow and stared at him.

"Your dad is aware of all that. But apparently, before they separated, Roark was getting death threats on his personal computer. His wife claimed it stemmed from a shooting in the line of duty a few years ago. There was an investigation, as there always is in cases involving death. His partner and the suspect were killed. Roark was cleared of all wrongdoing and put back on duty."

"Without counseling?"

He shrugged. "Don't know. But that's when the problems began. The report says a bullet from his partner's gun killed the suspect. The suspect killed his partner. But the e-mails claim Roark shot the suspect who was an enforcer for a large street gang and had a couple of prior run-ins with Roark. The bullet disappeared from evidence, so there is no proof except the report." He took a bite of hash browns, washed it down with a swig of coffee, and picked up a piece of bacon.

"My dad didn't know about this when he hired

Roark?" She poured a glass of orange juice. She motioned the jug toward him, eyebrow raised. "Want some?"

He picked up the empty juice glass and held it toward her. "Sure. It looked like Roark needed a fresh start in a small unknown town, so he didn't mention the emails. His record was spotless, other than the shooting. And that wouldn't deter your dad or council from hiring him. If I had to guess, I think he was planning to try to patch things up with his wife and move his family here if it all worked out. It didn't. When your dad contacted the wife about Roark's death, I don't know why his wife didn't mention the emails. Seems strange." Taking a bite of bacon, he chewed thoughtfully.

"I guess we better get over to Dad's and tell him. I'm sorry, but I have to ask, is this associate of yours reliable?"

"More than. He was part of my unit until he was wounded in an op."

"Does he have copies of the emails, or did he just talk to Roark's wife?"

"He talked to her—huh—after he got access to the emails. He has copies. Knows his way around a computer, not as good as you, but…"

"They were illegally obtained." She put a piece of egg on her biscuit, then popped it into her mouth.

"His copies. I am sure we could get them from the wife. Unless…"

"You don't have a good feeling about the wife, do you?" She mopped up her plate with the last bit of biscuit and put it in her mouth.

"I don't understand why she didn't say anything to your dad. Her husband is dead, so why not give him access?" He sipped at his coffee.

"Agreed. At the time Dad contacted her, we didn't have any suspects. He asked if she had any idea who would want him dead. It's standard procedure. My dad's a by-the-book kinda guy." She picked up her plate and walked over to the sink.

"That's what bothers me. I know the wife didn't just forget the emails." He shook his head and followed her over to the sink with his plate. "It doesn't fit, which gives me a bad feeling."

"What was your associate's gut feeling?"

"He figured if he went back to see her, she'd disappear. That's why he got a signed statement from her before he left."

"Well, at least we have that. Where's the statement?"

"Copy on my computer, original in the mail to your dad. If there is something not right here, I didn't want a trail to us. Figured sending it to your dad would be normal procedure in a murder investigation. No repercussions, as with a PI or former CIA operative."

"Dad is not going to like this one bit." She stepped to the door. "Terrabyte, come." The pup rushed through the dog door, stopped at her bowl, grabbed a bite of dog food, and charged to the front door, skidding sideways.

"She's getting used to our routine," Miacoh remarked, clipping the leash on Terra. "Come on, girl, out to the truck." He took the pup leaving Candle to lock up and set the alarm. "Hey, don't forget your computer."

She exited the cabin with her small backpack and her briefcase containing her computer.

Chapter Twenty-One

The Plot Thickens but No Resolutions in Sight

When they pulled up in front of her parents' house, there were no other vehicles in sight. Candle climbed out of the truck, looked up and down the street, opened the back door, hooked Terra's leash to her harness, and let her out.

"This is different." She walked up to the house.

"Convenient actually, given the information we have."

Hunter opened the door before they rang the bell. "You're early. Want some breakfast?"

"No, Dad, we just ate a big breakfast."

"Your mom made homemade cinnamon rolls." He waggled his eyebrows.

"Smells wonderful." She breathed in the aroma of cinnamon, brown sugar, and warm butter mixed with powdered sugar as it wafted through the room. She sighed, turning to Miacoh. "Wanta split one while they're still warm?"

"You betcha!"

Seated around the table, enjoying the fruits of Pekabo's labors, Miacoh repeated the information he'd discussed with Candle. Including the feeling that things were not right with the wife. Hunter agreed and reached for his phone as the blood vessel in his left temple pulsed.

Miacoh cleared his throat. "I don't think dealing with this situation over the phone is a good idea."

"I agree. I'll call my contact in Bozeman Police Department and see if he knew of those emails. If he didn't, it's probably best to let his department handle Roark's wife since he was a police officer on their force. If they're unaware, this may affect the internal investigation into that case, which I am pretty sure is the case. Otherwise, I'd been made aware when I did the background check on him. Or, at the very least, when I went up there to deliver the news he'd been murdered. Joey, a detective with Bozeman PD, went with me to break the news. That's who I'm going to call. Excuse me."

"Before you do that, you should know that my contact obtained the emails illegally but discussed them with the wife and had her sign a statement about their existence. That was all legal."

"Did she show him the emails willingly when he made contact?"

"Yes. Hunter, don't think I circumvented you in this investigation. I was just talking to my buddy, who happens to be a consultant for cybercrimes for the Bozeman Police Department. He was familiar with Roark's situation. I had no idea things would turn out like this."

"I wish you'd mentioned your buddy to me earlier." Hunter narrowed his eyes.

"To be honest, I didn't think of it. I only learned recently of his connection to the Bozeman Police Department. I knew he settled in Montana after rehab for his wounds. He'd been going through a rough patch, but he's doing much better now. Engaged to a nice woman."

"I understand." Hunter pushed up from the table. "I'll make that phone call to Joey." He stopped mid-stride. "You know, would your friend be interested in earning a little extra money? When I call Det. Joey Larson, it might be to our benefit to have Roark's wife under surveillance. Just in case there is more going on here than we know. I don't want him to make contact. Only watch. Clear?"

"Yep. I'll call him right now." Miacoh rose from the table and walked out the back door, accompanied by Terrabyte. A few minutes later, he returned. "All set. Give him an hour to get set up before you call Larson."

"Okay, but you two will have to accompany Pekabo to the salon while I stay here and take care of this. All right?"

Miacoh nodded. "Sure, no problem. If you need anything, call me."

"I feel like such a snitch, doing this to Bess." Pekabo stared at the floor then raised her gaze to Hunter.

"You volunteered," her husband reminded her.

"I know, let's get going."

"Wait. If you don't want to do this, Candle and Miacoh can handle it independently."

"No, I'm positive she is innocent of any wrongdoing. There is a simple explanation for her appearing in the picture with those men." Pek picked up her purse and stepped out the door, followed by Miacoh and Candle.

Hunter caught Candle's arm. "Don't let anything happen to your mother. And make sure her mouth doesn't get her in trouble."

Candle smiled. "No problem, Dad."

They drove separate vehicles to the salon. Miacoh

parked a couple of blocks away but in viewing range. They watched Pekabo park and enter the salon. Candle got out of the truck and strolled toward the establishment. Miacoh hung back, keeping an eye on the women. Pekabo exited the salon within a few minutes and held the door for a middle-aged woman with auburn hair and bright neon-pink nail polish. The woman wore a black pants suit with hot-pink athletic shoes. Candle walked up to them and started a conversation.

"Mrs. Wright, it's a pleasure to see you. I hope I'm not interrupting. Were you two going somewhere?"

"On no, dear, I have council business requiring my attention. Met your mother inside when she was making an appointment. Is there something I can do for you?"

"Yes, as a matter of fact, there is. I'm starting a security business in Aspen Ridge. The building center north of town wants a quote for my services. Their system is old and needs repair. They should invest in a new system. The outside surveillance cameras are so old that when you try to take photos from the video, the quality is so poor that you can hardly make out the people, not that they have ever had to do that, but…"

"You know you must have a business license? Have you filled out an application?" Bess peered at her inquiringly.

"Yes, my father is reviewing it."

Candle pulled out the photo of Mrs. Wright and the suspects. "Anyway, I'd like you to look at this picture to see what I mean."

She handed the photo to the councilwoman.

"Oh my, this is me." She held the picture closer and looked again. "That's the day those awful young men crashed their cart into me when I went to put the cart in the cart corral. I wasn't hurt, but I was sure mad and told them so."

She pulled on the edges of her coat, straightening it as red patches bloomed on her cheeks. "Not watching where they were going. Ran right into me. They mumbled something about looking for a street. I don't remember the road's name, but I told them best get a map and that the building center had nice ones. They never really looked at me, always at the ground, then a young dark-haired girl with a pixie cut came out waving a map, they all rushed to the truck and left."

Bess held the picture at a couple of different angles, then shook her head. "What a terrible picture. You are quite right. They need much better surveillance cameras. What if a crime had been committed? You could barely make out the persons involved." She looked at her watch. "Oh, my lord, I've got to get going. I'm late."

"Thank you so much. You've been extremely helpful. I hope you're not too late." Candle waved.

"Don't forget the business license," Mrs. Wright called over her shoulder as she hurried off down the street, coat flapping in the wind but not a strand of her hair out of place.

"Bess must have a can of hair spray on her hair." Candle turned to look at her mother.

"I can't believe you…oh, you are good, my girl," Pekabo said to her daughter, patting her on the shoulder. "Where did that story originate? Just make it up on the spur of the moment?"

"Yeah, kind of. I had to go over there last week to do repairs. I am talking to the owners of the building supply place about updating their equipment. Anyway, it's a skill I learned, saved my ass a couple of times."

"I guess I didn't realize just how dangerous your job was."

"Not really. Just a different lifestyle, or maybe mindset. We got the information needed. I'm good at reading people, especially if they aren't being honest with me. She was getting irate just thinking about her encounter. Did you see her?" Candle chuckled. "She wasn't lying to me."

"Yes. I have to admit that I'm relieved. Couldn't imagine one of our own doing such a thing." Pekabo blew out a breath. "I've got some shopping to do. I'll see you at home later?"

"Probably, I need to report to Dad." Candle ambled toward Miacoh's truck. She stopped and hollered, "Hey, Mom, how about you and Dad come over to my place for dinner? I made manicotti the other night and just stuck it in the freezer. A fresh green salad is in the fridge along with some cold ones."

"Okay by me, ask your dad when you report back." Pekabo hurried to her car.

Miacoh met Candle on the sidewalk halfway to the salon. "I was going to stroll closer in case there was a problem. But she's not involved. I could tell by her body language. What did she get all wound up about?"

"Apparently, the men ran into her with their cart when she put hers in the corral cart. Wasn't looking at her but at the ground." Candle laughed. "She wasn't happy with them. But she indicated that a young woman with dark hair cut in a pixie was with the men, rather than the blond we saw in the Pueblo Army Depot picture. Think we are dealing with more people than first thought?"

"Probably not. Probably a disguise. Colored her

hair, cut it, wig, you get the picture." He caught her hand in his as he walked beside her. "Wonder if the feds have picked Erin up yet?"

She snorted while climbing into the truck, "Right, that's likely."

Hunter was waiting at the front door when they drove up and parked behind a dark SUV. He stepped out on the porch and walked toward them.

"Nothing to worry about. The men ran into Bess with a cart as she put hers in the corral. Pissed her off. In fact, she started to get irritated all over again when she was telling us about it. I'm pretty sure she was telling the truth. They wouldn't look up at her when she was bitching them out, just looked at the ground, which is why they ran into her in the first place." She went on to tell him about the map and the dark-haired girl with them.

"That's a relief. I talked to Det. Larson. He claims not to know about any threatening emails. He indicated Roark was on edge before he left there, but he didn't think it was anything out of the ordinary, especially after being in a fatal shootout. Miacoh, any word from your guy in Montana?"

"Not a word, so I would take that as the status quo, but I can call him just to make sure." Miacoh pulled his phone out of his pocket and walked toward the truck.

Stopping just short of the porch steps, Candle peered at her father. "Dad, how about you and Mom join us for dinner at my place? Got homemade manicotti, garlic bread, green salad, and beer. Also have a bottle of nice wine. There are a few things I'd like to discuss with you. I don't want the feds privy to it."

"Involve the case?" he asked gruffly.

"No, not the local murder case."

"Are you involved in another murder case?" Hunter stared into his daughter's eyes. His forehead creased.

"I don't want to talk about it now. Nothing for you to worry about. Will you come? Mom said it was all right by her. By the way, she had some shopping to do. She'll be home later."

"Yeah, that sounds good. What time?"

"About five. Since you're coming over, as soon as Miacoh finishes talking with his buddy, we will head back to my place. Straighten up the cabin, let Terrabyte play in her backyard, kinda wind down.

"You and Miacoh serious?" He stared into her eyes.

"Don't know, taking it day by day. He told me you helped him out of some trouble when he was a teenager and suggested he join the military. Why didn't you ever tell me?"

"None of your business back then," her dad answered curtly. "I gotta get back inside. See if they have located the girl. You know she attends your alma mater."

"So I heard."

Miacoh came around the back of the truck and motioned for them to join him. "Jack said a Bozeman police cruiser showed up at Clare's house about a half-hour ago. Other than that, nothing different than when he talked to her a couple of days ago. The cruiser is still there. He didn't tap into her system, as you instructed, so he doesn't know if she is showing the emails to the detective or not."

"Okay. The good news is she didn't try to run after talking to you."

"See you and Mom tonight at the cabin." Candle climbed in the truck as Miacoh checked on Terrabyte, ensuring she was clipped in with the seatbelt to her harness.

Chapter Twenty-Two

Dinner At the Cabin—Secrets Spilled

Miacoh shoved through the door with another armload of wood. His nostrils flared at the wonderful aroma of manicotti and garlic bread that greeted him. Kneeling on the hearth, he filled the empty wood box. He then turned to the fireplace, tossed in crumpled newspaper, and piled kindling on top, framing it with split logs of aspen and pine.

Walking into the kitchen, he felt like he'd been transported to a cozy Italian restaurant, complete with red and white checked tablecloth, and matching napkins spread in wicker bread baskets ready for the bread.

Candle stepped back and surveyed her efforts. Two partially burned red and white candles in wine decanters had dripped hot wax in a flow down the side of the bottles in multicolored layers. She struck a match and lit the wicks.

A smile lit up her face as she sauntered across the floor, opened the oven door, and heat whooshed out. A strand of hair fell across her face. She blew it off and straightened. Untying her apron, she hung it on a wooden peg on the wall.

"Wow, secret agent turned homemaker, what a transition." He grabbed her around the waist, lifted her off the floor, and whirled her around. Setting her down on her feet again, he pulled her close and brushed his cold lips over her warm ones, nibbling along her jawline.

She shivered more from desire than the chill. "You're cold." Pushing him toward the warm oven playfully, she giggled. "I think we're ready here." She spun out of his hold and opened the refrigerator to check on the tiramisu she'd put together earlier and handed the bottle of wine to him. "Make yourself useful, open it and set the bottle on the table, please." The crystal wine glasses sparkled on the wooden table.

"I was starting the fire." He stopped at the sink to wash his hands and carried the wine to the table.

She tossed the box of long fireplace matches to him. "Thanks!"

A knock at the front door sent Terrabyte scurrying toward the door barking excitedly.

Miacoh opened the door to Hunter and Pekabo, ushering them into the living area. "Please sit down. Can I get you something to drink? I believe we have flavored iced tea, soft drinks, beer, wine, coffee, and hot chocolate."

"I'll take a beer." Hunter settled into the couch next to his wife.

Pekabo smiled, inhaling deeply. "It smells so good in here. So many choices. What kind of wine do you have?"

He grinned and held up a finger. "I'll be right back." In a blink of an eye, he was back with a bottle of red and a bottle of white. Giving a slight bow, he held the bottles out for inspection. "Your choice, my lady."

Pekabo looked from one to the other. "They are both wonderful, but I think I'll take the white wine."

He nodded and handed Hunter the beer. "Would you

rather it in a stein?"

Hunter raised an eyebrow. "What do you think?" He popped the top and took a swig. "Now that's good. What I want to know is just how bad the news is Candle brought us over here to tell." His gaze roamed around the room as he inhaled deeply. "By the looks of it—pretty bad."

Looking perplexed, Miacoh asked, "What do you mean?"

Hunter chuckled. "When Candle was little and had done something to get herself in trouble, she always picked up her toys and cleaned her room. But as she got older, she cleaned the house and made a wonderful supper. You get the picture."

He took another swig, setting the bottle next to the veggie tray on the coffee table. "It was funny because her actions were always a tip-off. Sometimes it was days before we figured out what she did wrong."

"Hunter, quit being like that. She is a grown woman, inviting us to her house for the first time. Of course, she's going to have everything perfect." Pekabo frowned at her husband.

Miacoh stood in place with his hands behind his back, holding the bottles of wine.

"What…we helped her move in here," Hunter said testily.

"That's different. The cabin is all set up now and ready for guests. We're the first. Now, why don't you go out and get the painting I brought with us?" Pek patted his thigh gently.

Miacoh peered from one to the other, then strode back into the kitchen and picked up a bottle of beer. He took a long swig, then a deep breath, glanced at Candle, and strolled back into the living area.

When he disappeared into the living room, Candle giggled, wondering what other tales her parents would tell of her childhood.

Hunter raised his hands in surrender, then pushed up from the couch and started toward the door. Turning back, he picked up his beer along with a carrot stick, scooped it in the ranch dip in the center of the tray, and took a bite. "Be right back."

****

Pekabo took a sip of wine and closed her eyes. "Mmmm that's good." She set the glass on the coffee table and padded into the kitchen. Miacoh followed her.

"Candle, it's not something terrible, is it?" Pekabo twisted her wedding band round and round her finger.

"Mom, what on earth are you talking about?" She tilted her head slightly, brows knitted together then turned to open the oven. Warm air whooshed into her face, and the aroma of manicotti filled the kitchen. Lifting the white ceramic dish from the oven with two new, red-flowered potholders, she placed it on a hot air balloon-shaped trivet in the center of the table. Leaning over, she took a long sniff, and her mouth watered. She nodded to Miacoh. "Could you put the garlic bread in the baskets?"

"Sure thing." He took the cookie sheet of bread, gave it a little shake then slid the pieces into the baskets without spilling a one.

When Candle glanced back over to her mom, Pekabo drew her bottom lip through her teeth still staring at Candle. "Mom, it's nothing. Just information dad should know as he is acting Chief. Relax."

Pekabo let out a breath and picked up a filled

breadbasket. "Want this on the kitchen table?" Her mom paused. "Beautiful table by the way."

"Thanks. I fell in love with it and the chairs at a log furniture place. First time it's been out of storage." She walked over to the table and ran her hand gently over the tabletop, her lips curved in a slow smile.

Four china plates rimmed in gold sat on the counter with napkins folded neatly beside them. Her mom picked them up and placed them on the table. She opened the drawer in the china closet and sucked in a breath. Glancing at Candle, she said nothing, moved the .380 aside, got out the polished silverware, replaced the weapon, and closed the drawer without a word.

"You sure keep your grandmother's silver in good shape." Pekabo held up a butter knife looking at her reflection.

Candle laughed out loud. "You should have seen them a couple of days ago. I polished them just before you guys came over."

Hunter walked into the kitchen, holding his empty beer bottle. "Could I talk you into another? It really hit the spot."

"Sure." Miacoh grabbed one out of the fridge and handed it to him.

"We're ready to eat. Take a seat wherever you want." Candle motioned to the table.

Pekabo carried her glass of wine into the living room. Checked the picture.

Miacoh gave a low whistle staring at a painting leaning against the wall of a chow puppy in a field of flowers to its right and a small cabin to its left. A mountain scape with snow on the highest peaks. "Candle will love this." He slung his arm around Pekabo's shoulders.

She jumped. "I didn't hear you come in."

"I can be quiet when necessary." He laughed and took another swig of beer. "Come on, let's get back to the kitchen before Candle comes looking for us and spoils the surprise."

Miacoh passed the garlic bread. Candle followed with the manicotti around the table until everyone's plates were full. Dinner conversation consisted of the day's activities. Candle cleared off the dinner plates, then brought out the tiramisu.

Her father licked his lips. "My favorite." After dessert, he leaned back in his chair. "Spill it, darling daughter."

"Dad, it's nothing to worry about." She paused, glancing around the table. "You already know about the accident that killed Carl, my boss. What you don't know is that in my opinion, it wasn't an accident." She glared over at Miacoh when he cleared his throat loudly.

"That's putting it mildly," Miacoh said around a mouthful of tiramisu. He swallowed and continued. "She insisted it wasn't an accident. Going so far as to request her former handler look into it, who was positive at that time it was an accident." He scooped up another fork of the dessert. "We met with him after Carl's funeral. He suggested that Candle back off. He'd handle it. And she did."

"Well, it wasn't an accident. Mark called back the other day. The second autopsy confirmed murder." Candle smugly dabbed her mouth with a napkin. "His neck was snapped in a twisting motion to the right, which was the cause of death. That injury was subsequent to the head trauma and whiplash from hitting the tree.

Witnesses found after the fact, but are unwilling to testify, indicated they saw two men dressed in white camo, skiing off to the left of the path heading toward the run. The witnesses skied down the slope a few minutes ahead of Carl."

"Suspicious," her father injected.

She nodded. "The two skiers that found Carl saw two men in black ski suits flying down the slope at a high rate of speed past them but were nowhere in sight when they stopped to help Carl. He was already dead. No one saw anyone dressed in all black at the bottom either. So, someone is lying."

"Wow, Mark's snooping paid off." Miacoh scooped up the last bite of dessert then popped it in his mouth.

"Yeah, but no one is willing to testify. They probably got messages like I did, or something similar."

"What kind of message did you get?" His eyebrows knitted together, her father took his last swig of beer.

She hesitated only a moment. "Someone tried to hack into my computer. My first layer of security caught them. Still, they managed to leave a message on my computer screen when I arrived home. Something to the effect that Carl's death was an accident. I should drop it." She looked around the table and stood. "Anybody want coffee?"

"Poking around where you don't belong is dangerous business. Carl's death was unfortunate but an accident. Leave it be or pay the consequences, is exactly what it said," Miacoh interjected. "I'll take some coffee."

Hunter nodded. "Me too. Didn't you move here to leave all the cloak and dagger behind you?"

Pekabo, turning pale, shook her head and pointed to her empty wine glass. "More, please. How did you know that was my favorite wine?"

"Thanks for that." Candle gave Miacoh an icy stare. "Mom, some things never change. Dad, I've dropped the whole thing in Mark's lap. He's better equipped to handle it. I don't want to bring trouble here." She gathered up the plates and stacked them in the dishwasher.

****

Miacoh started to get up, but Hunter motioned him to sit back down and then shifted his gaze from Candle to Miacoh. "How serious is this situation? Why didn't you tell me when it first started?" Hunter paced around the kitchen.

"Because when we returned, you were waist-high in a murder investigation. That's where your attention needed to be. Not on my problems which are under control. Mark has tracked down the computer IP and is on top of it. Dad, have you had a chance to see the new Christmas decorations the town maintenance crew put up? We threw out the old ones that were in storage."

All the talk of murder, threats, and investigations was wearing on them. She wasn't selfish but needed downtime. She was sure her father did. Police work never took a holiday. She'd learned that as a little girl. But with the FBI and Homeland Security taking the lead. Mark's chasing down the computer hacker. It seemed as good a time as any to step back and let others handle it for a while.

"What? Why are we talking about Christmas decorations when—wait—" Hunter paused for a beat and scrubbed his large hand over his face. "—how did you get into the town's storage?"

"I am the Chief of Police's daughter." Her lips

twitched in amusement. Then she paused for a second, seeing the thunderous expression on her dad's face. "Relax, Dad. It was Gabby. I invited you and Mom over here to discuss new Christmas decorations for the town. Not the investigation or computer hackers. I wanted to tell you how Gabby and I plan to jump-start the Christmas tree lighting celebration in the town square. Just like it used to be. This town needs some Christmas cheer. Gabby, Miacoh, and I are going to make it happen."

"Okay…but what…"

Her cell phone rang. She held up her index finger to silence her dad. "Hold that thought." She touched the screen on her phone. "Gabby, we were just talking about you, the Christmas tree, and town decorations."

"Well, it's about time. I've been trying to get a hold of you all day. Where have you been?" Gabby demanded.

"We had a few unexpected events. But everything is handled now, and its mission Christmas Spirit full steam ahead." She did her best to sound convincing. She wanted to put all this stuff aside just long enough to enjoy Christmas, but…

"You can't fool me, Candle Light Bearclaw. What's going on?" Gabby asked concern creeping into her voice.

She groaned rolling her eyes. Wanting to strangle Gabby through the phone, she hissed, "There better not be anyone within hearing distance of you, or Gabrielle Fern whatever your married name is…" She ran out of steam as she realized how silly she sounded. Besides, she really didn't know Gabby's married name. She looked over at her dad. . The left corner of his mouth turned up in a slight smile.

Gabby spluttered. "Or what? I'm over a thousand miles away and called you because I will be flying out of here the day after tomorrow to get an early start on our Christmas plans. But if you are still playing cloak and dagger, I'm staying put. Ben will be ecstatic at being relieved of twin duty."

"I'm not. I'll pick you up at the airport and fill you in. What is your flight number and what airline."

"Oookkkaay, if you are sure." Gabby hesitated only a moment and gave Candle her flight number and time of arrival. "I can't wait to see you."

"Me too." She looked at her screen as Gabby disconnected the call and sighed loudly. "That was Gabby, she'll be here the day after tomorrow." She bustled around putting cups, cream, and sugar on a tray then poured steaming coffee into the cups. Taking a long sniff, she sighed.

"So I heard." Hunter put his arm around his daughter's shoulder, watching her. He dropped his arm from around her shoulder and picked up the tray, carrying it into the living room. "Pek, don't you have something to show Candle?"

"Oh yes." She grabbed her daughter by the arm preventing her from entering the living room. "Close your eyes. I'll guide you."

Candle did as instructed. Hunter pulled the picture and put it on the couch.

Pekabo clapped her hands. "Open your eyes now."

Candle's eyes rounded as she stared at the picture. "Oh, it's absolutely fantastic. You captured Terra perfectly, and the landscape is reminiscent of your property." She flung her arms around her mother. "Thank you so much. We'll hang it tonight. Lest little teeth revise the painting.

"I've a hanger and hammer right here. Show me where you want it." Miacoh grinned.

After hanging the painting, he relaxed with a mug of hot chocolate as the evening conversation turned to Christmas decorations, lighting ceremony, and potluck arrangements. Her heart filled with pride each time her gaze wandered to the painting.

As the evening continued, on the surface, Miacoh seemed calm, but underneath that façade, she sensed he was uneasy and restless.

When her parents got ready to leave, she hugged them. Miacoh shook Hunter's hand and hugged Pekabo as they went through the front door and made their way up the path to their parked car.

Turning around to close the door, she asked, "Is everything all right? You seemed a bit distracted."

"No, everything is fine." He kissed her on the nose, turned off the porch light, and put an arm around her waist. "It's late, and we have an early morning tomorrow."

"Don't remind me. I have a meeting with a prospective client at eight in the morning. Don at the hardware store wants to revamp his security system, add real-time surveillance and monitoring ability from his home. I'm not sure getting a license to sell weapons was a good thing in his case." She glanced over at Miacoh as she put her phone on the night table, then wandered into the bathroom and showered before slipping into bed. "Night, Trouble."

The dog curled up inside her crate at the foot of the bed.

How the hell does she know? He checked his phone

for missed calls and emails before sliding it onto the nightstand. *Cayson should have reported in by now.* After returning from the bathroom, showered and shaved, he pulled back the bedding. Candle wore a very skimpy see-through, red negligee, and all thoughts of Cayson melted from his mind.

Chapter Twenty-Three

A Surprise Visitor

After a fitful night's sleep, Miacoh awoke to the aroma of coffee wafting into the dark bedroom. He rolled over, not surprised to find Candle's side of the bed empty. Bolting upright at the sound of a deep male voice mingled with Candle's, he yanked on his jeans, buttoning the top button as he sprinted down the hall, his bare feet silent on the wooden floors.

"What the hell are you doing here?" Miacoh demanded, glaring at a tall, well-muscled, tanned man who sat in a kitchen chair watching Candle scrambling eggs on the stove.

"Is that any way to greet your best mate?" Dressed in desert camo pants and a black T-shirt stretched tight over his rippled chest and biceps, he leaned back in his chair, grinning. "G'day to you too."

Turning to Candle, he growled, "Why would you let a stranger in the house?"

The man shook his head vehemently. "Oh, she didn't, mate. Came around from the side of the house, she did, while I waited on the porch for someone to answer the door. Suddenly a weapon is aimed at my head. She demanded I get to my knees and toss ID toward her. Keeping her gun trained on me all the time." He jerked his chin toward Candle, his pale blue eyes dancing. "Tough lady and smart pup. I wondered why the dog barely growled behind the door."

Candle smiled down at Terrabyte, lying at her feet in front of the stove. "I told her quiet and stay, while I went out the back door." She turned her attention back to the guys. "Cayson's ID and the fact he knew about Mac and the cafe convinced me."

Candle set the table for three and handed Miacoh a steaming mug of coffee. "Here, this will put you in a better mood." She dumped eggs from the cast iron skillet onto the plates. A tray of lightly browned toast rested on the table beside a large pitcher of orange juice.

"Talk about interrogation. What is she, CIA?" Cayson chuckled scrubbing a large, scarred hand over the day or two of butterscotch stubble on his face.

"Maybe. But you could have…" Miacoh began, then grinned, walking over to grasp his buddy's outstretched hand. "Good to see ya." He pulled out the chair across from Cayson and sat down, picking up his fork and eying the pile of eggs on his plate.

Cayson's eyes widened as if he considered the possibility. Then his expression went blank. "Yeah, I guess I could have, but she wasn't the enemy. Just surprised my best mate's woman." He scooped up a bit of egg on a piece of toast and slid it into his mouth. "Delicious." Picking up his fork, he pointed to the home-cooked food.

"Why thank you, Cayson." She moved the skillet to the sink and filled it with a squirt of dish soap and water.

Taking a swig of his coffee, Miacoh glanced at his friend. "I didn't expect you to show up here. Expected a phone call yesterday."

Cayson took a sip of orange juice. "Just got done

with an assignment, took some time off, and decided to see what I could do to help you. Chatter is serious. Something big is going down, not going to be far from here. Didn't want to discuss it over the phone. A substantial amount of C-4 went missing from…" Cayson cut his eyes to Miacoh, raised a brow, and reached for a piece of toast. "Pass the butter."

"Go ahead, as I told you, Candle is up to her neck in this mess, as well as the rest of us. However, a new development since I talked to you last. The recently murdered Chief of Police left Montana with a few loose ends dangling, which may have gotten him killed. But in my mind, it's still possible he happened along at the wrong place at the wrong time." Miacoh shrugged. "It's a big mess. FBI and Homeland are involved. Local police and county sheriff's department too. Law enforcement tripping all over themselves, trying to solve it."

****

Candle rounded the table and eased into her chair. She hadn't missed the reference to her as Miacoh's woman, nor the fact that he didn't deny it. A warm feeling in the pit of her stomach bloomed. She ignored it. "Speaking of that, if law enforcement hasn't located Erin O'Shea by the time Gabby arrives, I believe we need to find her. I've got a bad feeling about that one, and it has nothing to do with Roark's death." She scooped up a fork of eggs, deposited it on a corner of toast, and took a big bite. The events of the morning had left her starving.

"You can't leave Gabby alone to handle the decorations and prep for the Christmas Eve tree lighting ceremony and potluck." Miacoh waved a hand at her.

"She's counting on your help to get this thing off the ground."

She sipped her orange juice, took a bite of bacon, and chewed slowly. She forked up more eggs and paused. "Mom's got the church ladies to help with the potluck on Christmas Eve, reserved the church too. After we get things rolling, I can leave Gabby to supervise for a day or so while we hunt Erin down. Dad's got the maintenance division straightened away for putting up the new decorations that Gabby and I bought." Candle's eyes caught Miacoh's and held for a moment. Then she looked at Cayson. "You with us?"

Cayson leaned his chair on the two back legs. "Yep."

Candle glanced at the chair legs, then sternly at Cayson. He dropped the chair back down on all four legs. Terrabyte rushed in her dog door, stopped at her water bowl lapping for several seconds, then bounded over to Cayson, rubbed her mouth and nose against Cayson's pant leg, pranced over to Candle, and sat down.

"Did that dog just wipe his mouth on my pants?" A disgusted look crossed Cayson's face.

"First of all, Terrabyte is a female puppy. Yes, I'd say that's exactly what she did." Miacoh smirked. "If I didn't know better, I'd say that Candle put her up to it. But we all know that's impossible."

Unable to hold a straight face any longer, Candle roared with laughter until tears streamed down her cheeks. Eventually, her laughter subsided. She popped her final piece of toast in her mouth, gathered the plates, and put them in the dishwasher. "I gotta go. Don't want to keep Gabby waiting. Patience is not her strongest suit. Wanta ride along to the airport?"

"Thanks, but I think we'll go over to my place. I have a couple of PI files I'd like another set of eyes on. Want me to take Terra?" Miacoh raised his eyebrows.

"No. I'll take her with me to the airport. Gabby will meet me outside, so I won't have to leave the pup in the car. You boys have fun." She locked the dog door and clipped the leash on Terrabyte. "Lock up when you leave."

Miacoh nodded. "Call me when you and Gabby come up with a plan. See you two for dinner?"

"Yeah, I'll call with the specifics."

"Nice to meet you," Cayson called after her.

"Same here," she said over her shoulder.

The men finished their coffee and talked a while longer. They washed the mugs and cast-iron skillet and put them away. As Miacoh set the alarm and walked out the door, Cayson's phone rang.

Chapter Twenty-Four

The Christmas Spirit Alive and Well Until…

In front of the airport, Gabby stood beside a pile of luggage in the pickup and drop-off area. Candle pulled alongside her, and they loaded the bags in the back.

Gabby slid into the passenger seat of the SUV, reached behind, and stroked Terra's ears through the crate. "Where's tall, dark, and dangerous?"

"A buddy of his showed up this morning. They went over to his gram's house to review PI files. That reminds me…" She pulled out her cell and touched Miacoh's number. "Hey. Picked up Gabby. Going to drive through town so she can see all the decorations before going to my cottage and discussing Christmas plans. Be in touch later about dinner."

"Thanks for calling. We'll meet you at the cottage later."

"Sounds good. See you then." She tapped the screen ending the call.

"You're reporting your every move to Miacoh now?" Gabby teased.

"It's either him or my dad. Both are way overprotective. Miacoh is staying at the cottage with me." She guided the vehicle onto the highway.

Gabby's mouth fell open as she shifted in her seat to stare at Candle. "Really? Moving kinda fast, aren't you?

Your dad's okay with it?"

She shot a devilish grin at her friend. "He insisted on it. It's either that or stay with him and Mom." She rolled her eyes. "So much for a nice quiet life."

Gabby scrunched her face up in a mix of puzzlement and concern. "What's going on?"

The expression on Gabby's face was so classic from their high school days of boys, shenanigans, and nearly getting caught that Candle snickered. "It's not like that. Miacoh is acting as my bodyguard. He started out staying in the extra room at my cottage."

"But…" Gabby raised an eyebrow.

"Okay, things changed. Dad is cool with it. Too many loose ends. Roark's murder case you know about and…" She paused for a beat to decide how much to tell her best friend. "Seems my old boss plowed into a tree on the ski slope. First considered an accident, now it's a murder investigation."

"Sooo…what's that have to do with you?" Gabby's forehead creased, then a slow smile spread across her lips. "You didn't do it, did you?"

"Noooo. But my questions and statements made the investigators reconsider the accident designation." She shrugged. "Maybe I should have kept my mouth shut. At least that's what my handler thinks."

"You…Never happen." Gabby leaned forward in her seat, straining the seatbelt. "You have a handler? So, you weren't able to leave your life as a spy behind after all?"

"Had a handler. And not exactly. Someone tried to hack my computer. There's nothing sensitive on it. I left all that with the agency. But someone didn't know." She waved one hand in the air dismissively as she slowed down to turn into town.

"Not a very informed hacker, if you asked me." Gabby laughed. "You don't hack the best with limited info."

"Enough about me. Let's talk Christmas festival." Candle brought her up to speed on the arrangements. "There may not be a lot to do after my mom gets through. She's assigned tasks, and it appears everything is going smoothly. The townspeople are extremely excited. See." Pointing to the wreaths and garland hung on the streetlights, she slowed the SUV to a crawl. "Maintenance got the rest of the decorations up and tested a few days ago—without my prodding."

"What about a joint family Christmas? Are we?"

"Oh, your mom and mine have that under control too. They kinda took over when I kept getting involved in the cases. Speaking of that, Miacoh and I may have to disappear for a day or two to smoke out a suspect if the other agencies can't find her. She's a student at the School of Mines."

"Your old stomping ground. Isn't that coincidental?"

"More like fortunate. Nothing against the agents working the case, but I'm afraid they're out of their league. Their high-handed techniques will cause the students to scatter rather than cooperate."

"You and Miacoh can do better?" Gabby settled in her seat, watching the trees, houses, and fields zoom by the window.

"I know the layout of the college and where the areas students used to congregate when they didn't want to be found. Besides, I know the psyche of the students there." She drove around the cottage before pulling into the circular driveway in front. Terrabyte whined and pawed at the crate to get out.

Gabby bounded out of the vehicle and up the path. "Can't wait to see what you've done with the place."

"It's far from done. But since you're here, how about helping me decorate for Christmas?"

"Of course." Gabby rubbed her hands together in glee. "Do you have decorations?"

"Yep, I bought a wide variety in town a couple of days ago. Hoped to get it done yesterday. Didn't happen." She brushed her hair out of her eyes and opened the back of the SUV. "Had enough confinement, girl?" Opening the crate, she clipped on the leash, put the pup on the ground, and turned to Gabby. "How about turkey sandwiches for lunch?"

"Sounds good." She took her phone out of her purse. "I better let Mom know I'm here. Given the recent events, I don't want her to worry."

"Good idea." The lock clicked as she turned the key, and a beeping sound commenced. When she tapped in a code, a small scanner appeared. Touching her hand to the screen silenced the alarm.

Gabby, wide-eyed, let out a low whistle. "Wow, high-tech."

"It's brand new. Testing it out. Need the latest and greatest if I am going to convince clients I know what I'm doing." She grinned. "Make yourself at home while I let Terra outside."

While checking the yard, she grabbed a squeaky toy and threw it for the pup, who promptly pounced on it shaking it from side to side, growling.

She returned to the cottage, washed her hands, and got bread, sliced turkey, cheese, mayo, mustard, lettuce, and tomatoes from the fridge. "Want chips with your sandwich?"

"Sure." Gabby joined her in the kitchen. "Starting a security company, huh?"

"Yes. Cyber security. I can also hard wire home and business alarm systems, but my expertise is cyber security. Besides, for the first few months, it'll be just me. Don't want to spread myself too thin." She got plates out. Spread mayo on the bread, then stacked cheese and turkey on the sandwich.

"Wow. If I lived closer, I could help out with office stuff while the kids are in school." Gabby scrunched up her face. "I've been considering moving back here with the kids for a while."

"And give up the high society lifestyle you've become accustomed to?" She snorted and waved her hand prettily. "Grab glasses from the cupboard. Iced tea is in the fridge."

Gabby got to her feet and rolled her eyes. "Like you, things don't always appear as they truly are. I never fit in. The kids don't either. They have chores, bedtimes, and rules."

"Their friends don't?"

"Though Ben came from money, he's worked hard and made his mark in the business world. He believes in making the kids work for what they have, unlike the children they go to school with." Gabby reached into the cupboard, took out two glasses, and set them on the table.

"Must have been hard on you and Ben." She sliced the sandwiches and put them on plates.

"For me more than him. He simply ignored them. When we married, I agreed to try to fit in. I think ten years is long enough. Don't like the school the kids are going to or the social functions they are required to attend." She shrugged as a little line dug itself between her brows. "Ben is fifteen years older than me. To say his family had a fit when he announced our engagement is an understatement."

"Must have been hard. He's all right with you moving back here?" The rumble of a truck engine had her peering out the window.

"Yes. We've been seriously discussing it for several months. Even found a house we both love. It was going to be a vacation home at first, but then you moved back. I remembered what it was like growing up here. I—we want that for our kids. Aspen Ridge is only approximately twenty-five miles from one of his satellite offices in Aspen. He's willing to move his operations there and drive back and forth. Even work from home when possible."

"Wow. Good for you. Sounds like you married well."

"Yeah. He's wonderful—his family—not so much. When he's gone, it's lonely."

"Look out, world! Gabby and Candle are back. Things may never be the same." Candle dissolved into a fit of giggles.

Gabby snickered. "At least Aspen Ridge may not."

"Where's this house?"

"On the edge of town. The opposite end from here. It's being remodeled. We'll move in after school is out. Haven't told the kids, mom and dad, or his family yet. So don't say anything."

"Your secret is safe with me. What does the town council think? Word spreads like wildfire around here."

"You're telling me. We simply said it would be our

vacation home."

"Smart." She pointed out the window. "Looks like we are about to be invaded."

The door swung open. Miacoh and Cayson strode inside. "Lunch ready?" His eyes twinkled as he paused to kiss Candle.

"The fixin's are all still out. Help yourselves. You're just in time to help put up the Christmas tree and decorations. Afterward, we can take a stroll down Main Street so Gabby can see the town lit up at night."

"I'm game. How about you, Cayson?"

"Sure. Never experienced a small-town Christmas. Heck, it's been years since I was stateside for the holidays. Looking forward to it."

She took a bite of the sandwich, padded into the living area, and turned on Christmas music. "Tunes to set the mood."

Miacoh spread mayo and mustard on the bread, then piled meat and cheese. He took a bite and handed the other sandwich to Cayson.

After lunch, the gals cleaned up with Terrabyte's help. While the guys dragged the bags and boxes of decorations into the front room, the women set up the Christmas tree.

Candle clapped her hands as she surveyed the tree and boxes of decorations. "It's been…" She scrunched up her face, then put her hand to her mouth. "I've never decorated for Christmas since leaving home."

Gabby's mouth hung open. "Why in heavens not?"

"Usually, I was on assignment. Or just coming home and too tired to care." She grinned at her friend. "Such is the glamorous life of a spy. NOT."

Miacoh set up the stepladder. She placed the fiberoptic star on the treetop. "Plug in all the lights," she and Gabby chorused.

The room was bathed in multi-color lights reflecting on the walls, windows, and ceiling. "Do you think we have enough decorations?"

"You can never have enough decorations." Gabby spun around in a circle. "But I think you come close since you and Miacoh must have room to navigate." She giggled. "You may have a square inch of empty space next to the fireplace." Gabby paused. "What about…"

Terra came bounding in her dog door and headed straight for the tree. "NO." Candle grabbed the wire puppy pen, and Miacoh helped her set it around the tree while Gabby grabbed the pup by her harness.

"Whew, that was a close one." Candle surveyed the rest of the room. All the decorations were placed well out of Terrabyte's reach. "Well done, everyone."

The pup sniffed and pawed at the edge of the fence. Finally, plopping down with a huff, Terra tilted her head, ears flat, and peered at Candle with a disgruntled expression on her doggie face.

"Come, girl. Wanta go for a walk?"

Miacoh tossed the leash to her. He and Cayson grabbed the coats from the hooks on the wall. "Ready to check out the town's lights you so generously supplied?" He glanced at Gabby.

"Yes." She shrugged into her coat that Cayson held out for her. "Thank you."

Candle donned the coat Miacoh held for her, then pulled a knit cap and mittens out of the pockets. They all piled in her SUV. He drove through the neighborhoods first to admire the lighting displays of the locals. Turning on Main Street, Miacoh parked a few blocks from the town square. "Everybody out. We do the business district on foot."

Ice crystals floated on the crisp night air giving a snow globe effect as they meandered to the center of town. Multi-colored lights reflected on the ice crystals. "Wow, this is absolutely magical." Gabby took her phone out of her pocket and took pictures of twinkling lights twined in the garland wound around the lamp poles. Lighted wreaths hung on the streetlights with colorful gels covering their glass panes. "I have to send these to Ben. The kids will love them." She sent the pictures and pocketed her phone.

When they reached the town square, Gabby sucked in a breath as she gazed up at the huge pine tree covered in hundreds of red, blue, green, and yellow blinking lights. A solid blue star shone brightly on top of the tree. "Wow, what a wonderful display." Whipping out her phone again, she took more pictures.

"Completed without having to pester anyone." Candle put her hands on her hips. "Well done, everyone." Turning her face up to the star-strewn sky, the frosty ice crystals landed lightly on her face. A crescent moon hung in the sky, adding to the ambiance.

Smiling fervently, she hoped they made it through Christmas without incident. Not paying attention to the pup, she nearly went splat on the sidewalk as Terra wound herself and her leash between Candle's feet. The puppy yelped as the leash pulled tight.

Miacoh reached out an arm wrapping it around Candle's waist to steady her and chuckled. "You might want to pay attention to where you're going." He untangled the leash from her legs, and the pup immediately returned to exploring and pounced on a plastic bag that bobbed and weaved on the breeze across the sidewalk.

Her phone vibrated in her coat pocket before playing a lively tune about a devil in Georgia. She took off her mittens, jerked the phone out of her pocket, and stared at the screen. Her face crumpled as she put the phone to her ear. "This is Candle Bearclaw." There was a long pause as she listened and surveyed the faces of her friends. Terra strained on her leash. "I understand. We're on our way." She touched the screen ending the call. Sighing, she shoved the phone in her pocket. "Looks like we need to cut this enjoyable stroll short. Miacoh and I need to rendezvous at Dad's house. Cayson, we could use your help."

"No problem, I'm in."

She glanced apologetically at Gabby. "Sorry about this. We can drop you at your parents' or you can stay with my mom and dad." She peered at Miacoh. "We'll leave Terrabyte with Mom."

He nodded as the group turned around and double-timed it back to the vehicle.

Chapter Twenty-Five

Too Many Agencies Underfoot—No One Knowing What the Other is Doing

Expecting to see a multitude of official vehicles in front of the Bearclaw residence, Miacoh was surprised to find only one black SUV parked in the driveway. He slowly drove a circuit around the block then parked in front.

Rather than return home, Gabby elected to stay with Pekabo. She bounced out of the vehicle and rushed to the house, followed by Cayson and Candle with Terrabyte on lead. Miacoh brought up the rear of the group carrying the pup's crate. Her grim-faced parents greeted them at the door.

"What's going on? What's the urgency?" Candle walked to the back door and let Terrabyte out in the backyard, waiting at the door for her to do her business and come back in. Since the pup preferred to play outside with her squeaky toy, she returned to the living room where two unfamiliar faces met her. "And who are you two? Where's Caitlin and Jed?"

He set the crate in the corner of the living, glanced at Candle, and tossed the SUV keys to her. "Let's give them a chance to bring us up to speed."

Frowning, she shoved the keys into her backpack.

One of two FBI agents cleared his throat. "I'm

Agent Seevers and this is Agent Graham." He paused for a beat and glanced at his partner, who gave a slight shake of her head. Eying Cayson, Agent Seevers jerked his chin toward the man. "Who's he?"

"Cayson Eriksson, military special forces," Cayson answered ambiguously.

"He's a buddy I served with. Has connections that proved useful and provided important intel. He's on leave right now and offered his services in this case." Miacoh figured that's all they needed to know.

"I think we have enough civilians involved in this case," Agent Graham said haughtily.

Pekabo elbowed Gabby and quietly said, "Let's put the coffee on and fix snacks. This could take a while." Pekabo took Gabby's arm and walked into the kitchen.

"If that was the case, why'd you call us?" Candle moved toward the back door and whistled for Terra. This time the pup trotted inside with a squeaky toy in her mouth. She closed the door behind Terrabyte and whirled around to face Graham with hands on hips. "Huh? Cayson's not a civilian."

"Check him out," Agent Seevers barked. "Because Jed and Caitlin requested your presence at the School of Mines and at the moment they have the lead in this case."

"What are we waiting for?" She pulled her keys out of her backpack.

Candle's dad snorted. "One hand doesn't know what the other hand is doing. Both agents appear less than competent from where I'm standing."

Agent Seevers narrowed his eyes at the Chief and opened his mouth as if to speak.

Agent Graham returned to the room. "Erikssen checks out. Permission to grant him access was given."

"Okay then." Seevers paused, shoving his fingers through his hair. "Homeland Agents Adams and Rossy are in Golden. Thought we had the situation under control. Couldn't find Erin, but after surveilling the two men for a few days, we picked them up yesterday. They're not talking. We canvased the campus. Talked with nearly the entire student population and faculty before we discovered the names of Erin and the men's acquaintances."

"Really, all 4,532 students." Candle smirked. Her dad shot her a warning glance. She raised her hands in a gesture of surrender.

Seevers continued. "However, this afternoon, we ran across a document on Erin's computer."

Candle interrupted, "Where'd you get her computer?"

"She'd left it with one of her friends." He paused. "We had to threaten the girl with accessory to get her to give it to us."

"Yeah, our IT guys had a heck of a time getting access to it. Still don't have access to all the files that were encrypted." Agent Graham waved her hand. "Which is where you come in." The agent peered at Candle.

"May I finish?" Seevers frowned at his partner.

"Oh, sure. Sorry. Didn't mean…"

"We didn't catch the document the first time because it was buried in a bunch of chemistry lab assignments." He handed several pieces of paper to Candle, copies to Hunter and Miacoh, then hesitantly gave one to Cayson.

Candle gave a low whistle the same time he did. "This is more than a chemistry assignment." She cut her gaze to Miacoh then Seevers. "Did you question all the faculty? Tell them to stick around?"

"There were a couple of professors that left early for Christmas break. Otherwise, we've interviewed the rest. Yes, there was no reason to detain them—at that time. Why?"

"Because this document changes things. You guys are going down the wrong rabbit hole." Candle flipped through the papers again.

"I couldn't agree more." Miacoh grabbed his coat. "The sooner we get to the school, the better."

Pekabo came out of the kitchen with two thermoses and large bags of goodies. She held up one thermos. "Coffee." Holding up the other, she grinned at Candle. "Hot chocolate. Had a feeling you'd be leaving soon." She glanced at her husband. "You're staying here to man the command center—right?"

"Hadn't planned on…"

"Great idea." Candle took the bags from her mom. Kissed her on the cheek. Miacoh grabbed the thermoses and winked at Pekabo.

Cayson shrugged one arm into his coat. "Going or staying?" He raised an eyebrow and stared at Miacoh.

"Going."

"I need to stop by her cottage and grab my gear. It may come in handy."

"Will do."

Chapter Twenty-Six

Explosion, Debris Flying Everywhere...What Happened?

As Miacoh turned the SUV into one of the School of Mines parking lots, one wing of a building exploded with debris flying everywhere and flames shooting over sixty feet in the air. He slammed on the brakes, put his hand over Candle's head, and ducked over her as flying objects assaulted the vehicle. Cayson lay sprawled across the back seat.

The blast's concussion overturned vehicles and smashed them into other cars causing more explosions. Cars with shattered windows lined the rear of the parking lot just in front of their SUV.

Moments after the rain of debris stopped, Miacoh, Candle, and Cayson jumped out of the SUV and glanced around. They ran toward the scene, masks from Candle's first aid kit covering their mouth and nose. They coughed and choked as the scent of burning debris and heavy smoke filled the air. Their eyes teared as they fought their way toward the crater where the building had been. Due to the intense heat surrounding the crater, they stopped several yards from point of explosion.

"If there was anyone in the building, they were incinerated. Beyond help now. We should wait here for the emergency personnel." Cayson raised his mask, mopped his face with his handkerchief, and replaced his mask.

Pointing at the flames, "That's the Chemistry building," Candle screamed. "Could be noxious fumes. Need to let everyone know to stay away." She pulled out her phone and dialed Jedediah's number with Homeland Security as she ran back toward her vehicle, motioning the others to follow. "I've gas masks in my emergency bag in the back of the SUV." If their hunch was correct, this wasn't the primary target. She was sure of that. After four rings, she left a message and stuffed the phone back in her pocket.

"Who the hell did you call?" Miacoh fished out the keys from his pocket and touched the fob to open the back of the vehicle. Black soot rained down, covering everything.

"Jedediah. I left a message. Thought he should know what was going on. If he wasn't here already." Candle reached for the rear door release but was pushed aside.

It looked like ground zero in a war zone. Far off sirens wailed as people came screaming and running from other parts of the campus toward the building or what was left, now engulfed in flames. Soon reflections of the red and blue emergency vehicles spread across the parking lot. Fire engines rumbled up to the front of where the building used to stand. Firefighters rushed toward the scene as campus police vehicles blocked the entrances to everyone except emergency personnel.

Miacoh yanked open the back hatch. Candle shimmied in, grabbing the black duffel bag, tearing it open and tossing out the gas masks to Miacoh and Cayson, keeping one for herself.

"We need to tell them to get away unless they have

masks." Cayson pulled the mask over his head, sealing it against his face. The others did the same.

They rushed back into the melee to help the rescue crews evacuate the area. Candle's cell phone rang. She didn't have time to answer it but glanced at the screen. Jedediah returned her call. Was he enroute to the explosion? The message light blinked on. Someone screamed her name, and the phone call was forgotten. She whirled around to find a soot-covered Caitlin staring wide-eyed at her and swaying unsteadily. "Where's Jed?"

In a shaky voice, Caitlin began, "We'd finished evacuating anyone working in the building during the holiday break whether they were authorized or not. On our way out we were making a last check of the rooms when Jed discovered a device in the chemistry lab, taped underneath a corner table toward the back. It was counting down."

"It wasn't there during your initial sweep of the building?" Candle reached out and steadied Caitlin.

The agent pulled away, turning her gaze in the direction of the parking lot and building as support beams crashed to the ground sending embers flying into the sky. "If it was, it wasn't activated. At the time, we were intent on getting everyone out. There wasn't time to disarm the device. We ran for the entrance but got separated." Caitlin started toward the burning building as a second explosion erupted from the other end of the structure, shaking the ground and shooting flames and debris over thirty feet in the air.

Candle grabbed Caitlin's arm and ducked behind a vehicle. "You can't go any closer. It's not safe." No sooner than the words left her mouth, a burning piece of debris crashed onto a nearby vehicle's convertible top. The car alarm wailed while the fragments burned through the cloth and dropped inside the car.

"He's still in there," Caitlin screamed, jerking free of Candle. The agent attempted a sprint toward the chaotic scene with an unsteady gait.

She chased Caitlin, catching her around the waist and taking her down to the pavement. Miacoh raced toward them from a different direction and helped the women to their feet. Shoving a mask at Caitlin, he helped her put it on. "Fire department and local police have arrived and set up a perimeter to keep everyone at a safe distance. They're also evacuating the residential area around here as a precautionary measure. These winds could carry hazardous chemicals for miles."

Out of the smoke and confusion, a figure stumbled toward them. "Jed." Caitlin rushed forward as the man collapsed. His jacket shredded, a red stain bloomed through Jedidiah's shirt sleeve on his upper arm. His face was streaked with blood.

Miacoh jerked his first aid kit from around his waist and knelt at the agent's side assessing his injuries. "Jed—Jed—can you hear me?" He tore open a large sterile alcohol pad and gently wiped the blood from Jed's face. A long gash ran from his temple across his cheek. Glancing up at Caitlin, he shouted, "Appears worse than it is. Though jagged, the wounds aren't deep." The wail of sirens grew louder. Getting to his feet, Miacoh waved down an ambulance. In the reflection of the red and blue flashing lights, the paramedics took over.

With a gentle shake of Caitlin's shoulder, Candle tried to get her attention. "Did you find Erin or Professor James?"

The agent shook her head slowly.

In her mind, she quickly flipped through the hole-in-the-wall places students went to be "off the grid," making them difficult to find. One stuck out in her mind, "The Mud Puddle." If Erin or the professor were there, Candle couldn't legally detain either, but Caitlin could. Was the agent in any shape to assist in a capture?

Could she, Miacoh, and Caitlin leave the scene without repercussions? *Heck with this, Erin or the professor could be on their way or boarding a plane right now to who knows where. Never to be seen again. I can't risk it.* She leaned over toward Miacoh and pointed to her SUV and Caitlin.

He peered pointedly at the agent and shook his head, then pointed to himself, holding up five fingers. Yanking his phone out of his pocket, he texted and then said something to the paramedics working on Jed. Miacoh glanced at his phone. "Cayson will stay here and monitor the situation."

She nodded. "We'll meet you at the SUV. Come on, Caitlin." She pulled the agent along with her as quickly as possible. "I may have an idea where Erin might be." Opening the passenger door, she waited for Caitlin to get in and closed the door. Racing around to the other side, she saw Miacoh running toward her. She slipped into the driver's seat as Miacoh climbed into the back seat.

"Where are we going?"

"Mud Puddle. A little café the students use when they don't want to be found. At least they used to. It's worth a check."

Once they were all in the SUV, gas masks removed, she attempted to pull around a new barricade. A uniformed officer motioned her to stop. Caitlin showed her ID, and they were permitted to pass.

Fifteen minutes later, she drove past the café and parked half a block down the street. She turned to Caitlin. "You feel well enough to cover the back with Miacoh? Or do you want to wait here until we need you? Keep in mind. They may not be in the café at all."

"I'm not going to sit here and let you two do my job. I'm coming in."

Miacoh and Candle exchanged glances and shrugged. "Okay. Got your cell phone?"

"Yeah. It's the one we called you on."

"Copy that. Let's go." She exited the vehicle strolling up to the front door of The Mud Puddle as Miacoh and Caitlin made their way around back. Pulling open the door, she found the café filled with people talking about the explosion. Seated in a corner booth alone, her face half-hidden, Erin peered over a menu. She passed by the booth and pretended to wave at a person across the room, then doubled back, blocking Erin from sliding out of the booth. Candle lifted her jacket showing her weapon. "It's over, Erin. Where's Professor James?"

The woman's eyes widened and shifted left then right as if looking for an escape.

"Nowhere to go. Just sit here for a moment." Never taking her eyes off Erin, she pulled the phone out of her pocket and touched the screen. "Got her. Come on in."

At that moment, Erin pulled her feet up underneath her, stood on the seat, and rushed toward her knocking her off balance. Erin vaulted over her.

She caught Erin's ankle and yanked. The young woman face-planted on the floor. Scrambling to her feet, she put her knee in Erin's back, pinned the girl's arms, and pulled her gun, pointing it at Erin. "Settle down."

A short man with a gray braid hanging down his back shoved his way through the gathering crowd. He paused in front of them and pushed his round spectacles up his nose. "What the heck is going on here? The police are on their way."

"Good."

Caitlin strode in brandishing her badge and handcuffs, slapped them on the young woman, and read Erin her rights. Handing the girl off to Miacoh, Caitlin dumped Erin's purse on the table, sorting through the contents. "What do we have here?" She held up an airline ticket to Morocco. "Planning a trip?"

Caitlin narrowed her eyes at the suspect. "I believe you'll miss your flight." She pulled out her phone, touching the screen. "Check all flights leaving for Morocco today. Delay any on the ground. We're looking for a Professor Raymond D. James."

Erin clamped her mouth shut, her lips turning white with the pressure.

"If I were you, I'd start talking. It appears the professor has plans to flee the country without you. Leaving you to take the fall for everything." Candle smiled sweetly. "Not the first time a pretty girl's fallen prey to an older man."

"I have no idea what you're talking about." Erin squirmed under Miacoh's firm grip.

"You had some pretty interesting chemistry assignments on your computer, Erin. Once we deciphered them, your professor's plans were set out in great detail. What I don't understand is why?" Her forehead creased as she studied the suspect.

"Then there's the matter of the police officer you and your friends gunned down outside Aspen Ridge."

Miacoh jerked her around to face him. "Who panicked and shot the officer after he discovered what was in your pickup bed?"

Her eyes flew open wide, and she stared slack-jawed at him.

"Got your guys on dash cam."

She regained her composure, a sarcastic smile turning up the corners of her mouth. "Don't have any idea what you're talking about. I don't have any guys. I'm merely a graduate student working on my degree. One of many who are required to take Professor James's advanced class. He's quite helpful in furthering a student's education."

"I'll just bet he is." *To further his own agenda.* Candle glanced at Miacoh, who had Erin pinned up against the wall with his body and one hand. He was talking on his phone via a wireless earpiece. *Funny, I didn't hear the phone ring.*

He ended the call with a touch to the wireless headset and grasped Erin with both hands. "Cayson informs me that Homeland, FBI, and local police have things under control. Apparently, the chemical containment system recently installed worked fairly well. No dangerous fumes to surrounding neighborhoods. Additional agents are enroute to our location to take custody of Erin. Jedidiah's on his way to the hospital to get stitched up. He'll be in the hospital overnight for observation despite his objections.

"The concussion from the blasts scrambled his senses. Doctors are pretty sure he's concussed to boot. The paramedics assured Cayson Jed'll make a full recovery. Cayson's ready to go anytime we are."

"Where'd you get the earpiece?" Candle pointed

toward his ear.

"Courtesy of Cayson. Thought hands-free might come in handy. You rushed into the fray before he could offer you one."

Three official-looking men entered the café waving badges and made their way to Caitlin. "We'll take it from here. Agent Peters will take you to the hospital to get checked out." Caitlin opened her mouth to object, but the man raised his hand, silencing her. "Orders from the top."

Chapter Twenty-Seven

A Welcome Celebration and Surprise
Announcement

Miacoh, Cayson, and Candle trudged up the path to her parents' home. She reached for the door handle. Her mother opened the door. Terra pushed her way out of the door, barking, jumping, and circling the group as if to say, where have you been? Candle knelt, rubbed the wiggling pup's ears, and picked her up, burying her face in the pup's soft golden fur. "I'm happy to see you too."

The others skirted around her and into the house.

"It's about time you guys returned. We were worried sick. Especially after we found out the whole building exploded." Gabby hugged the group.

Candle's shoulders slumped, and she blew out a breath. "It's been a long day. Erin will join her compadres in lock up. Professor James appears to have escaped for now. Caitlin is at the hospital being checked out at her company's request. Jed is at the hospital being treated for injuries received in the blast. They'll keep him overnight for observation. He was the closest when the first blast went off." She glanced over at Cayson and Miacoh. "Anything to add?"

"It was lucky the explosion was over the holiday break. Cait and Jed cleared the building before it blew. Jed located the incendiary device on the last sweep through the lab. The good thing? Don't believe it's a terrorist activity, or it'd been timed to explode when the building was full of students for most impact and casualties. Our gut feeling is that the prof had an ax to grind and used his graduate students to do it. No proof."

"Some ax." Candle shook her head.

Her dad rocked back on his heels and stared at the group. "I'm just glad none of you were hurt." He directed his gaze at his daughter and gripped her by the shoulders. "Heard you did a good job thinking on your feet, locating Erin, and wrapping up that portion of the feds' case for them. I told 'em one hand didn't know what the other hand was doing." Pulling his daughter into a hug he kissed her on the cheek. "You two make a heck of a team. Heard Cayson wasn't a slouch either."

"Thanks, Dad."

"I've got a chicken enchilada casserole warming in the oven with tortillas. You guys must be starved. Come sit down." Pekabo herded them all to the dining table.

Hunter plucked three bottles of beer out of the fridge. "Who's driving?"

"I am." Gabby raised her hand. "They can drink whatever they want. They've earned it. Besides, I'm staying with Candle and Terrabyte tonight."

Pekabo set a wine glass in front of her daughter. "Red or white?

"Neither. I'd like a cola. I'd be sound asleep after a couple of sips of wine."

Miacoh grinned, an eyebrow winged up in surprise as he took the icy bottle from Hunter. "Gabby, you're amazing. I was going to suggest that exact thing. Cayson and I will bunk over at my gram's house. Or I guess it's my house now. Took it off the market yesterday.

Thinking about sticking around here for a while. Heard the town's looking for a new Chief of Police." He took a long swig from the bottle. "Hits the spot."

Hunter handed a beer to Cayson and cut his gaze to Miacoh. "Aww cut the crap—son. I saw your application in the new batch the town council is considering." He winked at Miacoh. "Put in a good word for you."

"What—Why am I always the last to know?" Candle took the soft drink bottle from her mom.

Gabby set the large casserole dish in the middle of the light oak table and jabbed two large serving spoons in it. She returned to the kitchen, brought out the orange and blue southwest design ceramic tortilla warmer, and set it next to the casserole. "Dig in. Pekabo, sit down. You've done enough pacing today for all of us. Worn a path in the living room rug, she did." Gabby snickered as Pekabo swatted at her and then eased into the chair next to Hunter.

"I was going to tell you at the Christmas festival you two have worked so diligently on. But after today, I didn't want to wait any longer. Besides, I didn't figure your dad would out me like that."

He reached for the enchiladas, dipped out a couple of large spoonfuls, and put them on his plate. Inhaling deeply, he smiled, returning the spoon to the dish. "Smells delicious." He glanced around the table hand still on the dish. "Anyone else want some?" Scooping up a huge forkful, he popped it in his mouth. "Mmmm. These are fantastic. You've outdone yourself, Pekabo."

"Pass the casserole before Miacoh eats it all," Cayson growled.

She snickered. "Great, by the time those two are finished, there won't be any for the rest of us."

"Don't underestimate me, young lady," her mother said sternly then broke into a wide grin. "I made two casseroles. Worst that can happen is we eat them all. You won't have any to take home with you." Pekabo reached for the tortilla container, took one, and passed the rest to her right.

Candle took a tortilla, rolled it up, scooped up a bit of enchilada, and popped it in her mouth. "Excellent."

"Thank you. But you all are simply starving. Probably haven't eaten since morning."

Murmurs of agreement floated around the table.

Pekabo took a sip of wine and set her glass down. "What are the plans for the festival? Want to meet here and go as a group? Cayson, you're sticking around for a while. Right?"

"Yeah. Until after Christmas, then I have to report for a new assignment." Cayson and Miacoh exchanged looks but neither said a word.

After dinner, Gabby and Candle helped her mom clean up amid jaw-popping yawns and heavy eyelids.

"Looks like I better get these guys home before they all fall asleep, and we have to carry them out." Gabby caught the keys that Candle tossed to her.

Hunter stood up and stretched pushing his chair back. "Good idea since none of us are able to haul them out to the SUV and then into their respective homes."

Terrabyte whined at the back door. Candle got up, shrugged into her coat, and hurried to the door. "Come on, girl, out you go then we're on our way home. She turned the door handle. The wind caught the door with a whoosh and slammed it back against the stop. Zipping her coat, she peered outside. "Looks like a storm is blowing in. Hope it doesn't spoil the festival tomorrow."

Taking a firm grip on the door, she stepped outside with Terra and closed it.

Chapter Twenty-Eight

Christmas Festival a Fun Time for All

The next day huge storybook snowflakes floated through the air as Candle lifted Terrabyte into her crate inside the SUV. Gabby rushed out behind her friend, one arm in her coat, the other sleeve flapping in the mild breeze. Her purse swung around her body as she tried to get her arm in the other sleeve.

Candle laughed. "Gabby, slow down. We've plenty of time. We'll make it to your parents' house in time for you to take their car and pick up Ben and the twins at the airport. Their plane doesn't land for three hours."

"I know. I know. But I can't wait to see them. The festival is going to be so much fun for the twins." Finally getting her coat tamed and on, Gabby turned her face to the sky. Wet sparkling snowflakes landed lightly on her cheeks and hair. "This weather is perfect for the holiday festival." She climbed into the vehicle and clicked the seatbelt. "I'm ready for hot chocolate. How about you?"

"You betcha. You'll have to get hot chocolate on the way to the airport." Candle smiled happily. "Good thing your family caught an early flight. We could have a lot of snow by tonight if this keeps up." The back hatch to the vehicle closed, she slid into the seat and started the engine. A lively tune came from her pocket.

The screen on her sound system asked her to accept

or decline a call from Mark. She blew out a breath and touched the screen accepting the call. "Mark you're on speaker phone. My best friend Gabby is with me so can I call you back in a few? I need to drop her off to pick up a car and head to the airport. We're kinda in a time crunch."

"Fine, don't take too long." He disconnected the call.

"Friendly sort. Business?" Gabby shifted in her seat.

"Don't know. Mark used to be my handler. He's okay…all business. Can't imagine what he wants two days before Christmas. Mark informed me about Carl's death."

"Carl was who? These last few days have been like living in a spy thriller."

"My ex-boss at the agency. He recruited me out of college."

"Oh, one of those if I tell you, I'll have to kill you kinda things." Gabby snorted.

"Turned out that way." She drummed her fingers on the steering wheel.

"That phone call isn't going to spoil Christmas. Is it?" The creases on Gabby's forehead deepened.

"Of course not. I don't work for the agency anymore. I asked him to keep me in the loop as to the investigation into Carl's murder, uh death."

"Murder. It was murder?" Gabby gasped.

"That's what they're investigating. Nothing to do with me."

"What about the attempted hack on your computer?"

"How did you know about that?"

"Your dad told me. He said your previous life seemed to have followed you here."

Gee thanks, Dad. "No, it's not like that. I left all that behind. I reported the attempted hack to Mark in case he wanted to check it out. The hackers probably discovered my computer wasn't an agency computer and moved on."

"But your dad said…"

"Too much. You overheard him talking to Homeland or FBI, didn't you?"

Gabby twisted her fingers together in her lap. "Sort of."

"Nothing to worry about. Christmas is going to go off without a hitch. What'd you get the twins for Christmas? The holidays are so much fun with kids around."

Gabby stared dubiously at her friend. "Okaaay… I see what you're doing, though—changing the subject. But I'll let it slide this time."

"Good choice. I appreciate it."

"We got Natalya a new computer. Nash wanted a tablet with a keyboard. He's not as techie as Natalya and does everything on the fly. Whereas his sister would rather sit in her corner of the world and use her computer. Those are the big things. Mom and Dad got them clothes and hiking boots. They're growing like weeds. And have probably eaten way too much candy by now."

She snickered, bringing the SUV to a stop in front of Gabby's parents' house. "I've heard kids do that—grow like weeds."

"Since we'll have to take two vehicles anyway, we'll meet your group at the festival by the evergreen tree in the town square, say…" She paused for a beat. "About six?"

"That'll work." Candle leaned over and hugged her

257

friend before she exited the SUV. Prior to pulling away from the curb, she touched the screen to recall Mark. The call went straight to voice mail. "Telephone tag. You're it." *He hated her leaving messages like that.* She snickered.

Big, fluffy, wet snowflakes continued to fall as her windshield wipers swished back and forth. The SUV's blinker ticked off and on as she pulled out into the street and turned the vehicle toward Miacoh's place. Even in her mind, his staying sounded strange and exciting all at the same time. He would remain in Aspen Ridge, maybe taking over her dad's position.

She pumped one fist in the air. "Yes." Butterflies fluttered around the knot forming in her stomach. *Were they ready to take the next steps in their relationship? Was his staying an indication he was prepared to settle down? Am I?* She slowed to turn into Rosy–Miacoh's driveway. Terrabyte woofed excitedly. By the time Candle got out of the vehicle and rounded the back end, Miacoh had the rear door open, and the pup leashed. He sat her on the ground. She took off sniffing and squatted to do her business.

Miacoh wrapped an arm around Candle and brushed his lips over hers. "About time you get here. Forgot there isn't any food in the house. Cayson and I are starving."

"You haven't even had coffee yet?"

He raised an eyebrow. "Of course, I have coffee."

She laughed, enjoying the cozy feeling of his arm around her. "Shall we go to the little diner on Main Street? They serve a dynamite breakfast all day."

Cayson jogged out the door. "Sounds great. But after yesterday, I can do without the explosive references today."

"Oh haha. Aren't we cute?"

"Well actually, I'd prefer handsome, studly, or something along that line," Cayson joked.

"Just get in the car." She gave him a little shove.

Miacoh rolled his eyes, lifted Terra into the SUV, closed the crate door, and sprinted to the house to lock up.

"Only a little while longer, girl, and you can run wild in Mom and Dad's backyard. We gotta feed these guys before they fade away from hunger." She snickered, checked that Terra had food and water then closed the rear door and tossed the keys to Miacoh as he returned. "Mark called while I was taking Gabby to her parents' house. When I returned the call, it went to voice mail. I left a message." Pausing for a beat, she fingered the phone in her pocket.

"So, I have to drive for you to take the call. Should he return your call."

"Yep." She scooted into the passenger seat and turned the blue tooth connection off on the phone.

Miacoh slid into the driver's seat and started the engine. "Heard anything from Homeland or FBI?"

"Not a word. I haven't been to Mom and Dad's yet. They may have some news. Figured we'd go over there after I picked you two up. Didn't count on a detour to the diner." She grinned.

"You've already eaten then?"

"Not exactly. But I could have. There is food at my house. Gabby was in such a hurry. We grabbed drinks and hit the road." Smirking, she pulled her phone out.

He put his hand over her phone. "If you call your parents, your mom will insist on feeding us. She's got to be worn out. So, let's wait until we've finished breakfast, then you can let them know we're on our way. Besides, if they have bad news, I want to have a full stomach first."

"How'd you know what I was thinking?"

"It's a talent." She waved her hand dismissively and pushed her hair over her shoulder.

****

An hour later, Miacoh parked in front of her parents' house. There were no other vehicles in sight. He took this as a good sign until Candle's phone rang as she let Terrabyte out of the crate. He glanced in her direction, and she nodded.

"You guys go on in. I need to take this call." She put the ear mic in, touched the screen, and clipped the leash on Terra. "Hey, Mark. Give me a minute." She glanced at Miacoh and Cayson. "I'll take her around to the backyard. Meet you in the house."

Miacoh and his friend trooped up to the house. Pekabo stood at the open door, watching her daughter walk around the house with the phone to her ear. "What's going on?" She wiped her hands on her apron nervously. Her gaze flicked to her husband, then back to Miacoh.

"She had to take a phone call. She'll be right in. No biggie. Is there anything we can help with for the festival?" He took the door from Pekabo shutting it behind him.

"Nope. The town council and Rita have it handled. We're to come hungry and enjoy ourselves." Pekabo untied her apron and hung it on the back of a chair. "House seems empty with everyone gone."

"Have you heard anything?" He looked to Hunter.

"Not a thing. After the agents cleared out last night, it's been kinda nice. Huh, Pek?"

"Let's hope it stays that way. Now the town needs to hire your replacement. So we can get on with retirement plans."

"On that front. Anything in your background since you left that I should know about?" Hunter's cop stare landed on Miacoh.

He hated that stare when he was a kid and didn't much like it now. "Nope. Not a thing."

"I can attest to his spotless military record," Cayson chimed in, picking out a piece of hard candy from the candy dish and popping it in his mouth. He walked over to the lounger and sat down.

"The admin is running a background check on you now. After that comes back, I believe they will offer you the job. If everything checks out, you'll start January first."

"Hallelujah." Pekabo squealed, clapping her hands together. "Bahamas, here we come."

"Now, don't go getting all excited. It's not a done deal yet. There's the subject of salary. We can't pay what government contractors do or the big city police departments."

"If I'd have wanted that type of lifestyle and compensation, I'd have sold Gram's house and moved on, which was my original plan. But things changed. As it turned out, what I'm looking for is right here." He returned the stare with as much determination as he dared. Backing down had never been in his wheelhouse.

Cayson's lips turned up in a devilish grin. He began whistling a familiar tune about another one biting the dust.

Miacoh chuckled. "Give it a rest, will ya?" Walking across the room, he eased down on the couch facing the

Tena Stetler

fireplace.

Cayson raised his hands in a gesture of surrender. "What?"

The door banged open, and four paws thundered through the kitchen. Candle sauntered in behind the pup. All eyes in the room turned to her.

"What?" She tucked the phone in her pocket.

"Spill. What did Mark want?" Miacoh patted the seat next to him. "Take a load off and fill us in."

Candle plopped on the couch next to him. "It was all good. I guess. My name is being scrubbed from the investigation into Carl's death. According to Mark, it could be a long one. Carl had his fair share of enemies, a lot of bad actors. In recently located files, Carl left instructions if something like this happened, I wasn't to be involved. He wanted me to have a great life. It's almost as if he knew something or someone was stalking him."

Miacoh raised a brow in question. "It's that easy to walk away from the agency?"

"I thought so at first. I struck a deal when Carl changed my status from independent contractor to CIA Agent. Now I wonder if it was all a smoke screen, and I was never really an independent contractor. The bottom line, my name has been redacted in all files. Only those with a top-secret security clearance will know who I was, what I did, and will have to go through Mark for any intelligence on me. Whatever Carl was mixed up in that got him killed, I didn't know anything about it."

"Basically, you're an agency ghost."

She shrugged. "Guess so. This was my last communication with Mark unless things go south in a big way. Even then, according to him, my whereabouts are unknown since the day I left the agency. No next of kin listed. I'll never know what really happened to Carl or if I had anything inadvertently to do with it."

"It's for the best." He slung an arm around her shoulder. "What about your investigation into Roark's murder?"

"Any agency avenues I used to research have been switched to appear as Homeland or FBI. Officially, I was helping Dad on his case as a civilian."

"Caitlin and Jed are in for one heck of a surprise."

"It will be their problem, not mine or ours." She glanced from him to her dad. A tune erupted from her pocket. "Now what?" Yanking the cell out of her pocket, she peered at the screen, then touched her wireless ear mic. "Hi, Gabby. Family arrive safe and sound?"

"Yep. Twins are fine. Ben may be a little shell shocked since this was the most time he's spent with them without me running interference since they were born." She snickered. "Probably be the last for a while. Wanted to let you know we're all on the way to the festival."

"Great. We're about to leave. See you at the tree." She ended the call. "Gabby and family are on the way to the festival."

"Thank goodness. I've had enough cloak and dagger to last a lifetime." Pekabo stood up, picked up her coat, and padded to the door. "If I'd known what you…" At her husband's warning glance, she waved her hand dismissively. "Let's go."

At those words, Terrabyte's ears perked up, she got up and stretched, then trotted over to the couch tail wagging. "Yes, you're going." Candle clipped the leash on her harness and shoved up from the couch. "What about the potluck? We don't have to bring anything?"

"Didn't I tell you? We decided to have food vendors at the festival so everyone could enjoy themselves and not worry about cooking, bringing a dish, and cleaning up afterward. Not to mention the scheduling nightmare. This time of year things are so hectic."

"Great idea."

Hunter doused the fire, humming a Christmas song under his breath as the others donned their coats, gloves, and hats.

****

Candle sidled up to her dad. "Could I have a quick word with you?"

"Your mom is ready to leave," he protested. "Can't it wait?"

"No, I believe it's waited long enough."

He raised his eyebrows. "Okay. Pek, Candle and I'll be right along. You and Miacoh go on to the vehicle.

"Dad, I'll cut straight to the chase. Why didn't you tell me about your, our genetic history? Especially when you knew Miacoh's."

He blew out a breath "Well, I have no confirmation of our line having shifters in it. More like rumors or legends passed down from our ancestors."

She paced in front of him. "Don't you think I had a right to know?"

"In retrospect, I should have told you." He shoved his fingers through his hair leaving little rows. "Would you have believed me? You've always been a prove-it-kind person. I couldn't. And I had no way of knowing that you would become involved with an individual who could prove that such creatures exist."

She narrowed her eyes. "I could pass that gene on to

my children?"

"Highly unlikely. It's been several generations since it surfaced, according to the ancestors. I'd say our line is a dead end as far as that goes."

"I don't like the way you handled it. But I figured it was something like this after Miacoh refused to divulge how or why you were able to help him."

"Did Mom know?"

"Of course. There are no secrets between us." He shrugged. "But Pekabo didn't see you and Miacoh happening, until recently. Her gift of sight is blurry when it comes to immediate family."

Miacoh knocked on the door, then opened it a crack. "Hey, guys, we need to get going before Pekabo explodes." He glanced from Candle to her dad. "Or maybe not."

Hunter put his arm around her and squeezed, then looked solemnly at Miacoh. "The family secret is no more."

"That's a good thing. It wasn't my tale to tell." Miacoh opened the door wider for Hunter and Candle to exit. She caught hold of Miacoh's hand and walked to the SUV.

****

After finding a parking place, Candle and her group bounded out of the SUV. The minute Terrabyte's paws hit the ground, she tugged on her leash in an effort to get to everyone. Candle reined her back with a quick tug on the leash and commanded, "Leave it."

Ears pasted to her head, the pup let out a huff and stared indignantly at her owner.

"It's for your own good. Don't want you getting into trouble. Not everyone loves dogs. Even if you are the cutest pup on the planet." She bent down and ruffled the fur behind Terra's ears.

The precipitation had stopped leaving a blanket of freshly fallen snow reflecting twinkling lights strung from the light poles and across vendor carts. The effect created a magical wonderland in the town square. Christmas music drifted from speakers set up around the area. Multi-colored lights adorning the giant evergreen tree in the town center shone brightly through the snow-covered branches.

She and Miacoh meandered down Main Street exchanging greetings with several people, admiring the twinkling Christmas lights and holiday scenes decorating the store windows. When they came to Magic Treasures Book Store, she stopped fondly remembering all the afternoons spent inside the store, lost in a world each book brought to life. "This was one of my favorite places growing up."

"I spent quite a bit of time here researching the myths and legends of my people. It was a quiet place away from the town's prying eyes." He pulled up on the leash as she reached for the door handle. "It's all right to take Terra inside?"

"Sure, Sorcha is an animal lover." She waved through the window to a woman with graying hair done up in a bun with a pencil stuck in it, then tugged Miacoh through the door. The old brass bell above the door rang merrily. "Merry Christmas, Sorcha. The store looks fantastic."

Miacoh swept the pup under his arm. "Happy Holidays, Ms. Cohen." He glanced at the wiggling Terra and scratched her ears. "Best not track snow and mud in the store."

"Oh, thanks for picking her up." She turned her attention to Sorcha. "Could we get a paper towel to wipe her paws?"

"Of course." Ms. Cohen handed her a roll of paper towels. "She is a cutie. What's her name?" Sorcha rubbed behind the pup's ears.

"Terrabyte." Candle wiped the dog's paws and took the leash from Miacoh. "Okay if we put her on the floor? We won't let her get into anything." He put Terra on the floor, and Candle wound the leash around her hand until the pup had to stand right beside her.

"No problem. I love puppies." Sorcha leaned back, reached behind the counter, and pulled out a puppy biscuit. "Can she have a treat?"

"Sure. No freebies. Ask her to sit."

Terra's gaze never left the small bone-shaped treat as the shop owner said, "Sit." Terra complied, and Sorcha handed the pup her treat.

Surveying the store, Candle pointed across the room. "The new shelves are a great addition. I love the comfy chairs arranged in the cozy reading corner." Strolling to the children's section, she lightly touched the wall decorated with bright-colored faeries, unicorns, and other mythical creatures frolicking in the magical garden. Then turned her attention to the opposite wall where renderings of spaceships destined for far-off planets would call young scientists. "These murals are wonderful. I bet they spark youngsters' imaginations. Did you paint the wall yourself?"

Sorcha laughed, waving her hand in dismissal. "Heaven's no. Cally, an art teacher at the high school, made the wall her class project last year. All had a fun time, and we've had more students visit the store since.

It was time for an upgrade." Sorcha smiled wide. "What brings you in?"

"Lots of fond memories. We're on our way to the festival and decided to wander Main Street first. The merchants really outdid themselves."

"Yes, we did. You girls' enthusiasm to bring Christmas back to our tired old town inspired us. Not to mention the Halloween celebration." Sorcha shook her head. "It's been a rough couple of months."

"It has, but things are looking up." Miacoh grinned, picking up a worn book, turning it over in his hand, and flipping through the pages.

"So I've heard." Sorcha's eyes twinkled. "Things are a changing."

"Will you be joining the caroling around the Christmas tree?" She glanced out the window at the gathering crowd around the tree. "We better be going. Gabby and her family are meeting us at the tree."

"Yep, I'm closing up now and will be there shortly. You two go on. I'll see you there." Sorcha put her hand on Candle's arm. "I'm glad you're back."

"So am I."

Walking toward the door, Candle craned her neck to look up at the shiny bell above the door. "That bell's been there since I was a kid."

"Yep. It'll outlast me, I'm afraid." Sorcha cackled as she followed them to the door, flipped the open sign to closed, and locked the door behind them.

With her arm through Miacoh's, they ambled through the growing crowd. "Looks like we've got a great turnout. Gabby'll be pleased."

"The wide smile on your face says the same about you." He bent down and kissed her on the nose. "You've been good for this town."

"Right back at ya. Funny how things work out." She snuggled closer to him as they strolled toward the town's Christmas tree, their boots crunching in the sparkling snow.

"Hey, Miacoh." One of the town council members, Boyd, rushed up to him and paused looking from side to side. "You didn't hear it from me, but I wanted to be the first to congratulate our incoming Chief of Police." The man grabbed Miacoh's hand and shook it vigorously. "Mum's the word. Don't want Tressa, Madam Chairman, to get her knickers in a twist."

"My lips are sealed." He made a zipping motion across his lips as they turned up at the corners.

The man waved and hurried off toward another group of people gathered near the tree.

She giggled. "Chief. Congratulations."

"Hey—it's a secret." He gave her a stern look then his easy-going smile returned.

"Not for long in this town. It'll be old news by morning."

"Don't I know it." He chuckled, glancing toward the sound of voices singing traditional Christmas carols.

"Come on. They're starting without us." She tugged him toward the tree where Cayson, her mom and dad, Gabby's family, Tressa Harper, and Boyd Bently stood together, singing their hearts out and waving at them.

Terrabyte bounded forward first to greet the group. Tressa put her hand on Miacoh's arm, leaned over, and said something in his ear. He grinned and bobbed his head up and down.

Chapter Twenty-Nine

A Christmas Surprise and the Beginning of a New Era

Miacoh slowed the SUV to a stop in front of Candle's cabin. Cayson reached up and tapped him on the shoulder. "I'll check the backyard, then wait at your truck."

He nodded and handed the keys to Cayson. "Start the truck so she'll get warmed up."

Cayson nodded and ambled toward the backyard.

Candle jumped out of the vehicle and sprinted around to the back to release Terrabyte. "Are you really going to let Terra and me stay in our own home alone?" she teased, lowering the pup to the ground.

All wiggles, Terra sniffed around then spied Cayson. She raced to the end of her lead, barking.

"Quiet," Candle commanded.

"Not my first choice, but I've been a terrible host to Cayson. Once I secure the house and walk your property's perimeter, you're on your own. The threat seems minimized from what you told us of your conversation with Mark. Your dad relieved me from bodyguard duty—for now."

The feeling of foreboding that hung over him recently was gone, replaced by unknown anticipation he couldn't put a name on. Being unable to voice a reason for concern, he'd no choice but to allow her and Terra to spend the night without his protection.

"Roark's murder investigation is just about wrapped up though it's doubtful the professor will be tracked down anytime soon. Think his students will talk?" Candle unlocked the door and stepped aside, allowing him to enter first.

"Doubtful. Besides, I'd be shocked if he confided his real plans to them. He wasn't sleeping with Erin. No weak link there. The professor is long gone." He finished checking the cabin and returned to where she and Terra stood. "Good to go."

Cayson rounded the corner of the house. "Perimeter and fence line secure. You can let the furry princess out." He snorted a laugh. "Night, Candle. Meet you at the truck Miacoh."

"If there are any problems, call me." Miacoh pulled her close and kissed her.

"You know that I took care of myself for the last fifteen years, and I'm still alive to tell about it."

"Yeah, yeah, yeah, even a blind squirrel gets a nut once in a while." He ducked to avoid the punch she sent his way. "Seriously, I know you can take care of yourself, but there is still safety in numbers. See you in the morning." He strolled down the path to his truck. Terra's barks of joy and constant squeaking of her toys told him she was happily playing in the backyard under the watchful eye of Candle.

Glancing back once more, he was surprised to see her standing on the porch. She blew him a kiss and went inside, closing the door. He waited a couple of minutes more until she called Terrabyte inside and the beep of her setting the alarm eased the knot in his stomach.

When he climbed into the truck, Cayson shifted to face him. "You're serious about this woman and her dog." He grinned.

"Yep. They're a package deal. She's the one." The street clear, he pulled out and headed for home.

"Wow, I never would have thought." Cayson shook his head and settled into the seat.

"When I arrived in Aspen Ridge, I planned to sell Gram's house, settle the estate, and move on. But it didn't turn out that way." He stopped the truck at the grocery store. "I need to pick up a few food items. Be right back."

"All kidding aside, I'm happy for you, bro. I can see how this town could grow on you." Cayson exited the vehicle. "I'll join you. Need junk food. I'm going through withdrawals."

A half-hour later, they returned, several bags of groceries in hand, to the truck. Miacoh turned to Cayson. "Offer still stands. If you tire of the high adrenalin life, you've got a place here." He tossed the bags in the back and started the engine.

"I'll keep that in mind."

Coasting to a stop in front of his house, he grabbed a few bags, and Cayson took the rest, carrying them into the house. After putting the groceries away, he reached into the fridge. "Want a cold one?"

"Naw. I'm beat. Mind if I turn in?" Cayson stretched his hands over his head and yawned wide.

"Some party animal you are." He laughed. "I'll be right behind you." Wandering into the living room, he plopped down on the lounger and relaxed, sipping on a cold drink. Headlight beams flashed through the window. He got to his feet and looked out. A car's red taillights bobbed in the distance. "Huh?" Before trudging up the stairs, he set the alarm, paused to flip the light switch, and continued to his bedroom.

The next morning the doorbell rang before he was even out of bed. The heavenly aroma of coffee wafted from the kitchen, and Cayson called up, "Want me to get it?"

Who the heck is here this early? "Sure. I'll be down in a minute." He yanked on jeans and ran a brush through his hair. As an afterthought, he grabbed the shirt tossed across the back of the chair. Taking the stairs two at a time, he stopped short on the landing. A tall woman with long light brown hair streaked with gray stood in the living room, peering up at him with blue-green eyes. "What are you doing here?"

An uncertain smile curved the corners of her mouth. "I told you I'd think it over. I'm done thinking."

"Fine. I'll get the envelope." He wheeled around and started back upstairs.

"I don't want the money. I'm here to talk." His mother's gaze wandered over the room and landed on Cayson standing in the kitchen doorway.

He cleared his throat. "Anyone want a cup of coffee?" Cayson waved his hand toward the coffee maker. "Fresh brewed."

"Yes. I'll take a mug. Mom?"

"Okay," she said quietly.

At the bottom of the stairs, he paused to pull on his shirt. "Mom, this is my buddy, Cayson. We served in the military together. Cayson, this is my mom, Tamber Zane." He glanced over at her. "It is still Zane?"

"Yes. Of course." She stiffened, then sighed. "You're the spitting image of your father."

"I didn't mean anything. It's been a long time. I'm sure…" He trailed off, scrubbing a hand over his face. "Got your eyes."

"True." She paused for a couple of beats. "Your father was the love of my life. That will never change. No one could ever replace him. But after the accident, things were difficult."

He walked over and hugged her. "Come on in and grab a mug. I'll get breakfast started. Eggs, bacon, toast okay?"

"Sure." She walked over and eased down in a chair.

Cayson looked from Tamber to his friend. "I've some errands to run."

"Don't be ridiculous. You're starved—as always. Breakfast is ready in a minute. I'll loan you the truck afterward, and you can run your errands."

"Talked me right into it." Cayson took the loaf of bread from the cupboard and popped four slices into the toaster. Reaching into the fridge, he brought out the butter dish and set it on the table with a knife.

"You boys are quite handy in the kitchen. Miacoh's dad couldn't boil water without burning the pan." She smiled sadly.

"I remember Gram doing most of the cooking." At his mother's dispirited expression, he added, "You worked a lot."

"True. Wish I could have been here for you. But your father and his mother took over raising you. Said it was in your best interest. Guess as it turned out, you weren't what they expected."

"If you are talking about our people's legends, Mom, that's not exactly true. I was exactly what they expected. Shapeshifting or furry creatures on moonlit nights—were my destiny. Learned to handle it with the help of Chief Bearclaw." He glanced at Cayson, hoping his friend would take it all in stride and not freak. "It's Dad's genes I have to thank for my exceptional athleticism, hearing, sight, and intuition—the rest—well." He shrugged. "Can't have everything."

Wide-eyed Cayson swallowed hard. "Oh, so that's how you outperformed all of us regularly in training." He shook his head. "You know the guys in the unit were always—never mind—not important."

"Trying to beat me. Level the playing field. Finally, wised up and let you guys score higher than me on occasion." Grinning, he flipped the eggs and turned the bacon out onto a paper towel. "Breakfast is ready."

Cayson caught his friend's arm. "You and me—we gotta talk soon."

"Agreed."

After they ate, he tossed the keys to Cayson. "Don't be gone too long. This afternoon, we're expected at Candle's parents' place for last-minute tweaking of Christmas plans."

Cayson sent him a thumbs up, picked up his coat, and hurried out the door.

"Candle. Isn't that Hunter and Pekabo's girl?" Tamber's brows knitted together in an uncertain expression. "Didn't she leave here to pursue a hush-hush government position straight out of college?"

"Yes, she's Chief and Pek's daughter. She did leave, but she's back. We met again when I returned to settle the estate and sell Gram's house."

Her gaze scanned the house again. "Doesn't look like you are readying it for sale."

"I'm not. Plans change." He was unreasonably short

with her, but he couldn't help himself.

"Are you involved with her? If you don't mind my asking."

"I don't mind your asking, but involvement in my personal life—it's a little early yet. Don't you think?" Pausing, he wondered how much to tell her. Was she even interested in his life now? *Aww, com'on give her the benefit of the doubt. She's here, isn't she?*

She smiled knowingly. "I understand. Just so you know, it's written all over your face. And I'm happy for you. The Bearclaws are a great family. You were always close to Hunter after your dad died. Candle's had a crush on you since she was in junior high."

"How'd you know that? When I never noticed."

His mom laughed. "You were too busy trying to live up to some standard you set for yourself to notice what was right in front of your face. But she was too young for you then, and you had—needed to prove something. And I took the easy way out. I'm sorry."

"I have to ask. What's with the money Gram left for you?"

She took a deep breath and blew it out slowly. "After his accident and we moved here, your father made Rosy promise to take care of both of us."

He nodded in understanding.

"You were her last hope and connection to the tribe's heritage. Legends, so you call them. She believed in them to her dying day and blamed me for diluting the bloodline. I heard it so often I began to believe her and that your defiance was somehow my fault.

"Now I realize you were searching for a male role model you found in Hunter. Rosy and my arguments drove you away from home. I considered leaving here

276

and taking you with me but couldn't bear to take the only thing Rosy had left, so I stayed and endured."

"Gram was mean to you? I never knew."

"No, no, it wasn't like that. She—blamed me, and I let her. If I had stood up for myself, things would have been much better. But I missed your father so much. I failed to see how much you missed him too. Your grief and hurt turned to defiance. If Hunter hadn't been there for you…"

She shook her head and stared at the floor for a beat. But when her eyes met his, a spark of hope glimmered. "That's all in the past. A past I want to—I'd like to salvage. No—I'd like to be a small part of your life now if you'll let me."

"Mom, of course, I want you in my life. I didn't reach out because I didn't understand what I did wrong to cause such a family rift. As I grew older, I realized it wasn't me but figured you'd made a new life for yourself." He shrugged.

"I had enough problems dealing with the fact the legends were true, lived on in me, and learning to cope with them. Hunter was my savior. He wasn't shocked at my transformation into a wolf, nor was he derogatory. Chief did insist that I learn to control it.

"When I finally did, he suggested the military might be a good fit. I was still terribly angry. The gene exists in his ancestors' bloodline too but didn't surface in Hunter's recent generations." As the words left his mouth, he had a startling thought. *What if by combining our genes, the legend would spring forth?* He shook his head. *I'm getting way ahead of myself.*

"No wonder he stepped in. Believe me, I never stopped thinking about you or loving your father. He was one of a kind."

"Why did you leave Aspen Ridge before I got here?"

"It was easier than explaining. Or at least that is what I thought until you called. Besides, the last I heard was no one was sure where you were or when or if you'd be back. Rosy's attorney wasn't helpful."

"Yeah, Hunter tracked me down. The lawyer wasn't much help to me either, mostly concerned about getting the estate settled and his fee."

"I figured Hunter would locate you and help get things handled. So I left."

"Enough of this. We start a new page today." Surprised at how big his hand looked as he placed it over her small one. "Christmas is over at Hunter and Pek's house along with Gabby and her family. Cayson and I are meeting Candle over there to see what help they need. You're more than welcome to join us."

"Oh, I don't know. Hunter and Pek never approved of the way I handled…"

"Mom, believe me, they don't judge and would be happy to have you." He glanced out the window and saw Candle's SUV pull up in front. Smiling, he started toward the door as she let Terra out of the truck. The pup strained toward the house, all wiggles and barking excitedly.

Snapping his fingers, he rushed toward the bedroom. "Mom, give me a minute." He dug through his drawer until he pulled out a purple velvet box. Sprinting back to the door, he opened it and enveloped Candle in a bear hug. He'd been waiting for the right time. Now was the time.

"If this is the kinda greeting I get for showing up unannounced I'd been here sooner." She laughed as

Terra tangled herself and the leash around his feet.

"Sit." The pup's butt hit the ground. He leaned down and scratched her ears. "Candle, there's someone here I want you to meet." Twining his fingers through hers, he pulled her into the kitchen. "My mom, Tamber, stopped by unannounced too."

Never missing a beat, Candle reached her hand out and grasped his mother's hand. "So glad to see you again, Mrs. Zane. It's been a long time." She grinned. "I'm the little girl that used to stand on the sidewalk outside your house with my friend Gabby waiting for a glimpse of him." Candle pointed a thumb in his direction. "Thanks for not shooing me away. That would have been terribly embarrassing at that age."

"He was oblivious at that time. So I didn't see the harm. I remembered being young once." His mother withdrew her hand from Candle's and smiled. "As it turned out, I was right."

"Mom, if you'll excuse Candle and me for a moment. There's something I need to do." He slipped on his coat and took Candle and Terra out on the back porch.

"What are you doing?" She quirked a brow questioningly.

He bent down on one knee and tossed a new squeaky toy to the pup. Terrabyte promptly pounced on it, squeaking it as she ran across the yard. Turning his attention to a puzzled Candle, he looked into her eyes. "If the last few weeks have taught me anything, it's that life is short. You have to take it by the tail and wrestle it to the ground if you are going to be successful." He reached into his pocket, pulled out a deep purple box, and flipped the top open.

"Candle Bearclaw, would you do me the honor of

becoming my wife?" He hurried on searching her face as if afraid of her answer. "We don't have to set a date anytime soon. Lots of changes in our lives are imminent, but I want you locked in—" *Oh boy, wrong choice of words. I should have practiced this.* He stared at the ground for a beat, then glanced up. "Let me rephrase that. I want you by my side, sharing whatever life may throw at us." *Geez, that wasn't much better. Third time's the charm. Keep it simple.* "Please marry me."

A twinkle of amusement sparked in her eyes as she took the box from his hand. "Well, not exactly as I imagined, but entertaining all the same." She caressed his cheek, and slipped her hand under his chin, gently tilting his face to hers. "Yes, I'd love to be your wife and share your life."

Inside the velvet box, a square cut garnet winked in the sunlight between two diamonds in a gold setting. He took the ring from the box and slid it onto the finger of her left hand.

"Now, let's go back inside where the whole world isn't watching." She jerked her head toward the fence where Cayson stood, a grin spreading across his face, dangling truck keys from his finger.

"Way to go, bro." His friend held two thumbs up.

Two neighbors behind his house smiled, waving as they returned to their homes.

He got to his feet, ignoring them all. "I want everyone to know you're mine," he said nonchalantly again, twining his fingers through hers. They walked hand in hand back to the house.

The wind rustled through the dry leaves swirling across the ground. Pausing for a couple of seconds, he could have sworn he heard his Gram's laugh. Whether or not it was his imagination, in his heart, he knew she was looking down on him, wishing them well.

Candle glanced back to check on Terra, who was oblivious to the monumental moment, only intent on making as much noise as possible with her new squeaky toy.

****

Rather than make an appearance at Candle's parents' house, they called, explained that Tamber had stopped by, and asked if there was anything they needed to bring to Christmas dinner tomorrow.

Hunter immediately answered, "Bring yourselves, Cayson, and Tamber, then we'll be all set."

Miacoh and Candle spent the rest of the evening catching Tamber up on the recent events in Aspen Ridge and her son's life. Cayson unabashedly told stories of his and Miacoh's experiences in the special forces, careful to leave out classified information and traumatic events.

Tamber glanced over at Candle. "What brought you back here?"

"The glamorous life of a CIA agent wasn't all it was cracked up to be." Candle smiled and shrugged.

"Welcome to the family, Candle." Tamber turned her attention to him. "What are you going to do now that you've asked Candle to marry you?" Tamber glanced uncertainly at her son.

"Oh, I guess we didn't tell you in all the excitement, I'm taking over Hunter's position as Chief of Police on January first."

Tamber's mouth fell open momentarily. "Wow, I guess I have missed a lot."

"Don't worry, tomorrow you'll learn more than you ever wanted to know if Gabby has anything to say about it. The information pipeline will include my best friend's family and Mom and Dad."

Chapter Thirty

Christmas Feast, Stories & Updates Galore

On Christmas day, their little entourage strolled up the path to the Bearclaws' home. Candle glanced over at Tamber. The woman looked terrified. Miacoh's hands were full of packages. He nudged his mother with his elbow and smiled reassuringly.

For once, Terrabyte trotted obediently beside Candle as she leaned over and whispered, "Mrs. Zane, everything is going to be fine. You'll have a wonderful time." In a conspiratorial tone, she added, "Though I must warn you, Gabby and her twins can be overwhelming. They don't mean to be, just the way it is."

Tamber smiled. "I remember you and Gabby were a force to be reckoned with as children. I can only imagine now."

"Would you believe they single-handedly resurrected the Christmas festival and convinced the town to put up Christmas decorations? Now I'll admit that Gabby and her family donated the new decorations to replace the worn-out ones." Miacoh winked at Candle.

"That's not exactly true. We just got the ball rolling. The whole town pitched in to make it a success." Heat bloomed on her cheeks.

Her mother flung open the door bouncing out to hug

everyone. "So glad you could join our family's holiday celebration, Tamber. You too, Cayson."

Her dad stood smiling behind her mom. "Welcome to our home." He gave Tamber a quick hug, clapped Cayson and Miacoh on the shoulder, and kissed Candle on the cheek. "Come on in, make yourselves comfortable." Glancing at her, he did a double take, his gaze locked on her left hand. A knowing smile spread across his face.

No sooner than Hunter closed the door, Gabby dashed into the living room. "I heard—hi, Mrs. Zane." Gabby extended her hand to clasp Tamber's. "What a wonderful surprise." She glanced at Miacoh and then over to her best friend. "Oh—oh—my!" Gabby's hand flew to her mouth. "Is there something you want to share?" The woman was nearly vibrating.

"As a matter of fact—" Was all she got out before Gabby grabbed her hand and raised it for all to see.

"Look everyone—" Gabby said excitedly.

Miacoh dumped the packages under the tree and hurried to stand by Candle's side, grinning from ear to ear. "Before Gabby explodes, Candle and I have an announcement. He peered lovingly into her eyes, then shifted his gaze to their friends and family. "Candle has agreed to be my wife." He paused as cheers and congratulations filled the room.

Holding his hand up to quiet everyone, he continued, "Before you ask, we've not set a date. Figured in the coming months, we'd have a lot of changes in our lives. When things settle down and we decide on a date, all of you will be among the first to know. Fair enough?"

Hunter cleared his throat. "As long as we are making announcements. I'd like to officially introduce you to our next Chief of Police, Miacoh Zane."

The room erupted in applause and more shouts of congratulations.

"If the announcements are completed for the day, everyone grab a chair at the table. Let's eat." Hunter motioned everyone into the dining room.

Pekabo brought out the turkey. Miacoh followed her with the ham. Dishes of candied sweet potatoes, stuffing, and deviled eggs lined the middle of the table. Candle removed Rita's cranberries from the refrigerator, dumped them out of the Christmas tree mold, and carried it out on a crystal serving plate.

As Pekabo took her seat, the doorbell rang. She glanced around the room. "Are we expecting anyone else?"

"Not that I know of." Hunter set his napkin on the table. The others around the table shook their heads.

He got up and strode to the door and checked the peephole. "It's Jed and Caitlin." He swung the door open. "Merry Christmas." He reached for Jed's hand, shook it, and did the same to Caitlin. "I hope it's not official business that brought you to my doorstep." Opening the door wider, he motioned them inside.

"We are flying out tonight and thought we'd update you before leaving. From all appearances and information we obtained, Professor James has already escaped the country. After digging into his background, we believe he set this whole plan in motion to get back at his department head and the committee that oversees the tenure of professors.

"Apparently, he received negative decisions over the years and appealed, some were reversed, others were not. This last go around, the internal evaluations of his research, teaching, service, accomplishments, and potential garnered several negative decisions, and he was on the brink of being dismissed. He decided to go out with a bang," Jed said.

"But you already knew this—didn't you?" Caitlin stared in Candle's direction.

Her face flushed as her father's attention switched from the agents and riveted on her. Miacoh's lips twitched as he raised his hand to his mouth to stifle a cough that may have covered a snort of laughter.

She grimaced. "After our recent experience with your IT people, I wasn't sure… I wanted to verify my hunch before I said anything to anyone. You know, no more going down the wrong rabbit holes, so to speak." At her father's disapproving expression, she raised her hands in a gesture of surrender. "The search was all legal and above board after talking to his department head. I still have a few ins at the school."

"So we discovered. Our techs followed your trail, one I presume you left for them, and they reported back to us." Caitlin peered at Candle.

"Just so you know, the previous file we had on you no longer exists. Therefore, any search you initiated would never be found unless you wanted someone to find it," Jed added.

"Interesting. Where do we go from here?"

"You keep your nose out of government business. Our agency will watch and wait for the professor to resurface."

"Did you find which of his graduate student's info he used to procure a false identity? He had all the information at his fingertips and may not be traveling alone." Candle quirked an eyebrow in question.

"Not yet. But we'll find the info and him or anyone else involved. Don't worry," Caitlin said. "Sifting through that many student records and comparing them with passenger logs for that time frame will take quite a bit of time."

"Okay—You know he could have used more than one," Candle said pointedly.

"We are aware and are handling it." Jed glanced at his watch.

"When does your plane leave?" Pekabo peered at the agents. "Got time to join us for Christmas dinner?"

"We don't want to intrude."

"You already did." Hunter motioned toward the table. "Might as well make it worth your while."

Miacoh got up and grabbed a couple of chairs from the kitchen and set them at the far end of the table across from him and Candle. She brought out two more place settings.

"Thank you. We appreciate your hospitality—again," Caitlin and Jed chorused.

A devilish grin spread across Hunter's face as the agents settled into the chairs. "By the way, let me introduce you to Aspen Ridge's new Chief of Police, Miacoh Zane." His eyes twinkled with amusement.

Caitlin sighed and glanced over at her partner with an I told you so expression. "Congratulations, Miacoh."

Jed grinned. "I thought you were leaving town?"

"Things change. I grew up here and wanted to ensure our little town recovers from this unfortunate incident."

"And you." Caitlin stared pointedly at Candle. "What are your future plans?"

"I'm staying here. Terrabyte Security will provide

residential and business security systems and cyber security based in Aspen Ridge. At Dad's and Miacoh's suggestion, I'm moving the company out of my cabin and into the storefront Delta, my real estate agent, found for me next door to the police station."

Caitlin narrowed her eyes. "No interest in agency business?"

"Nope. I'm a small-town girl returning to her roots. As you discovered, I've been scrubbed from the agency. I want to keep it that way."

Caitlin leaned over to her partner and said something in a whisper.

Jed grinned and nodded. "Please pass the turkey."

Candle turned to Miacoh knowing he'd have overheard Caitlin. "What did she say?"

"Fat chance." He chuckled. "Oh, there is one more announcement. Pekabo and Hunter leave on their inaugural retirement trip to Hawaii on January 2nd. Followed by a cruise to Alaska in March or April." He raised his wine glass. "A toast to Hunter's well-deserved retirement."

Everyone raised their glasses and chorused, "Congratulations!"

As the guests lowered their glasses, Candle leaned over, kissed Miacoh, and raised her glass again. "I have another toast." She gazed at him lovingly. "To us and our new life together. No more spy games."

A word about the author…

Tena Stetler is a best selling author of paranormal romance. She has an over-active imagination, which led to writing her first vampire romance as a tween to the chagrin of her mother and delight of her friends. After many years as a paralegal, then an IT Manager, she decided to live out her dream of pursuing a publishing career.

With the Rocky Mountains outside her window, she sits at her computer surrounded by a wide array of witches, shapeshifters, demons, faeries, and gryphons, with a Navy SEAL or two mixed in telling their tales. Her books tell stories of magical kick-ass women and mystical alpha males that dare to love them. Well, okay there are a few companion animals to round out the tales.

Colorado is home; shared with her husband of many moons, a brilliant Chow Chow, a spoiled parrot, and a forty-five-year-old box turtle. When she's not writing, her time is spent kayaking, camping, hiking, biking, or just relaxing in the great Colorado outdoors. During the winter you can find her curled up in front of a crackling fire with a good book, a mug of hot chocolate, and a big bowl of popcorn.

http://www.tenastetler.com

Thank you for purchasing
this publication of The Wild Rose Press, Inc.

For questions or more information
contact us at
info@thewildrosepress.com.

The Wild Rose Press, Inc.
www.thewildrosepress.com

www.ingramcontent.com/pod-product-compliance
Lightning Source LLC
Chambersburg PA
CBHW070057030726
47506CB00002B/501